RACHEL LOUISE DOVE is a mum of two from Yorkshire. She has always loved writing and has had previous success as a self-published author. Rachel is the winner of the Mills & Boon & *Prima* Magazine Flirty Fiction competition and won The Writers Bureau Writer of the Year Award in 2016. She is a qualified adult education tutor specialising in child development and autism. In 2018 she founded the Rachel Dove Bursary, giving one working-class writer each year a fully funded place on the Romantic Novelists' Association New Writers' Scheme.

Also by Rachel Dove

The Chic Boutique on Baker Street
The Flower Shop on Foxley Street
The Long Walk Back
The Wedding Shop on Wexley Street
The Fire House on Honeysuckle Street

The Second Chance Hotel

RACHEL DOVE

ONE PLACE. MANY STORIES

HQ
An imprint of HarperCollins*Publishers* Ltd
1 London Bridge Street
London SE1 9GF

First published in Great Britain by
HQ, an imprint of HarperCollins*Publishers* Ltd 2020

Copyright © Rachel Dove 2020

Rachel Dove asserts the moral right to be
identified as the author of this work.
A catalogue record for this book is
available from the British Library.

ISBN: 9780008375829

MIX
Paper from
responsible sources
FSC® C007454

This book is produced from independently certified FSC™ paper
to ensure responsible forest management.

For more information visit: www.harpercollins.co.uk/green

Printed and bound in Great Britain by
CPI Group (UK) Ltd, Melksham, SN12 6TR

To all the fellow women out there, PCOS warriors
&
*to everyone who makes the world a better place, one kind
act at a time and never, ever give up*

Prologue

To You

If I was writing this letter under better circumstances, I could have written a much better opening. I'm sitting here on my bunk trying to think of what to say. I don't even know what to call you. I know we have to be careful. If I could, I would say your name over and over for the rest of my life. How lucky people who see you every day are, for they get to say it willy-nilly.

For you, nothing seems appropriate, or enough, so I decided that You will have to do. My You. My one and only You.

I have the shell you pressed into my hand that night, and I haven't stopped looking at it. It smells of you, of home, and it makes me feel like my recurring nightmare was just that, and that my real life is still there, at Shady Pines with you.

How long do we have left, till the letters have to stop? I fear the day, yet I know it must come. You must live your life, and I should at least try to start mine. Even with the huge You-shaped hole in my soul. Don't tell me, not till you have to. While you're free, let's pretend, just you and Me.

G

Prologue

Chapter 1

April Statham sat as close to the steering wheel as she could get, nudging herself and her clapped-out brown Ford Escort along the road, turning slowly into the entrance to the chalet park. Unfortunately, a few seconds earlier, a horse rider had passed, and now his steed was going to the toilet in the middle of the road, leaving a huge steaming pile of horse plop right in the entranceway. April wasn't really one to believe in signs, but this was kind of hard to miss.

'Er ...' She wound her window down. 'Excuse me?' The horse, and the rider, a thin man whose long features mirrored that of his thoroughbred, dipped their heads to look at her. 'Could you possibly move your horse? I need to pass.'

The horse snorted loudly. Or was it the rider? Both parties looked equally nonplussed, but the man nodded once and the horse trotted away, leaving his ... offerings. April turned the car into the lane, avoiding the pile, and headed for the large wooden hut marked 'Reception'.

'Bloody great pile of steaming poo in the entrance, great advert for the place,' she muttered under her breath, her eyes flicking down to her petrol gauge, which was pointed straight at zero. Past zero, truth be told. She could feel the change in the engine,

3

the car chugging along on petrol fumes. She pulled into the space marked 'Management' in between the reception hut and a small chalet. She yanked up the handbrake and turned the key in the ignition to off. She could swear that her car breathed a sigh of relief as the engine cut out. They had made it, her and her little car, all the way from Yorkshire to the tip of the Cornish coast. She sat back in her seat, her limbs and back stiff and wizened, as though she had been tied in a knot somewhere along the A38 and had driven bunched up like a pretzel ever since.

She was just easing the knots out of her neck when a sharp tap on her window made her jump. A woman stood there, her face pinched up tight, her dark hair tied into curling rollers on her head. She was wearing a pink dressing gown and dark green wellies, and looked more than a little crazy, even at 8 a.m. on a Monday morning. April wound her window down wearily, plastering a patient smile on her face.

'Are you lost?' the woman said pointedly, looking from inside the car to the boxes and suitcases strapped to a roof rack that April had nabbed from a Freecycle site. Her suitcases came from there too, with her not wanting to take the monogrammed luggage set she had been given as a wedding present. His and hers. She'd left it next to Duncan's in the detached garage. Camped out in her late mother's house. They'd looked so pathetic sitting there together, never to be used again, as they once were on honeymoon, and on their exotic holidays and horrifying business trips he'd dragged her along on.

'No,' said April. *Yes, I am a bit. I think I've made a big mistake.* 'I'm not lost.'

The woman looked again at the worldly belongings strapped to the roof and sighed, a small unsympathetic sigh that made April feel about an inch tall.

'Well—' the woman raised her eyebrows again '—you look lost. Can I call someone for you? We're expecting the hotshot new owner at some point today.'

4

'I'm the new owner,' April tried, her voice a faint whisper. 'I own this place.'

The woman, having caught the gist now, looked at her with wide eyes.

'You?' She leaned into the car window, her head floating there like a balloon. 'You—' punctuated by a jab of the finger in her direction '—actually bought this place?'

April nodded slowly. The woman began to laugh.

'Pull the other one, love, it's got bells on.' She guffawed, her face looming in April's window like an animal in a safari park now. A camel sprang to mind. Something that could spit at you from ten paces if it saw fit. Yanking her head back out, the woman tapped twice on the top of April's car and carried on her way, disappearing as quickly as she had appeared.

April was suddenly alone again, wondering what the hell she had gotten herself into. *Hotshot new owner? What had the camel … er … the woman heard?* April didn't want to ruffle any feathers here before she had even unpacked so much as a solitary toilet roll. Why did she think April was a hotshot? *Oh God.* She'd said 'we'. 'We have been waiting for the new owner.' Who were 'we'? The woman had obviously found her lacking, and once more, April's eyes turned to her phone, sitting there innocently in her handbag. It looked so normal, but April felt as though the damn thing was a ticking time bomb waiting to explode on her frazzled brain with an influx of messages. Posts on social media of 'you okay, hon?' People commenting on her life, strangers and people who didn't know her well at all. Not the real her, and nothing like the post-divorce her. Emails from old acquaintances. Purchase reminders for occasions she didn't need to be reminded of at all. Ever. It would all be in there, lurking.

It had been bad enough already, without her sudden departure from everything and everyone. Divorce was a great vehicle for gossip, her mum had told her. Boy, was she right, as ever. April had turned all her notifications off. If she didn't need to use the damn thing to navigate, she would probably have pitched it into the nearest and deepest river she could find.

Soon, news of her escape would spread around her hometown, and the gossip would start again. *She couldn't have kids, you know. Tried for years, they did. Broke them apart. Still, his new girlfriend seems lovely. Child-bearing hips, that one. Shame about April, though. She never did quite fit in.* They chatted on social media as if they were in the hairdresser's or in the Post Office queue. *What was it that Gran used to tell me? Oh yeah. Loose lips sink ships. No wonder I feel like a crap second-hand dinghy with a Hello Kitty plaster holding in my deflated soul.*

They'd be feasting soon, beaks sharply stuck in everyone else's business. Just like the buzzards to return to a carcass in the hope they'd missed a piece of flesh, a strip of soft underbelly to rip from the bones of her failed life. She had failed as a wife, as a—

April stopped that train of thought by grabbing her phone and jabbing the off button hard, till the screen powered down. She didn't need her map app now, so why would she leave it on to tick away like a telltale heart? She felt instantly better. She was gone, out of their reach. She'd rather thought that being 'off grid' would make her feel a tad edgy or a bit hippyish, but instead, she just felt relief. Bone-deep relief. Un-contactable. Freeeeeee! Relief that she wouldn't have to endure their pitying stares and sympathetic nods, complete with the 'little rub'. People thought that rubbing your arm or your shoulder was comforting, but it was just a bit too condescending for April. She hated it more than anything. She felt like a simpleton half the time after they had descended on her. What a joy life could be After Duncan. AD. Life after husband.

Zipping up her oversized handbag, she looked once more out of the window at the corner of the world she would now call home. It looked a little like how she felt: neglected, empty, peeling at the corners. Muted against the blue of the sky above. She pulled herself out of the car, her bones popping and cracking as her body unfurled itself. She could feel the shale beneath her feet, her black and white sneakers crunching as she looked around her. The Shady Pines Chalet Park was perched on a beautiful strip of land near Lizard Point, Kynance Cove a short distance away. From the park, April knew from memory that there was a direct walkway to the beach area, for the use of her guests. It had been there for many years and was one of the biggest selling points to her, the thought of waking up and having her toes in the water to start her day right.

Stretching her legs, she walked slowly to the reception hut, brand-new keys in hand. She'd picked them up from a key safe at the estate agent's that morning, and now here she was, about to start her new life. Taking a gulp of the sharp sea air deep into her lungs, she unlocked the door. The key slotted into the metal housing like a glove. There was a slight resistance, salt in the old locks making the mechanisms stick, but then she felt it turn, and the lock click open. It was times like this, right now, that April felt like she had done something right, for once. She'd done this; she was here. It was all hers, a new life for the taking. If she hadn't sworn off social media, she would have snapped a photo of the moment for Instagram with a witty hashtag like #divorcerules or #suckonthatduncanyouutterwan—

Maybe not. Not like she threw herself a divorce party, was it? She'd spent half the day crying, the rest feeling completely out of her depth. She obviously wasn't feeling #blessed quite yet, but she could fake it for now. This was her new life; it was time to get cracking. Pushing open the door, she took a step forward … and hit the deck with a very loud and dusty bang.

'Ouch! Broken boobs!' April shouted, or tried to shout. Since her face was smushed into the now broken wooden door, it came out as a muffled humming sound. Prising her lips off the peeling paint, she pushed herself up on her arms and inspected the damage. The whole door had collapsed, the hinges still attached to the door beneath her. Standing, she inspected the wooden frames and saw that the wood was old, brittle to the touch. It crumbled to dust and fell through her fingers.

'Great,' she grumbled under her breath. 'Better find a carpenter pretty sharpish, before the rest of my life turns into the bottom of a rabbit hutch.' She heaved up the door, resting it on her face at one point to get a better handle on the heavy wood. Placing it to one side of the room with a loud bang, she looked at the dust on her plain black T-shirt and old blue jeans and sighed. She brushed herself down, gingerly around the already bruising chest area.

'Well,' she said to the room, looking around. 'Cheers for the excellent welcome, new home. Be careful, or I will use the last of my money to have a wood chipper party, right here.' She pointed her finger to the centre of the floor and braced herself, but the ceiling didn't fall in. Phew.

The reception hut was deceptively large, a square room with a desk off to the left-hand side, complete with a counter in the same faded white-painted wood as the rest of the place. Off to the right, against the wall, were rows of shelving, all empty and filled with dust. The floor was the same white wood, giving the whole room a cube-like effect, and making April feel a bit hemmed in for a second.

There were windows behind the desk on the left, and on the back wall opposite the door was a large set of glass-panelled doors, leading out to a grassed area out of the back. The chalet park ran on the green grass like a horseshoe, twenty blue-and-white trimmed identical chalets, all with their own porches and back patio areas for dining out and sunbathing. Where the ends of the horseshoe met, on the left was the sign indicating the park, with a rack that must have once been used for bicycles alongside it. It was metal and had been painted cream at one point, with pretty shell details around the lettering. Currently, it looked a little worse for wear, the paint peeling and rust-coloured. There was a lone rubber tyre and a dented shopping basket using the facilities, and the sign was tilted to one side, looking as though it was hanging on with the one rusty protruding nail that was still attached. To the right of this was the reception, and on the other side of this, her chalet. It matched the others and looked just as dilapidated. Through the dusty doors, she could see the blue sky and the grass expanse beneath, leading off to the track to the beach. The beach where her mother had taken her, that first night here all that time ago.

It had nearly been dark, the sun setting slowly on their first long day in Cornwall. April had been tired. She remembered how cloudy her head had felt, how she'd moaned when her mother wanted them to see the sunset together.

'When are we going home?' She could hear her little voice now, remembered how her mother ignored her at first. Her back to her, facing the fading sun, head tilted up like a flower head. Her mother's fists clenched when she asked again, her voice whinier, higher. It sounded at odds to the crashing of the waves, the laugh-like call of the birds ahead.

The clenched fists were only there a second, but April thought of her father and shrank back. Her mother turned, but her face was kind.

'April, come here, petal.' April went to her mother, and she turned them back to face the chalet park. Other families were in the chalets, or out on their patios. Playing cards, having a glass of wine. Laughing as the kids played. They passed them on the way to the shore, and the happy noises of life filtered down to the beach.

Hands on her daughter's shoulders behind her, her mother spoke. Her voice sounded different. Louder, somehow.

'You hear that?' she asked, gentler now.

'The sea?'

'The people, April. You hear the people up there?'

April looked past the dunes, where the lights from the park

could be seen. She could hear the sounds of people talking, laughing, kids screeching with joy as they played and ran about.

'Yes,' she said, her mouth curving into a smile.

'That's what life is supposed to be like, April. I want you to look around you, my girl, soak it in. I want this for you, all of this. We're not going home, April. It's just going to be me and you from now on, and we'll be just fine.' Her mother squeezed her shoulders, a loving gesture that warmed April through as the words washed over her like the waves behind her. 'This is our second chance hotel, sweetheart. New life starts right here.'

April's feet were moving, heading for the glass doors, key in hand, before she even registered the urge overtaking her body. This was what had been keeping her going, thinking of seeing that beach. Feeling the wind whip her shoulder-length brunette hair around her face, walking barefoot along the sand. She loved the beach, and always had – she thought back to the long summers she had enjoyed growing up. Crabbing off the docks, swimming in the clear blue waters, curling up with a fire and a hot chocolate on a dark night. After that summer at Shady Pines, the two of them had visited every beach they could find. She envied the child she had been, all innocent and full of hope. What did she have now? Besides wood rot, of course?

This, that's what.

As she pushed on the doors, they resisted at first, stuck fast with dirt and grime, but then she gave them a shove and she was outside, half running across the grass as she shoved her keys into her bra and picked up the pace. Walking out of those doors felt like stepping out onto the moon's surface. The grass led to a path cut out of the rocks and wild tufts, the thick carpet of green blades giving way to sandy dunes the closer she got. She kicked her shoes off, not giving a toss where they landed, and once her bare feet hit the wet sandy beach, she whooped with delight.

'I'm here, Shady Pines!' she yelled, her jean bottoms getting flicked with the sand she was casting off in her run to the sea. 'I'm really here!'

The sharp shock of the cold water took her breath away momentarily, and she squealed to herself. After a few gentle steps, she felt her whole body sigh with the pleasure of the sensations. This was her favourite place, by the sea. She loved it, had always loved it, and once more she found herself marvelling at the journey she had just undertaken. A year ago, she would have laughed in the face of anyone who told her the story. It would have seemed so unbelievable, so daring. Like a lifestyle piece in the magazines she used to read, once upon a time. Before they seemed to mock her, show her what she was missing. When your life didn't follow the usual expected path, where did that leave a modern woman? The knackers yard? Spinsterhood? She wasn't ready to start knitting a straitjacket just yet, thank you very much. She still felt twenty-one most days.

Not today though. Today she felt about eight years old, holding her mother's hand while she paddled in the sea, tiny toes wrinkling in the water. She felt brilliant. Right now, standing there in the sea, her old life miles away and out of reach, she felt amazing. This was day one of her new life. Peeling paint and broken doors be damned. Duncan seemed like a bad dream right now. Hoping the feeling would last once reality set in, she smiled to herself, turning to walk further along the shoreline, to leave her footprints in the sand, and make her own mark.

Chapter 2

Cillian O'Leary followed the sticky blobs of raspberry jam as they led a trail from the worn lino of the kitchen to the scuffed wooden floor of the lounge. He was spraying and wiping away the globules as he went, moving from the floor to the doorframe, where red seeded fingerprints were stuck to the white-painted wood. A cartoon pig was jumping into a puddle on the television in the corner, and a pair of bush baby green eyes followed the movements on screen.

'Orla,' he said softly, causing her brown wispy head to turn into his direction. 'Daddy can make your toast, poppet. I told you, I'm here to look after you.' His daughter regarded him as she often did these days, with a blank, open expression that made his heart break. He looked at the slice of toast, half eaten on the plate, buttered better than any girl her age should be able to achieve.

Orla's eyes were already back on the screen, watching the pink, animated animals live their perfect, happy lives. What a crock we teach our children growing up. White picket fence, smiling parents, happy children, perfect homes. Baddies wear black, and the good guys wear white and always win, no matter what. White hat or black hat. Right or wrong. Good or bad. In Cillian's world, the grey areas had overlapped, encircling him in a storm that he couldn't see through, let alone get out of. Except, he did get out of it. They just needed that next step now, that little lifeline. Something to break them out of this rut and get them moving again.

He put the dirty cloth straight into the washing machine and flicked on the kettle, flicking it off a second later once he realised that the coffee jar was empty. He didn't get paid till Friday, and he was staring down the barrel of a full five days with the tenner and change he had in his wallet. Thank God he had diesel at least for his van. He could still take Orla to school nursery and pick her up after. At least there she would get snacks of fresh fruit, and a hot lunch. By the weekend, he would have money to feed and clothe her, at least until Monday rolled around again.

He only got paid from the agency, and with the benefits taking time to transfer to him, he was struggling more than he ever had without the sole care of a child to consider. The sting of having to ask for help wasn't nice either. He'd always been lucky enough to be in work before, well and able to provide for himself. Once more, he thought of Tina and silently cursed her for not being there. Judging by her social media update, she was doing just fine. Back in her old job, picking up her old pre-family life. Erasing it completely for the most part. Hard to believe they'd lived in the same place, but were strangers now. *Bully for you, Tina. Hope you are enjoying yourself there, without a care in the world.*

Of course, that was always the problem. She never wanted the whole domestic life, not really. She'd told him enough times. The problem with people was, they heard what they wanted to hear sometimes, no matter what's actually said. It was up to him now, to move on too. Once the pit of what felt like battery acid stopped swirling in his stomach. He needed to let go, but the anger was all he had to fuel him right now. That, and sodding *Peppa Pig*.

His phone buzzed in his pocket, and he fumbled for it, desperate to answer it before it rang off. They often rang on withheld numbers from the employment agencies he was registered with, which wasn't exactly helpful if you needed to call them back. Not that he could, given his lack of phone credit. The money he had left was in case of emergencies only, for ringing the school, the social workers.

'Hello?'

Thirty minutes later, and he was pulling his van up outside Martha's place. A light sheen of sweat sticking his clothing to his back, he squirmed in his seat and looked around at the park. He could see no signs of life, and other than the tatty car with all its baggage, nothing looked any different. Walking around the other side to the reception hut, he saw the broken door that Martha had called him about. Inspecting the hinges, he felt relieved that there was no sign of forced entry. The lock was intact, not smashed off. No tool marks. Whoever had come through the doors had a key.

Grateful that Orla was at nursery, he stepped over the threshold, noticing that the patio doors at the back were wide open. Other than the door, there wasn't any damage. The place was empty, and he shook his head. The old manager really had stripped the place. Whoever was taking over had their work cut out. He was just heading back out of the door to inspect the car when he spotted movement out of the patio doors. He backed up against the wall and shimmied along as quickly and quietly as he could, listening for the footsteps getting closer and closer. There were no voices, no communication. Was it just one person? They didn't seem to be in a rush.

He looked around him on the dusty floor for some sort of weapon, but other than dust bunnies and junk mail piles, he was out of luck. Someone was coming in, right now. He pushed himself flat against the wall, his whole body coiled behind the patio doors. The footsteps got closer and louder, and then a leg came through the door. WHAM!

14

Cillian wasted no time at all, springing on the intruder in a flying frog-like leap, just as a mature woman wearing a murderous expression and what looked like a butcher's apron came running through the front doors whooping at the top of her lungs with a large cricket bat clasped in her raised arms.

'Martha, run!' Cillian shouted at the bat brandisher, his leap descending till he collided with the shape, knocking them both to the ground and hearing the person beneath him grunt loudly in pain. Martha ran all right, but not to the door. She sprinted over to the counter nearby, and bringing the wooden bat down hard on the surface, she screamed, 'Eat dirt, pussbag! I've called the rozzers!'

'Get off!' a voice screamed, and Cillian and Martha both whirled around, looking for the source.

'It's me, down here! Can you get off me? Your knee is jammed in my ribs!' A female voice. A rather startled female voice.

Cillian looked down and saw an irate brunette staring back up at him. A brunette with huge brown eyes, that were now glaring at him in shock. She was blinking rapidly, and he was just admiring how long her lashes were, when he realised she was trying with all her might to shove him off her.

'Oh sh— sorry!' He scrabbled to his feet, or tried to, but they were a tangle of clothes and limbs, and it took a second or two to get separated from each other. He caught a flash of pale midriff as her top rode up, and he shook away the distraction from his thoughts. *Dark lashes, hot body. Nice one, Cill, first sniff of a woman in months and you slam her to the floor like a prop forward.* Finally managing to stand, he held out his hand to her. Lying there on the floor, her hair windswept and clothes thick with dust, Cillian thought her the cutest burglar he had ever seen. She eyed him, but finally pursed her lips and put her hand in his.

'We thought you were an intruder,' he said by way of explanation, his Irish tones fuelling the echoes in the room. It also amplified her indignant huff back at him.

'So you thought you'd crush me to death?' The woman was rubbing her ribcage, and Cillian felt a pang of guilt. Maybe he had overreacted, but Martha had been so sure that there was trouble.

'Who are you, anyway?' Martha asked the woman now, bat still firmly gripped in her charcoal-streaked hands. The two women locked eyes, sizing each other up. Cillian watched them both, waiting for the first strike to come. It would kick off in three, two—

'Hello, I'm sorry I startled you earlier.' It seemed the cute burglar had other ideas. 'I'm April Statham.' She held out a hand out, but it was to Cillian. He went to shake it, tactfully brushing off the spider web that was hanging from her fingertips. She blushed, and Cillian felt a faint bloom of warmth in his chest. She met his eyes before she spoke again. 'I'm the new owner.'

Yes! a little voice inside his head said. Cillian opened his mouth to welcome her, maybe even ask her what the plans for the place were, but Martha was in like Flynn with her questioning.

'Yooouuuu?' She dragged the word out as her voice got higher and higher. By the end, dogs were heard barking outside. 'You bought this place? Just you?' April nodded patiently, looking from one to the other with a tight expression plastered across her features. 'With what, brass buttons?'

'I don't really think that this is any of your business to be honest, but—'

'Well, whose business is it then? As a resident, I have rights, I'll have you know! It's not right, picking on a vulnerable woman alone!' Cillian and April both looked at her, not a drop of sweat dripping from her brow, her clothing and hair still immaculate, apron streaked with what Cillian could now see was paint, in different shades of pinks and reds. She looked a little like Leatherface, still swinging the hefty bat in her hands. In comparison, looking at dusty, dishevelled April and her rather haunted expression, Cillian was pretty sure it wasn't going to end well.

16

'Resident?' April echoed, looking bewildered. 'Resident of what?'

Cillian heard the gulp of air Martha took in, and he intervened before she got back into full flow.

'Er yes, a resident. The old manager had an arrangement with Martha. She lives here year-round, rents chalet 1, across the way.' He pointed in the vague area of Martha's chalet, not trusting the women enough to take his eyes off them. 'I thought you would have known that.'

April sighed heavily. 'No, I didn't, but it's not the first time I've been duped. So do you have a rent book?'

Martha's eyes narrowed to tiny slits. 'Yes, of course I have, and I pay in advance. Will that be a problem?'

April brushed her hair back from her face, and Cillian noticed that she had a spider crawling down her elbow. He leaned in a little, brushing it off with his arm. April jolted at the side of him, but didn't move. She was still looking at Martha.

'That's fine,' she said eventually. 'I can sort out the paperwork and everything once I'm settled in.' Looking around her at the derelict office, which didn't have a scrap of paper, let alone a phone or a computer, her words tailed off. 'It might er … take me a minute.'

Martha made a high-pitched 'huh' sound in her throat.

'Thank you for coming, Cillian, I do appreciate it. Miss Statham? It is miss, isn't it?'

April thought for a moment, before nodding. Cillian found himself releasing the breath he was holding captive in his lungs. He thought for a second his face had been injured in the kerfuffle, but then he realised he was grinning. He dropped his face back down into neutral before anyone noticed.

'Miss Statham, I shall be ready with my rent book whenever you want to call on me.' She went to leave, but paused as she eyed the broken front door. 'If you are truly the owner, I would recommend hiring young Cillian here. He worked here before

17

the old manager Tim ground the place down. He knows his way around.' She looked around her, and Cillian noticed the way her whole body sagged as though defeated somehow. 'It would be something to see this place nice again.' She was nearly out of the room, when she turned. 'Don't forget, Cillian, this isn't just any live-in position. You deserve to be paid well too. I shall be checking, Miss Statham.' Giving Cillian a sideways look, she left. The two of them were left alone and Cillian felt obliged to fill the silence.

'I'm sorry about the misunderstanding, I really am. Martha called, told me that there was an intruder.' Nothing. April was still staring at the space that Martha had just left. 'Are you okay?'

She turned to him, and he could see she was there, but her mind was very much elsewhere. He pulled one of his last remaining business cards out of his back pocket.

'I am looking for work as it goes, so if you do need anything, let me know.'

She looked at the card, then back at him.

'You really worked here before? As what?'

'Bit of everything really. I moved here from Ireland a few years back, picked up some local work. I'm qualified in most things. Here I just did maintenance, bit of renovations here and there, heavy lifting, that sort of thing. The chalet park was a quiet place; the reception used to house the onsite shop, selling the bits the clients wanted, dealing with bookings, check-ins, you know. There used to be a games room too, but over time Tim got lazy, and the owners not being around to check on it, it just got … tired I suppose. When I asked, the money was never there for anything more than a patch-up. When are you reopening?'

One look at his prospective new boss, and Cillian knew she didn't have a clue. The woman hadn't even unpacked, let alone launched a revamp.

'Err … I don't know, soon, I know that! I need this summer to go well. I'm sort of banking on it.'

March already, Cillian thought to himself. It would take a hell of a lot of work to get this place up and running. Long days, most nights even. Great for money, if it was there, but what about Orla? He could barely work as it was, begging favours from people to get a couple of extra hours of pay, and for what? To live in a shitty flat, barely surviving?

'I do have a few hours to spare ...' he began, hoping it would be enough, and that he could pull off the juggling single dad act just a bit longer. 'If you can pay.'

'When can you start?' She cut him off, gripping the card in her hands so tight Cillian could see her fingertips turning white. 'I have a bit of a tight budget, but I can pay you.' He could feel his heartbeat in his ears. Was this it? Could he actually have a job, one he genuinely liked? He was suddenly very glad indeed that he had answered Martha's call that morning. He looked across to her chalet, and Martha's words pinged into his head. April was still talking about hourly rates, and long hours. He cut her off.

'Which chalet would be mine then?' he asked, as nonchalantly as possible. It looked like this poor lass was well out of her depth, but needs must, and he and Orla needed this. Besides, it wasn't like he wouldn't do the work. He loved being busy. 'I don't mind, as long as I have a room for my daughter.'

April was looking at him in a state of confusion now. He could see her as he flicked his head around the park, trying to be calm, cool and collected.

'Chalet? Daughter?' She was lost, and he knew it. He walked to her and held out his hand. 'I'll take the one next to yours, if you don't mind. Out of the way a bit there, handy for the equipment shed.' Another blank, worried look. 'You didn't know we have an equipment shed, did you?' She shook her head at him slowly, and he laughed gently. 'No problem, I can start today, and you have me till half two. Tomorrow, I can do more. Sound good? We can sort rates and rent out later.' He pushed his hand out a smidge closer, but she didn't take it.

'Cillian,' she said, an odd look crossing her features. 'I think I've made a big mistake, coming here. I don't really know what I'm doing.'

Her voice cracked a little, and his heart went out to her. What was she doing here, all on her own? By the look of her car, she had driven here with her whole life packed up. What was she escaping from? His hand twitched with the effort of not reaching out to touch her shoulder. He didn't want her to freak out completely – he had just body-slammed her after all. She might not be quite ready for a cuddle yet. Not that he would have tried.

'Don't fret too much yet. It's a lot of work, but most things are when they're really worth it. Let's just take it a day at a time. That sound good? You got a kettle in those boxes?' He pointed behind her at the car, and April nodded sheepishly. He grinned in response. 'First things first then, let's get the kettle on, eh?'

For the first time that day, Cillian saw April smile. She was quite cute when she did that, little dimples appearing in her pale cheeks. The sun split through the bank of clouds, lighting the grass around them outside emerald-green. The green tint came through the windows, lighting the reception area up and high-lighting her curvy body. The whole thing looked like a photo shoot, and he looked away before she caught him gawping. He didn't have the time for any of that. There was only one lady in his life, and this was all for her. All the hassle, the stress, and worry. Looking around him now though, he couldn't help but think that maybe Mondays weren't so bad after all. He couldn't wait to tell Orla all about it.

Chapter 3

'Well, that's that then.'

Martha Rodgers swirled the remnants of tea around her teacup, muttering to herself as she half leaned out of the kitchen window. 'We've had it. No hope.'

Martha's chalet was at the opposite end of the horseshoe of chalets that formed the backbone of the place. It was directly opposite the reception hut, so she had been camped out there most mornings of late, breaking her fast closely with fresh tea, hot buttered toast and jam … and a little light spying. Things were changing, and Martha wasn't one for change. Especially not now, when everything was just settling down again. The old owners had been good, sure, but they weren't exactly hands-on. It seemed like the longer they left between visits, the less they cared to return. The live-in manager Tim had always been a touch lax in his duties, and Martha had seen a marked decline in both the standards and the customers coming to holiday there.

Eventually, the tide had turned a little too much, and the owners had sold up and got rid of the manager. Martha had tried to find out who had bought the place, but the estate agents and solicitors were both depressingly tight-lipped about the whole thing. She'd expected to have to fight to stay there, but with no one to oversee, she was just … forgotten about. Her rent was paid till the end of the year, but after that, who knew what?

All she'd known before her foray into being a rather brutal batter was that it was a cash buyer, and no plans for the park or the land had been announced. She'd hated that. It had robbed her of sleep and peaceful thoughts ever since. The unknown worried her. She'd finally settled somewhere again, since her Charlie had passed, but now she felt powerless, at the whim of others. She had felt like this once before, many years ago now, but the heartache and the feeling of being trapped had never left her. She felt it just as acutely, and the pain was just as fresh. *Not this time.* She could feel herself bristle at the very thought. No one would ever tell her what to do again.

Bat safety stashed away in its hiding place, Martha carried a cup of Irish'd-up tea and her toast plate through to the second bedroom in the chalet, the one she used as her work room. After the morning she'd had, she felt rather out of sorts, unsure about her future and what the hell she was going to do with the new owner. Truth was, she could have probably bought the place herself, but who'd want to take that on? This April woman had obviously read too many 'I changed my life forever' pieces in the women's magazines and lost her marbles. It was probably a midlife crisis, given her worried and rather sweaty demeanour.

Some people had more bloody money than sense. She should have just bought herself a potter's wheel and saved herself a boatload of stress and expense. Martha had rather hoped someone with a bit of get up and go would have taken it on, seen the history and simplicity of the place for what it was. What it meant then, and now. If a place could talk … She would love to be able to have that conversation. Either way, the park wouldn't do well under Miss Statham.

Her car was barely in one piece, let alone her! What would they do now, with her at the helm? Martha couldn't bear it if the park got worse. The season was opening soon, and things were looking grim. For the first time in her life, she was glad her parents had passed on. That they didn't have to bear witness to the park's shabby state, as she did. It would have broken their hearts, given that their summers and family time were intrinsically linked to this patch of beautiful Cornish coastline. Lizard Point was home to them. It was family, and love, and enjoying the holidays that they had saved so hard all year for.

Chapter 4

April stretched her arms wide, sleep slowly leaving her body as her brain whirred and clicked back into life. She smiled to herself as she felt the sun on her face, heard the birds singing to each other in the trees. Bliss, she thought to herself, turning over to feel …

Bang. She hit the deck, having rolled off the sofa in the sitting room of her chalet. The WORST chalet out of them all, bar none. Tim's old bachelor pad. She'd only spoken to Tim on the phone, but if she had the previous manager in front of her right now, she'd have more than a few choice words to share with him. It looked like a cross between a meth lab and the bottom of a budgie birdcage. It was rank, and when she had opened the bedroom door late the night before, exhausted after a long and frantic first day, she had gagged and promptly closed it again. If she'd had the energy, she would have boarded the door up for good, or petrol-bombed the lot.

She'd brought all her bags and boxes in from the car, and they all sat around her now. She'd have slept in one of the other chalet, had she not felt the need to protect her meagre life possessions. Standing up in the *Jungle Book* themed short shorts and tank top she had managed to grab out of one of the suitcases last night, she flicked on the kettle, washing up one of the two mugs from yesterday. Cillian had been true to his word, helping her sort the reception hut out and cleaning it up as best they could. He'd been quiet but chirpier than earlier, and she had been grateful for the help, as awkward as it was.

The whole place looked unloved, but April could see the potential deep down, just as she did when she'd read that listing online. It was such a beautiful spot, perfect for family holidays, and her new life. She'd dreamed of living by the coast since she was a girl, and now here she was, where she had first felt safe as a child. Fair enough, she was single, hormonal, flat broke, hiding from all her friends and family, and currently living on a couch, but still. Chin hairs and stocky hips aside, she was the new owner of the Shady Pines, and she was going to make it work or bloody well die trying.

Which was all good talk: I am woman hear me roar! The problem was, before she could actually put her war paint on and get to work on her dream new life, she had to deal with her old one. Which meant turning her phone back on and dealing with the fallout of her moonlight flit. At thirty-five, she knew that she should be feeling rather more adult than she was currently feeling, but that was half the point of her leaving in the first place. People seemed to think her lack of fertility and loss of husband meant that she was a barren, useless husk that would be found crying and sweating in a muumuu in IKEA because she had no significant other to lug the stuff home and put it together. Her friends were all treating her differently.

Angela, one of her old work colleagues, had unfriended her on social media before sharing her baby news, then re-added her once the hubbub had died down. Did she think April was too stupid to scroll down? Did she not realise that her pregnant bump and resulting tiny human would give it away? In all honesty, being ignored or pandered to when she didn't need or want it just made her feel like a failure, a child even. It made her awkward around children.

The last time she was accosted in a coffee shop back home by an old friend and their new baby, she had felt so on show, she had ended up gabbling and patting the baby on the top of the head, as though she was a French bulldog or something. The mother and father were decidedly unimpressed, leaving April to run to the nearest shop door, mortified at her own actions, and crying at their reactions. Didn't they realise that avoiding the issue was just giving it oxygen to breathe instead?

The truth was, April had never been overly bothered about having children. Not till the moment she was told that she couldn't have them. When she was in her twenties and pictured her future, she always imagined herself by the beach, living her life, happy. Meeting Duncan at work was something she'd never expected, and so the picture had changed. When the children didn't come, the picture fell apart altogether. Now she was here, by herself, and whether she felt the need to defend her life choices or not, she would have to. Single, childless women of a certain age were treated as anomalies back in her old social circle, and she was glad to be away from it.

Picking herself up off the floor, she headed to the bathroom. It wasn't too bad in here after her earlier scrub fest. All the chalets were in good condition; they just needed a bit of a makeover, a deep clean that would make Kim and Aggie get a sweat on, and some home comforts. The skip that was Tim's chalet was one of the worst things about the place, and given that it was her home, she could put up with it. There was of course the odd collapsing door and rotten window frame, but Cillian seemed to be on the ball with everything, so she was trying to keep her panic levels low key. Martha, the resident she had seemingly inherited along with the park and a pile of problems, was obviously not impressed with her being the new owner. At one point, April thought that Martha might actually nobble her with the bat, but she had been decidedly quiet that afternoon.

She'd been surprised to find herself agreeing to Cillian's live-in position. She hadn't envisaged many people in the beginning, and now she had a grumpy octogenarian with a violent streak and a family living next to her. The thought of Cillian's daughter coming to live here made April feel a little odd. She couldn't imagine having a kid around, although she knew she was being stupidly naive. Holiday parks meant families, grandchildren, school trips. There was no avoiding seeing the tiny human portion of the population, no matter how she tried. Who could? They were everywhere, like flies around manure or bees around honey. The fact that she compared children to insects flying around a turd wasn't lost on her, and she was glad she was alone and couldn't blurt it out to anyone.

Why did the fact she couldn't have children make her this way? Some days, she wanted to scream at all the pregnant women moaning about their aches and pains. She often saw fraught parents shouting at a crying child on the street back home, or in the supermarket, the mother looking hollow-eyed and miserable, the child crying and shuddering with emotion. Didn't they realise how good they had it? Would she have been that person?

She knew it wasn't like that, not really. She got that motherhood was hard – hell, her own mother had shown her real strength, just by being out there, trying to live her life. She had been in her mother's shoes, packing up her life and driving to Shady Pines for a new start. She'd felt the connection so keenly at times that it felt like her mother was actually sitting in the car with her, listening to CDs and crying at the sad songs. How her mother had found the strength to go on, to raise her child and still keep smiling, she'd never know. It made her love and miss her all the more, so much her heart hurt. She wished she could talk to her now, tell her how grateful she was. *Thanks, Mum, for making me at least half as brave as you.*

Thinking about growing a new life inside her body left her nothing but cold now. She would never know that joy, so she shut herself away from it. Some days, it was easy. Days like today, dreading the arrival of a small person who had done nothing wrong, it wasn't so simple to understand. She really didn't want to pat another child on the head like a cocker spaniel any time soon. How old was his daughter anyway, and what about the mother? What did she think about moving to a chalet here again, and her husband working for a tearful woman who couldn't hang a front door? The whole thing had her stomach in knots. It made her think of Duncan, and a day some months back, when she'd felt just as anxious.

'God, I'm so depressed,' April murmured to herself, kicking a frilly grey scatter cushion off the bed with enough force that it propelled across the huge white and grey room, hitting Duncan's trouser press that sat to one side of the large bay window. From the walk-in shower in the en suite, a voice called out.

'You say something, honey?' His deep rich voice echoed against the tiled walls, the water still running as he showered for work.

'No, nothing,' she lied, lying back against the plush sheets. 'Just falling apart quietly over here.' She said it so he wouldn't hear, of course. He was already in work mode, his suit laid out on the dresser, the jaunty cherry-coloured cufflinks she'd bought him for their wedding anniversary sat on top.

Her phone beeped at the other side of the room, where it sat on charge. The sound set her teeth on edge. She'd had the foresight to book the day off, but she hadn't told Duncan why. She couldn't tell him; she felt embarrassed. More than that, she just knew he wouldn't understand either.

'So, what are you up to today?' he asked, finally turning off the power shower and walking into the bedroom with a fluffy white towel around his tight little waist. Duncan was ... well ... buff, for lack of a better word. She couldn't help but think about the day they'd met, and how taken she'd been by him. He'd been seated at her table for a business meeting, and it wasn't the only deal he clinched that day. That night, they'd had their first date, and the rest was history.

'Not much,' she muttered. 'I might go to the gym.' *Spend half my life there anyway, trying to stay clear of the chub rub the fancy dresses always cause. Sweatpants were created by the god of comfort. Sometimes, a couture gown leaves me feeling like I've spent a night on the rack in the Red Room. Chance would be a fine thing these days.* Baby making was more about the quantity, not the quality.

'You should,' he said, coming to sit on the bed and reaching under the sheet to pinch her midriff. 'You could do with a bit of toning up, less air in the old tyre!' April shrank away from him, and he laughed. 'Oh come on, I'm only kidding. The gym would be good though, get you out of the house. I do worry about you, rattling around here all day when you're not "working".' He air-quoted 'working' with raised hands, and April said nothing. She loved her job at the hotel, and it had been a lifeline to her over the years. It wasn't up to Duncan's swanky job, but she didn't envy him that either. There was more to life than sharp suits and flash cars. She supposed it was why they worked. She felt safe with him, and he felt secure that she was with him for him, and not the trappings

Why they had worked, a tiny little voice that sounded suspiciously like hers whispered in her head. *Had worked.* Lately, she wasn't quite so sure. Everything that once appealed to her angered her now. His ability to shrug things off. Lose himself in work, and statistics of conception techniques. Not sexy. Her phone pinged again, and Duncan stood up off the bed and fetched it for her.

'Here, maybe it's one of the girls.'

She smiled weakly, but didn't take it from him. His smile dimmed, just for a second, and he dropped it onto the bed next to her. 'I'd better go, early conference call from London.'

He leaned over her, taking her face between her hands and looking at her earnestly.

'April, you will get through this. I promise. Get outside today, please. You need any money?'

She scowled at him, and he pretended to jump in fright.

'Okay, okay, I was only asking. Have a good day.' He brushed his lips against hers, the tiniest scrap of a kiss.

'Love you,' she told him.

'I know,' he said, tapping the end of her nose once with his index finger. 'Best be off.'

He left her lying in their huge plush bed, staring at her phone. With a resigned sigh, she picked it up, looking through her notifications. The usual discount emails from the online clothing shops she used in favour of braving the harsh strip lighting and stick-thin shop assistants, trying on gorgeous clothes that made her look like sausage meat the second she donned them. Another email offered her a penis enlargement for only $2000, and the next one told her that she had won £18 million from a distant cousin, an African prince no less. Perhaps she could afford the penis enlargement then. A good day.

Then came the social media notifications, and she skimmed through them as quickly as possible. Nothing much really, but Hayley from work had posted, tagging her, and she clicked on it by accident. A photo popped up, with a caption.

'Lottie's first day at big school! Thanks so much **April Statham** for the gorgeous book bag! Can't believe my baby is so grown up!' It was followed by an alarming number of emojis and hashtags, crying faces, a school icon and a little girl emoji. Hashtags like #thanksauntieApril #biggirlnow #dontcry #mybaby and the one she always dreaded: #blessed.

#blessed was April's arch nemesis. She hated it. She used to use it herself, back in the day. She'd even set up an Instagram account to document her new married life with Duncan. Pictures of sunsets and fancy cocktails from Duncan's work trips, her tagging along and reading half the airport bookshop's paperbacks by the pool while he worked in the day. Now she barely went online, let alone posted anything. What would she post today? Social media was full of little children and young adults, all beaming in uniform, nervous smiles to the camera as their parents stood them against front doors and in front of houses and fireplaces around the country.

How on earth could she tell Duncan she just couldn't face the day? He would coo and make all the right noises, but she knew he didn't get it. Not really. The fact was that her front door was empty of tiny humans, and she just couldn't bear it today. She pulled the cover over herself, turned off her phone, and went back to sleep. The one thing she consoled herself with, as she drifted off, was that she had Duncan, and they were in this together. Had she known the truth, the tears might just have fallen that bit faster.

When Duncan had first suggested having a baby, she'd known it wouldn't be easy. Duncan was so upbeat, so utterly convinced that having enough money to throw at a problem was the answer. It wasn't though, and every failed attempt and test result turned to a wedge between them. While April researched, and obsessed, and worked out secretly at the gym, Duncan worked. He got busier and more distracted. Secretive even. The elephant in the room was the missing baby, and the fact that Duncan longed for it so much. Every day, April disappointed him more. Rejection chokes out intimacy, and right now, April could barely breathe.

Chapter 5

It was well past lunchtime when April's stomach started to growl so loudly she could hear it over the portable radio. She straightened up, her vest top and denim shorts splattered with paint, and admired her handiwork. She was systematically painting the outside of the chalets to brighten them up, and had decided to paint each one a different colour. She wanted them to look like beach huts, all jaunty colours and themed chalets. At present they looked rather like the remnants of a concentration camp, instead of somewhere that people would love to holiday at.

April knew that in this business, word of mouth and repeat custom were paramount, and made all the difference. She had sunk every penny she had into this place, and the pitiful amount she had left in her personal bank account needed to last long enough to cover the repairs and get the place up and running. She needed to live cheap and make the most of the money in her new business account. She needed this place to be what it once was, what she remembered as a girl, and not only that, it had to be better. It had to work, because otherwise she would … well, she didn't even want to think about that. After everything she had been through, she refused to go home with her tail between her legs. She had no home anymore. This patch of Cornish land was her hill, and if she had to die on it, so be it.

Placing the lid on the paint pot she was using, this one being a gorgeous mint-green colour, she took her brushes and went to head home. A voice called out to her. Martha.

'You shouldn't just rinse those brushes you know. It's best if you get them cleaned properly. That cheap outdoor paint tends to dry into horrible little globules on the budget brushes.'

April looked down at her brushes, then walked over to Martha. She was sitting outside the front of her chalet, in an egg-shaped chair. A sketch board and a few pencils sat next to a pitcher of lemonade on a side table next to her.

'What would you recommend, Martha?' April held out her brushes and Martha reached for them. Turning to her side, she lifted a small bin and unceremoniously dumped the brushes straight into it, slapping her hands together for effect.

'That,' she said bluntly, tossing her head towards the bin behind her. 'Buy new brushes and get better paint. That chalet you started looks like a huge ball of snot. Lemonade?'

April took a deep breath, winded by the sheer number of putdowns that Martha had expelled with pure finesse, and found herself nodding yes. Martha kissed her teeth and stood up, rubbing at her knee.

'I'll get a glass. The pitcher in the fridge is colder.'

April's sneaker-clad feet stood just outside the threshold, toes a half inch away from entering the chalet. Martha glanced back and rolled her eyes, making the little half moon glasses sitting on the end of her nose lift and drop back down.

'I suppose technically it's your property, so do come in.'

April checked the bottom of her feet for any stray paint flecks before walking in.

'Wow,' was all she could say. It was as if she had stepped into another world. The inside of the chalet was unrecognisable from the others on the park. Here, art hung on every available wall

33

space, on the cushion covers, even the rug was a rug hook version of 'The Scream', and it spanned the hallway area, making the whole place colourful. April's eyes were on stalks. She just couldn't take it all in fast enough. 'Did you do all this?'

Even Martha smiled now.

'I did, for the most part. Cillian is a dab hand with a hammer, he helped when he could.'

April was still scanning the room, trying and failing to be polite and not look around the place like she was an eager burglar.

'Well, it's beautiful,' she breathed eventually. Her gaze fell on a photo frame near a large flat-screen television that sat on a whitewashed wood dresser. A wedding photo, black and white, of a young man in a suit, and a tall determined-looking woman in white at the side of him. Martha saw her looking, but neither spoke a word.

Martha pulled a large glass pitcher out of her fridge, pouring two glasses out and filling them with ice.

'It's homemade, but I don't like it too sweet,' she warned as she passed April a glass. April lifted the glass to her lips and waited for a tangy taste on her tongue, but it was beautiful. She hadn't realised how thirsty she was. She'd drained half the glass without even trying. Martha held out the jug and refilled her glass. Pointing to the outside chair, she started to walk back outside.

'I have a recliner, in the corner. Just pull it out.'

April did as she was asked, and soon the pair were sitting like old friends, looking out at the park, drinking their lemonade. They were sitting like old friends, of course, but that was where the similarity ended. Martha was sitting rather dourly, looking at April as though she was looking for a label.

'Something wrong, Martha?' April asked.

'Why did you come here?' Martha countered at the speed of light. 'Why did you buy this place?'

'It's an investment opportunity,' she trotted out, as she had to ninety-nine per cent of the people back home. 'I wanted a challenge, a change of pace.' Martha snorted, and April's eyes widened.

'Did you get that from one of those daytime programmes? It sounds like a script.'

It is a script, April agreed silently. *That's exactly what it is. It hides my pain.*

'Nothing of the sort,' she said nonchalantly. 'I've worked in hospitality for a long time, and it was time for something new to sink my teeth into.' That part was true, at least.

'Oh?' Marta replied. 'What jobs have you done?'

This is feeling more and more like a job interview by the second. I own her home, and yet I feel like I haven't earned the right to be here yet. Why do I feel out of place everywhere I go?

'I worked in a hotel chain for many years.'

'Worked in one? As what, the manager?' Martha opened her sketchpad, angling it away from April, and started working on it with a pencil. Her eyes never left April's.

'Well … no but I did work in many different roles there. I learned a lot.' She was mumbling into her neck now like a naughty schoolgirl who'd been dragged in front of the headmaster.

'No?' Martha asked, an incredulous note in her tone. 'Never managed anything, have you? Chin up when you're speaking, dear.' April raised her chin, and Martha gave her an approving look. One that you would get from your nan when you remembered your P's and Q's.

April opened her mouth to plead her case, but then she realised she didn't have the experience on paper, so there was no point in lying to herself, or anyone else for that matter.

'I have the paperwork and insurance I need, and once the guests start coming, it will be fine.' She didn't know whether she actually believed that herself, or whether she was just telling Martha what she thought she wanted to hear. 'And I have Cillian now. He has the knowledge and background of the place. I'm sure we can get organised soon enough.'

Martha said nothing, just sat staring out at the chalet park. April looked across at the half-painted hut. In the sunlight, half-wet, it did have a certain bogey-like tinge to it. Hopefully once it was dry properly it would settle a little lighter. The tin had declared the colour to be Green Tea. Maybe the cheaper paints *were* a bad idea. The truth was though, her car had barely made it to the DIY store and back, and she had nearly fainted at the price of the higher end paint pots. Laughable really, since her old home was all designer wallpaper and Farrow & Ball paint. *How the other half live, eh.*

'This place used to be glorious,' Martha said, half to herself, half to April. 'The chalets were all painted fresh every year, and at the end of the season, the owners would throw a huge beach BBQ and party, to round the year off. All the locals would attend – it was a big highlight here, ending the summer off properly. Those parties were such fun, everyone together.'

April watched Martha's face light up as she talked about the old days here, and she found herself even more determined to bring the place back to its former glory, to get those days back, to build a sense of community here, just like she felt in the rest of Cornwall. How she'd felt when she'd come here with her mother.

'It ended not long after the last party I went to. The owners decided to take a step back. They got Tim in, and that was that. The next year, the party just didn't happen. Of course, I was married by then.' April saw her expression change, a flash of pain evident on her face. Maybe Martha needed this place to work just as much as she did.

'Is that why you moved here?' The words fell out of her mouth before she could stop them, but Martha didn't flinch.

'When my Charlie died, I was left in a big old house, full of memories and draughts, and cobwebs in corners I just couldn't reach anymore. I was gathering dust myself I think. It just made sense.' She tapped her hand on the wooden doorframe next to her affectionately, as you would a faithful hound. 'I work better here, always have. I started renting the chalet as a workspace at first, but then gradually, there was so much of my stuff gravitating over here that it didn't make sense to keep the other place. What did you run from?' Her blue eyes focused on April like a hawk would on a field mouse.

'Husband.'

'Still?'

'No. All finalised.'

Martha nodded. 'Anyone else back home?'

April thought of her mother, who'd travelled with her in the boot with her worldly belongings. She had friends, sure, but even those had drifted of late. Without her job, her world had gotten a lot smaller back in Yorkshire in those last few weeks.

'No, not now. My mum passed a few months ago.'

It felt as if Martha patted her hand, just once, the lightest touch. By the time she had looked to check, Martha was back scribbling in her sketchpad.

'Do you have anyone?' April asked, with a genuine longing to know the answer. Martha looked at her over the top of her glasses.

'I have friends, but no, not really. Not since Charlie. It seems like we are on our own, eh?'

It was a throwaway comment from Martha, but it felt like a javelin to the heart to April. She felt as though it was embedded in her chest, leaving her wholly unable to speak, or to protest that she wasn't alone. Not like Martha anyway. Martha was bitter, April wasn't. Not yet. There was still time for her to change her life. Martha seemed perfectly happy living in her bubble.

'For now perhaps, but I'll be busy soon enough.'

Martha pursed her lips. 'Well, that depends on what you turn this place into I suppose. I for one will be watching with interest.'

She was still scribbling away, her pencil making long sweeping lines. Other than the sound of the sea, it was all they could hear as they sat regarding each other.

'I'd better get back to it I suppose,' April said after a time, feeling more and more awkward by the moment. It felt like Martha had dismissed her like a schoolmarm. Martha gave her a curt nod, and she was almost out of earshot when Martha spoke again.

'About Cillian? He's a good man. Heart of gold. Fiercely loyal. Look after him.'

Look after him? An odd thing to say.

'Er, I will. I'll make sure he's paid the going rate, minus a bit for rent of course.'

Martha snorted with laughter. It took a few seconds for April to realise it was laughter, and not a stray biscuit crumb down the wrong hole.

'You'll see, love. We here at Lizard Point are a close-knit bunch, but secrets hide in plain sight like ornaments on a hearth.' She lowered her sketchpad a little as April stared at her open-mouthed. 'Look after him, that's all I'm saying. He's had a rough time lately.'

April found herself nodding along, wondering what secrets hung on the hearths of the people she'd met so far. What did she mean?

A van pulled into the chalet park, and April's worries fell out of her head. Her first delivery was here for the chalet shop, the basics, with more stuff coming later. She was going to get this place up and running, and keep her head down. As she smiled a greeting at the affable delivery driver, she was aware of how her guts churned at the thought of home, and what she had left behind. Maybe she shouldn't have left at all. Maybe this was the biggest mistake of the whole tragedy that seemed to be her life. She padded over to the office, to let the man deliver the boxes, and pushed the terror she felt down into the depths of her mind. She would focus on what she could change, not what she couldn't. After today, she would have a neighbour, and a helper, and she was determined to make the very best of both.

'She's so annoying! I mean it, Paddy – it's not going to work! I was better off in the crummy flat.'

Paddy rolled his eyes back in his head as he lifted his pint glass to his pouting lips. Cillian started to speak again, but Paddy held an index finger up to pause him, and kept drinking. Once half of the glass of amber liquid had been drunk, he reluctantly placed the glass back on the table and wiped the froth from his moustache.

'Really? Old Shady Pines that bad? Surely she can't be any worse than Tim. You put up with him long enough.'

'She doesn't have a clue.'

It was true, she didn't. He'd felt bad about going along with Martha's plan of him living in, but when they'd gone into the reception hut and discussed her plans, he'd realised just how skittish she was. How much she needed things to work out. Which meant pressure on him, to come through for her. What was she doing here? He couldn't help but feel like he had to help her now. The thing was, he couldn't get attached. He was already thinking about what she was doing now. What she would look like when he rolled up to live next door. He needed to keep her at arm's length. Focus on how bad a boss she was at the moment, all fingers and thumbs. His head was in a quandary, so being annoyed by her seemed to be easier. In his head anyway. The male brain was a wonderful thing. *Who said all we think about are boobies and football?*

'Tim didn't.' Paddy's raised brows said it all, but he said more anyway. Typical Paddy and his *Dr Phil* obsession. 'The man was a charlatan, and a lazy eejit to boot. This woman sounds like she's just out of her depth. Sound familiar?' The brows went again. 'We've all been there, mate. Shit happens, and we have to make a life.'

'She's not from round here.'

'Neither are you. Neither was Tim. What is this, the Mexican border?'

'She's a woman though.'

Paddy guffawed at that one.

'Oh no, a bloody woman! You should have said! Aren't you raising a future woman, single-handed? Come on, Cillian. You're not sexist. What's really the problem?'

Cillian huffed, straightening up in his seat, ready to give his friend what for, and list all the numerous reasons he had for not liking the new owner. Except, now Paddy had dismissed his concerns, he didn't actually know why he wouldn't like her. Maybe it was because she had up and bought a great big whack off chalet park single-handed, with seemingly no experience or help. Who did that? Cillian just couldn't understand it. Was she some sort of trust fund kid, spending her parents' money on some frivolous whim? She didn't look it, and her wheels weren't exactly posh. What was she doing here? This question just went around and around in his head, and all signs pointed to her not sticking around. All the more reason to focus on the negative and shut off his heart. Which, annoyingly, seemed to be beating that bit faster around her.

Paddy was watching him with a tiny little smirk on his face, and Cillian glared at him.

'All right, fair enough now. So she's not a total horror, but still, I ask you. Who just turns up in Cornwall with a car full of stuff, and nothing else?'

Paddy's eyes glinted with suppressed mirth. 'Er … you … me, half the bloody pub. People change their lives all the time. We did.'

Paddy was Irish too, but contrary to popular belief, they didn't know each other from Ireland. Paddy had moved here after his first marriage ended, and he needed a fresh start. He worked on the fishing boats, and years later, he was still here.

'I know, but I still don't like it. What if she just ups and leaves, and the place turns to shit again?'

Paddy stood up, taking both their pint pots and heading to the bar for a refill. 'Mate, it was shit before Tim left. She has to open properly first, and keep it booked up. You at least have the season to save some cash up for you and the little one.'

While Paddy went to get the drinks, Cillian sat and thought about what Paddy had said. It was true, he was there for the next few months anyway, provided the wages kept coming. They were out of the grotty flat, into a chalet that needed work but was still far better. They had heat, and food, and he could finally begin putting some money aside. If he could save enough for rent and a deposit, they could finally move into a little house somewhere. Orla deserved a home, and she had never really experienced one before. Not like other kids had at least, and even then not for long. He picked up the beer mat in front of him, distractedly pulling at it, lost in thought. His phone rang in his pocket, and when he saw the screen his heart sank. Not today.

'Where the hell is my daughter?' an angry voice screamed out the second he hit the green button. He turned the volume down on his handset and lifted it to his ear. 'I got a letter from the Child Benefit people today. You're trying to take the money!'

'Well, good afternoon to you. It's not your money, it's for the benefit of the child. As in Orla, not the landlord of the Lamb and Flag. Our daughter is fine, thank you. She's got an extra afternoon session today.'

Orla was going to full-time nursery in September, but because of the unsettled year she had endured, her anxiety was sky-high. The teachers were helping her as much as possible, including giving her extra time there in school to get her used to the huge change that was coming her way. Ideally, he shouldn't be moving at this time in her life, but they needed to get out of where they were, and fast. Orla needed her own room. She deserved to have a space that was just hers. She deserved a proper bed of her own, not a second-hand one shared with her dad. Shady Pines was the way out, and he had seized it with both muscular arms. He knew Tina wouldn't be happy, but it was Orla's money. She needed it far more than her feckless mother.

'What does she need extra time for?'

Cillian didn't answer her. If she didn't know about her own daughter by now, that was on her.

'For Orla's benefit, that's why. So she feels settled when she goes full-time. I did tell you, Tina. She starts in September. Did you want something, other than to yell?'

There was a pause on the line, and across the pub, Paddy raised his brows, questioning who was on the phone. Cillian mouthed *Tina* at him, and Paddy's face turned dark. He made a motion at Cillian with his hands, pretending to end the call on his own imaginary mobile phone. Bev behind the bar looked on, giving Cillian a little smile as she caught his eye. Cillian nodded at Paddy, knowing he was right.

The truth was, he was never sure just how fast things were going to get nasty, so he needed to keep the peace. He hadn't told her that they were moving yet, and he didn't want anything to stop that. Now the social workers were backing off, he didn't want them getting involved again. He wasn't the problem, and the move would be so good for them both. The social workers had agreed too, given his past employment there and Orla knowing the place a little. He needed to be there, the whole thing a done deal, before he even thought about telling Tina.

He headed outside, away from ear-ridden walls. The smoking shelter was empty. He sat on one of the painted wooden benches, getting a waft of old cigarette smoke and ash, and the smell of the flowers that were in planters dotted around the garden area.

'I did actually. I wondered if I could see her.'

Cillian didn't say anything himself this time. He felt like his tongue had been glued to the roof of his mouth.

'NO,' a voice said, stern. 'Not a chance.'

He'd hit the red button and was on his feet and back through the doors of the pub before he even recognised that the voice belonged to him. His legs felt like jelly, and the rage and sheer shock was fizzing through his whole body. Just the sound of her

42

voice did that to him. He couldn't imagine facing her in real life any time soon, but it was coming. He just knew it.

Paddy was sitting with his pint in his hand, Cillian's on the table, sitting on a new beer mat. Paddy took one look at him and turned to Bev.

'Bev, we will need that packet of pork scratchings after all, and lend us the phone, will ya?'

Bev nodded, taking the cordless phone off the hook on the wall and bringing it over with two big bags of pork scratchings. Her gaze lingered on Cillian, but to be honest, the Duracell bunny could have been standing in front of him, and he wouldn't have known. Paddy took the phone from her, shooing her away and handing Cillian the phone.

'Mate, I love you, but you're being a prize berk now, and enough's enough. Ring the damn number already. Get this sorted before it gets worse.'

Cillian thought of Orla, a little scrap of life, huddled between her old bed and the bedroom wall, reading in the near pitch black because she couldn't reach the light switch. His chest clenched, and he took the handset from his friend. He was right, as usual. It was time. Cillian needed to protect his daughter, and he needed to make it happen now. He needed to tell people. When the brown stuff hit the fan, and hit it would, he would need them. Even the confusing Yorkshire woman who had unknowingly handed him a paddle to get him out of the creek.

Paddy smiled when Cillian started to dial a number from a piece of paper in his wallet, and he patted his friend on the back of his hand.

'Proud of you, mate, you're doing the right thing.'

Cillian smiled back, and made all the right noises, but as he waited for the call to connect, he knew the only thing he felt was crushing disappointment, and the weight of the world on his tired and aching shoulders. He felt like he was betraying Tina once more, but it was down to her. The pressure and isolation of motherhood had turned her to drink, and away from him and their small daughter. When she'd left Orla alone, that had been the final straw.

He'd thought so at the time. Till now. Now, he was going to use the law to protect a daughter from her mother and protect their family from going under altogether. He was finally going to listen to those around him. He just hoped that Orla would understand when she was older. If he lost her anyway, that would kill him.

Chapter 6

Cillian left the pub in search of mints and a little bag of sweets for Orla. He'd only had two pints of shandy, but he still felt like he had been dipped in a brewery. Like the nursery staff would smell it on him and whisk Orla away to some rosy-cheeked Walton family. He had these irrational thoughts daily. He knew why, and the earlier conversation with Tina hadn't helped any. He could feel his fists clench at his sides, as he thought of Tina being in Orla's life again. It made him feel sick to his stomach, so sick and helpless that he wanted to scoop up his daughter and run away forever.

The fact was, men walked away from children all the time. It was part of life, seemingly. Cillian's own dad hadn't been much cop, and he didn't even know where the old fella was now. His mum was happy back in Ireland, busy with his sister's kids, loving life. He'd thought about going home, but Lizard Point felt more like home now, and Orla had always lived here. Besides, he didn't put it past Tina to have him arrested at the airport the minute he tried.

Heading out of the little corner shop, he waved at Sue, the shopkeeper, and she waved back jovially, her tight curls not moving on her head as she went about her business. Everything was packed up at the flat, their worldly belongings amounting to a toy box and a few boxes and bags. All of which were now sitting in the back of the van. The flat had looked so forlorn and empty. The stark reality of their situation wasn't lost on him.

Tina still lived in their old flat, but even with his key, he wouldn't go back there again. Not a chance. It wasn't his home anymore, and it definitely wasn't Orla's. He drove near there a few weeks ago, and Orla had tried to take off her seatbelt to hide in the footwell. Cillian had ended up having to pull over and sit with her in his arms until she stopped crying, and the shaking stopped. That's why he could never forgive Tina. She didn't see just what damage she had caused, and now she was calling again, demanding money, to see her daughter. For what end, he had no idea but he wasn't interested.

All he wanted now was to protect his child and give her the home that she'd almost had and needed badly. Tina could come at him with whatever she had, but Orla would never relive a time like that again. Fifteen minutes later, when he pulled the van into the nursery car park, the promise rang in his head like bells as he saw who was at the nursery gates.

Clicking a button on his car phone kit, he waited till Paddy answered.

'She's here, Pad. School gates.'

Paddy took a beat to answer. 'They know not to entertain her, right?'

Cillian nodded.

'Cill?'

'Sorry, yeah they know everything. They have her photo in the office.' He wiped his palms down his trousers distractedly.'

'Right, mate, so you're covered. Stay calm and get our little girl. If you have to wait or you need a lift, ring me.'

'Thanks, mate, ring you when we're home.'

'Home already, is it? Good, get there in one piece then, eh? Keys in hand, mate, phone stuck to my arse. K?'

'K,' Cillian repeated, hanging up. Taking a deep breath, he reached for the van door handle.

The chalet next to April's was looking great. She'd been scrubbing every available surface inside, making sure that the huge pile of bedding had been freshly washed and put on the beds. It was a beautiful chalet now, if a little bare. In the other chalets, which she was going through slowly, there was scope to add some personal touches to the rooms, but she didn't want to intrude too much in this one, given who was going to be staying there.

She had cut some wild flowers from the large patch she had on her land, and they looked lovely in one of her vases from home. In truth, it was a rather expensive cut crystal vase that she had received as a wedding present, but she had no need or want for it to be in her new home. She just hadn't wanted to leave it for Duncan to enjoy. He loved it, and it was one of the little victories that she took solace in. When she thought of that vase, or saw it, she would remember that tiny win. The vase looked beautiful here, the vibrancy of the flowers lit up by the light streaming through the window. It shone through the glass, painting pretty patterns across the living space. Without the taint of where it came from, the vase actually looked at home here, and it made April smile.

Walking through the chalet, she looked around the tidy kitchen, the dining area, the lounge. The sofas were perfect now that they were cleaned up, and the whole place was looking brighter already. She was planning to paint the outside yellow and call it the Sunflower Chalet, but of course Cillian might not be a fan. It seemed to her that he wasn't a fan of much, for in the limited time they had spent together working on the park, he hadn't done much more than grunt at her and offer up the odd helpful nugget of advice, before going back to silently working again.

Of course, it had only been a day. They'd only had the one afternoon together, and his stony face when she told him of her plans couldn't be missed. Given that all she'd done so far was paint a chalet to look like a bogey and clean the place, she couldn't blame him for thinking she was an airhead. They had a long way to go before things were shipshape. She didn't mind the quiet working either; it suited her fine. Given her own hormonal mood swings when her polycystic ovarian syndrome decided to throw her a heavy period, she could understand feeling a certain way. Hating people a little. Hell, when her hormones were in full flow, she pretty much hated the world and wanted to lock herself away with a hot water bottle and the latest weepy saga book to curl up with.

She understood moods, and feeling angry and frustrated about things. She had an idea that he was going through something but what, she didn't know. Everyone else around here seemed to have an inkling. Martha had dropped enough hints at it. Maybe it was having to move again. No one liked that. She herself had cried half the journey down here, part relief and part grief. Her life as she knew it was over, but she didn't realise how much in limbo she had been back home. How unsettled she'd felt. Maybe Cillian felt the same. Plus, she'd only been driving with the remnants of her old life, and her dead mother in the back. She had moved with family, but it wasn't remotely the same. Maybe Cillian was just making the best of a bad situation. Maybe he was just grumpy.

Martha sure was a prickly pear at times. Perhaps the famed Cornish air was a little off today. Or maybe it was she herself, her Yorkshire ways rubbing others up the wrong way. She'd felt that way at home, like she was surplus somehow. On the fringe of life, watching others live it and never quite being part of the gang. Her mother would despair at her thought pattern if she knew. She shook herself out of her reverie and went to check the bedrooms.

This chalet was a two-bedroom one, with twin beds and a double in the master. The sheets were all on now, and the rooms smelled clean and fresh. She'd even found a little pink teddy among her belongings, one that her mother had given her as a daft present one birthday. They were always doing that. Her mother was obsessed with cows and birds, so she'd often woken to a phone full of pictures from her, from the Yorkshire Show, or her daily dog walks. One of the last photos she'd sent her was of a robin, a little red-breasted fellow that had come to visit her mother daily in the hospice. On the last day, it had appeared again. Her mother's eyes had flickered when April told her, her head moving towards the window, as though her soul was searching for it.

The day after, when April had dragged herself, alone and numb, back to say goodbye to everyone she'd looked out of that window for the longest time. The robin didn't show. April liked to think it was because her mother was gone, and the robin had done its job.

Realising that she was looking at a teddy, crying her eyes out, she sat down in the easy chair she had installed in the room. It was a dusky pink colour, which matched the bedspread she'd dug out of the storage she'd bought along with the rest of the place. The previous manager might have been a really poor employee, but the storage reflected how the management had planned the place to be. Their loss, her gain.

From the chair, she could see the beach off in the distance, and it was away from the front, looking out not onto the other chalets, but on the landscape around them. It was a beautiful room for a little girl. She found herself choking up again at the thought of the new arrivals, but the sound of a van stirred her into action. Shit! They were here, and here she was crying in their child's new room like some kind of crazy Miss Havisham stereotype.

She was out of the back door a mere second or two before she heard the front door open. She pushed the back door closed as quietly as she could, hoping that the air wouldn't whoosh through the cottage, and give her away as an intruder. Listening for a moment, she heard something heavy being put on the floor, and the low rumble of a single voice. Peeping through the kitchen window, she saw a tall shadow, and ducked under the sill. Shimmying across the chalet wall, head dipped, she crab-walked the length of the chalet. Peeking around the corner of the building, she could see the van, the doors open, blocking most of her view.

She took a deep breath and jumped across the space between the chalets like a long jumper, lengthy desperate strides propelling her into the back of her own chalet, and safety. She was so involved in her Tom Cruise impression, *Mission Impossible* Cornwall edition, that she didn't see the woman standing some distance away, beach side, with a rotund brown chicken under one arm and a box of eggs under the other.

As April flattened her backside to the back door of her chalet, reaching desperately for the doorknob so she could pretend to be a grown-up, and not a gibbering idiot who seemed to thrive lately in social faux pas, she spotted her. The hen the woman was holding let out a 'bawk' as if to say 'what the hell are you doing, woman?'

'Hello again,' the woman said jovially. 'Settling in?'

'Oh, hi!' April tried to stage whisper across to her, while trying to appear like she was just hanging out on her land, casually leaning against her door. And not, as she was, trying to avoid making a total tit of herself in front of the man she had just hired to help the place stay afloat. While not crying over his family or offending his wife by basically being some kind of interior designer in a home that wasn't hers to make. Although technically, it was her home. And now she was rambling in her own head, as the chicken woman looked at her with an amused half-smile on her face. Even the chicken looked like it had a better handle on the situation. 'Yes, thanks. You know, busy busy!'

'Yes.' The woman smirked again as a noise from the front made April jump and her hand reach for the back doorknob ever more frantically. 'Listen, I want you to come see me.' She pointed towards the edge of April's property, where in the distance a bright blue wooden gate could be seen. A goat was looking through it, bleating occasionally at them all as it peeked through the slats of wood.

'Yes, Elvis! I'm coming; stop being pushy!' the woman blurted, stepping forward and placing the egg box onto the grass in front of her. 'That goat will be the death of me, I swear.' April looked at her again, and then it clicked.

'You're the woman who was here the day I arrived!' she exclaimed dumbly. The woman nodded at her, no expression on her face.

'Yes that's me. Congratulations for remembering what happened yesterday. More brains than a goldfish at least! There is hope after all. Judith Canter. Come see me, okay? Whenever you're done here?' April opened her mouth to say that she couldn't, she had her first 'guests' coming and she needed to get things in some kind of order.

'I don't like people being late, so think on.' She dipped her head towards the box. 'The eggs are on me. Come along, Petunia.'

April could swear the chicken clucked back at Judith in agreement. The goat was still watching at the gate, his lip curling up at one side comically. April slid down the wall, throwing her legs out in front of her and wincing at the sharp pains that ran through her half-asleep limbs.

'Mum,' she half whispered to herself, the occasional muted thud and skitter of shale being heard behind her over the sound of the sea. 'I know this is supposed to be an adventure, but I really could use you about now.'

She waited a few moments, not waiting for her mother to answer exactly, but just feeling better thinking of her. She remembered the summer they had spent here, and her mother had spoken of it so many times over the years. It had been just the two of them all summer. Her mother had collected her from school, early on the last day of term. April remembered feeling worried. Her mother never collected her early, but there she was. She'd bundled her and her school bag into the back of the car, where blankets, pillows, toys and clothes sat packaged up. They'd driven all the way down to Cornwall, arriving long after dark, not stopping once. She still remembered the sign she'd woken up to as they arrived at their destination. Her mother's headlights bouncing back off the sign, showing little April where they were to spend their summer. Shady Pines Chalet Park.

April thought back to that night, when she'd sat swaddled on the back seat, wondering where Dad was, why Mum hadn't mentioned him. And now here she was, back here again, and still feeling like the confused little slip of life in the back seat. The difference was, this time she really was alone, and she was still hiding. She clenched her fists, and dusting herself off, she got back up, picked up the egg box, and headed into her chalet to go and meet the new arrivals.

Coming out of her front door as though she was just hanging at home, she did a pretend double take at the van. Cillian, a box of food in his hand, turned and looked at her. For a moment, neither spoke.

'Hi!' April said shrilly. 'Oops, sorry. I was a little loud then. I've been indoors cleaning.'

'Really?' a voice across the park called. 'I thought I just saw you commando rolling between the chalets.' April's eyes flashed to Martha's and she winked at her. 'Must have been a trick of the light. You okay today, Cillian?' Martha's expression softened when she looked at Cillian. She almost smiled. The mere thought of Martha smiling was enough to unsettle April. She didn't miss a trick, that one.

Cillian, box in hand, was looking from woman to woman, a half-smile playing on his own lips.

'Good thanks, Martha – what are you working on?' Martha was sitting on her porch, sketchpad in her hand. She pulled it closer to her chest, just a fraction.

'I'm not sure yet, my dear. It's still a bit raw.'

He nodded genially, but April heard him mutter 'ain't that the truth of it' under his breath. She warmed to him instantly. Maybe he wasn't so unapproachable.

'So, everything okay with the chalet? I cleaned a little before you came.'

Saying that she had cleaned a bit before they came was like Mrs Hinch saying she ran the duster around once a fortnight, but April went with it.

Cillian nodded once, muttering his thanks before striding across to the chalet with the box and going inside. April waited outside for a while, but no one came out. They didn't seem to have a lot of stuff for a family. Cillian's van wasn't huge, and it was the only vehicle that had shown up.

'Okay, so I'll just wait here then,' she called to the door. 'In case you need anything.' She looked across at Martha, who was looking very amused, despite her apparent concentration on her work. 'Afternoon, Martha.'

'Stop trying so hard,' Martha said softly. 'Just let them settle in. There're no surfaces left to polish in the place. It's clean. Cillian's a grown man; he and Orla will be fine. If you need something to do, the shop needs to be open again, the games room smells like something died in there, and the whole place needs people. Or are you planning on staying empty all season? My rent won't keep you in Cornish boltholes for long.' She gave her a stern 'think on' look and pointed a pencil-smudged finger towards the van. April whirled around and standing next to the van, staring at her with huge almond eyes, was a little girl. April felt her whole body freeze, her stomach dip. *Please don't pat her on the head, dear God. Please don't let me pet this child on the head.*

'Hi!' she said, at a high-pitched level only dogs could hear. A couple even barked in the distance. Possibly speaking dog for 'shut that woman up!'

'Hi,' she tried again, cautiously taking a step towards the little girl. She was wearing a mustard-coloured top, with denim blue dungarees and a pair of little white trainers. She looked adorable, and April felt herself smile at her. 'I'm April. I'm really happy that you've come to live here. Your daddy is helping me make Shady Pines a really nice place for people to come and have a lovely holiday.' She sounded like an air hostess now, not herself at all. She took another half step and kneeled before her, getting down to her level. 'What's your name?' she asked even though she already knew the answer.

Orla looked her up and down, but said nothing.

'Her name's Orla. She doesn't speak much at the moment,' a gruff voice said. Cillian was striding towards them, a concerned look on his face. He looked different, tense.

'Oh,' April said, nodding to Cillian and looking back at Orla. She didn't get up from her kneeling position. 'Hello, Orla. Nice to meet you.' She held out her hand, offering the little girl a handshake. She didn't take it, so April crossed her arms instead.

'You know, Orla, your daddy and I are going to fix up the games room, and I was thinking that we could decorate the walls with some cool stuff. If you have any ideas, you let me know, okay?' April could feel Cillian's eyes on her, big almond eyes that matched the gaze of the little girl before her perfectly. 'I'm really glad you came.' She'd said it to Orla to try to make her feel at ease. Moving to a new place reminded her a little of how she had come here as a child, escaping their home life, bundled in a vehicle with possessions and promises of happy times. She found herself wanting to make Orla happy here, to make her feel at peace here. Just as she did, all those summers ago.

'Orla, come on, darling.' Cillian swooped in now, picking Orla up like she was a dried leaf in his broad arms. Broad, muscular arms, April noticed now as he effortlessly hoisted a box, holding Orla to his chest with his other arm. He nodded awkwardly at April.

'She's had a busy day. I'll get in and settle her, if that's okay. I know we have a lot on …' He looked around him at the park.

April waved him away with a flick of her hand.

'No no, it's your time off; you make yourselves at home. You don't start till tomorrow. What time is the other van arriving?'

Cillian blinked. 'Other van?'

'Yeah.' She pointed to the box in his hand. 'With your wife, and the rest of your stuff?'

Orla whimpered a little in his arms, and Cillian's face darkened.

'It's just us,' he half spat at her. 'Everything we need is here. Now if you'll excuse me, I need to see to my daughter.' He turned to go.

'I'm sorry, I didn't mean to offend. I just …'

'It's fine, thanks. See you in the morning.' He cut her dead and left her flailing for words outside as he stomped off like a moody teenager. Orla's huge eyes never left hers, following her as she held her dad's arms, her little fingers curled round his T-shirt. She watched till they were out of sight, the front door banging closed just a fraction louder than was necessary. Great, now she'd annoyed the one man she had left in her life even more. She was starting to see a pattern occurring.

'I told you so,' Martha sang, and April felt irritation wash over her. Standing up straight, she turned and fixed the fiery retiree with what she hoped would come across as a hard, businesswoman of the year stare.

'Well, thanks. I'm going to see Judith now, so if you know *everything*, do me a favour. Man the phones.' She threw the keys to the office across the park. They landed on the grass just off Martha's wooden porch. 'We're open for bookings from the end of the month, even if it kills me.'

'Man the phones?' Martha asked, incredulous. 'I'm not a receptionist, I'm an artist!'

'Yeah?' April countered, feeling her rage spike to back-home levels. She could feel the anxiety well up in her, and she needed to get away. Then thinking of getting away made her remember her last yearning to do a bunk. The very bunk that had landed her here, hanging off the edge of the earth with people surrounding her who seemed to actively dislike her, just for existing. It was a lot, and after the last two years, April could sense that her ability to cope wasn't made magically better by the Cornish air she was taking huge gulps of. The difference was, though, that this time she was here for good. She was here because she had chosen this. Just her, no one else. She had started this adventure, and she realised, standing there, that she no longer had to answer to anyone. This was her life, and she needed to jolly well step out from the shadows and claim it.

'Well, I'm a glorified hotel waitress, and this place is kind of my last stand. We all have our bloody crosses to bear.' She didn't wait for an answer, but she knew enough about Martha by now to realise that she wouldn't be up for taking it lying down. She could still hear her chuntering as she reached Judith's gate, but she would rather die than give her the satisfaction of looking back. She thought of the look in Duncan's eyes all that time ago, the last day she'd set her own two eyes on the man she'd thought she would grow old with. She remembered every detail. Even the ones she didn't wish to.

He'd looked so different standing there in front of her that day, his hair styled in a way she'd never seen before. His colour was darker, his greying hairs hidden away with dye, his clothes modern, younger. Perhaps a little too young, if anything. Duncan had always dressed so dapper, but now he looked like a politician out of a suit. Alien in his surroundings.

'Hi,' he'd said, as if that could possibly cover the years between them. As if one word would ever be enough to address each other. It sounded feeble to her ears, and looking at his expression, April knew with a pang that he was thinking the same. *How is this person a stranger now? How does that happen to two people in love? If love just isn't enough, then what is the point? In us, in anything?*

'Hello,' she said, finding herself wanting to look away. She hadn't wanted to come in the first place, but she'd told their mutual friends she wouldn't miss it. The last time they'd seen each other, it was at their divorce hearing. When they'd signed to separate their lives. 'I didn't think you'd be here.'

'Er, well no.' He looked down at his feet. 'Actually, it was a last-minute decision.'

April nodded once, lifting her chin a little higher and forcing herself to look him square in the eye.

'Yes, well …' She turned to leave. She'd already put her present on the pile and greeted Sasha, their expectant mum friend. She was more Duncan's friend really, but the two had got on from the off. Sasha was about the only one who kept calling after he left. For her. Before Mum got so sick so fast, and she was left alone. April was happy for Sasha and Elliott; in fact, it was the one baby she could tolerate talking about. The fact that she was at a baby shower was an achievement in itself. Six months back she had punched a hole in a box of nappies on a supermarket shelf, making a toddler sat in a nearby trolley cry, and her mother look down the aisle in desperation.

'Hormonal woman, clean-up on aisle 3. Rocky Road, Kleenex and Pink Gin required immediately. We thank customers for not approaching that aisle, until the situation is contained.' That was right after they'd signed the papers. She'd left the office, and for lack of anything better to do, she'd gone to buy food.

'April, she's here.'

He might as well have shot her. Right in the back with an arrow of broken, irretrievable love. It would have hurt less.

'She's … she's … here?' April half turned, one of her feet steadfastly pointing towards the front entrance and the safety of her car. The other was wavering in between. 'Why?'

Duncan lifted his hand and tucked his hair behind his ear. It was a move she had seen him make countless times, his muscle memory realising all too late that his hair was different now. There was no cute little curl to tuck in. The thought of that missing curl made April unspeakably sad.

'Well, Sasha has met her, and the divorce is do—'

A woman's voice called his name, and he turned in its direction instinctively. April's foot finally met the other, and she started to walk away. She couldn't see her, she just couldn't do it. She would lose it right here, right now.

'Wait, please,' Duncan said, his hand closing around her arm, just above the elbow. She flinched, caught between her own hurt and the social-event etiquette she never quite got right. She stuck to her gut, elbowing him off and herself free.

'I'm not interested, Dunc, you knew I was invited. Sasha told me she told you!'

Her voice was raised now, and people were diplomatically giving them the side eye while milling around the boutique hotel, moving from onesie-making stations to waitresses serving buck's fizz.

'Please, just let me explain.'

'No, Duncan, no. I'm not interested. How could you put Sasha in this position? Let alone me!'

Duncan sighed heavily, his hand in the air halfway between them. Behind him, April could see Sasha looking across the room nervously, her hands cradling her bump protectively.

'The thing is, April …' He closed his eyes a fraction too long before answering. 'She's here because she and Sasha have become sort of friends recently.'

April snorted. 'Really, a pregnant happily married woman and a homewrecker? They have a lot in common? Pull the other one.'

'Sasha's our matron of honour,' he blurted out. 'We're getting married, April. I'm sorry to tell you like this.'

The air around April seemed to shift and sway.

'Married?' she echoed, marvelling that she could even still speak. She caught sight of a woman standing with Sasha, the pair of them speaking in muted tones, and she knew it was her. The woman saw April looking and studied the floor.

'Yes. We were waiting till everything was finalised. I was going to tell you.'

'Really?' she said, her voice sounding tired and hollow to her own ears. 'When exactly? You're a liar, Duncan. Get out of my fucking way, right now.' She saw him roll his eyes, and just about resisted the urge to punch the flash little ponce in the face. She looked across to Sasha, to try to show in a look how sorry she was that she'd caused a scene, but her blood ran cold when she looked around the room. Some people were openly staring now, a sea of faces, all turned to the pity setting. *They feel sorry for me.*

Suddenly she could barely hold herself up. She made it out of the doors and into the car park before she threw up at the side of her car, tears streaming down her face as she dry-heaved on the pavement. Broken and spent.

The very next week, researching old haunts for the perfect resting place for Mum, she saw the advert for Shady Pines, and she'd put in the offer in two minutes flat.

Chapter 7

Beyond the blue gate was a long winding stone path, leading to a huge house. There were outbuildings all around it, the same brickwork and architecture design throughout, making it look like a Cornish picture postcard. Elvis the goat was in a large pen to her left, and he sprang to the fence when he saw April approaching. He was seemingly saying hello, quite loudly too.

'Hello, Elvis.' It came out flat, even to her ears. If she couldn't muster up the enthusiasm to say hello to a friendly goat, then what chance would she have with Judith? She huffed glumly as she passed the little fella, already wondering how long she would have to stay before she made a quick and hopefully more dignified exit than the last time they met.

Chalet hopping and commando rolling across the Cornish coastline wasn't quite what she had planned for her new life here. She had thought it would be easier, granted, to fall off the face of the earth and, quite literally, live on it in peace and solitude. The thing that she hadn't thought about, not once through it all, was the fact that wherever she went, the rest of her followed. Her bloated stomach, her muffin top, the 'tyre' that Duncan teased her over. Her general feelings of despair at being left with a life that she never asked for, and a constant feeling like something was passing her by. Did you get FOMO at the end of the world? It seemed so.

She was doing her own head in with her moods, but she fluctuated from sheer panic to the pits of despair and back to blind optimism four times before her first coffee hit her system. Given how things were going, she was amazed that she was able to get out of bed at all. The mood to do so certainly hadn't embraced her yet. Every morning was met with the same 'meh' feeling, and it was starting to get boring. Back home, would she have been any better? She doubted it, and the thought of going back to her old life … it made her chest feel just that bit tighter, her resolve just that little bit stronger. She wasn't about to fall on her face here, despite the continual worry that she felt.

She needed to shake herself out of it, she knew. She could hear her mother in her head. *'My girl, get yourself back up. Don't let them see you cry, or they've won.'* She was the toughest woman, in the end. The dark moments of her illness were lifted by her herself, simply and bloody-mindedly choosing to ignore how sick she was, and embracing every second of the life she had left. Even then, on the worst days, it had reminded April of when she became this woman. When the strong, fiercely protective woman dying in front of her changed from the mousy woman who watched her take her first steps. The woman who had dragged her only child out of bed in the small hours and made a run for her life.

'That woman,' April muttered to herself, looking up at the blue sky above, 'would be kicking my behind right now. Right?' She threw the question to the clouds, already knowing the answer to her question.

'April! You're late!'

Judith came bounding over to her, sans chicken this time. She was clad head to foot in a rather sexy-looking tracksuit, a bit Juicy Couture with a hint of country garden. It was a look, and topped off with a bright yellow sweatband and a pair of pink DayGlo trainers, it looked like she was off to be a backing dancer for a weird exercise video.

'I didn't think we'd said a time actu—'

'No matter!' she said brightly, stopping abruptly in front of her and lunging forward to touch her toes, her arms stretched straight and wide from her body. 'Just a few of these and we can start the run.'

April looked behind her, and back at Judith, puzzled.

'Run?'

Judith grinned. 'Yes, city girl. A run. If I know anything about living here, I know you need to run. Do something for yourself.' Judith checked her pulse with her fingers, frowning at the screen of the get-fit activity watch on her wrist. 'Bloody thing, it's never worked right. Curse Tim and his bloody dodgy deliveries.' She jabbed it a few times with her finger, eventually just glaring at it and giving up altogether. 'Ah well, sweat equals workout. Right?'

April was staring at her as if she was deranged. 'Well, yes I suppose …'

'That's the ticket!' Judith slapped her on the shoulder, in a friendly way. It made April feel a bit like a piñata, but she shrugged it off. 'You might need to get changed first though. What were you thinking? You can't run in that!' Looking down at her scruffy clothing, smelling of Zoflora, she started to apologise even though she'd had no idea about the planned run. It was a bit of a run by ambush. A Runbush. Sounded like an after-curry event, rather than a sporting one.

'I know, I should have thought. I can go back, get something else?' *And maybe something will arise when I get back to the park, something that will make running with this stranger suddenly impossible.*

Judith was already waving her away.

'No, no I'll have something. I gained a bit of weight last spring. I have something to fit you.'

April opened and closed her mouth, not knowing which part of what Judith said had ruffled her feathers the most.

'Judith, I appreciate you trying to look after my health.' She said this through gritted teeth. 'I do have to get back to it today though. Was there something you wanted in particular?'

Judith looked at her and smiled. Not just any smile though. This one left her looking a little like the Grinch. It began small, barely there, and then her mouth opened, showing so many little pearly white teeth that April began to think she would just go on and on. Her whole face was grinning now, and it didn't look quite natural.

'Well, actually – yes, there was. Come round back, and I'll show you.'

They walked around the side of her house, which was an impressive detached house that looked at home among the backdrop, almost like the sea had been built around it. Rounding the corner, she opened another gate and waved April through.

The garden spread out before them, and April didn't know what to focus on first. It was all so … busy. Judith chuckled, brushing past her, and headed to the house.

'What is this place?' April breathed, taking in the various pens housing a variety of creatures, all looking pretty happy and well fed.

'Well, it was a working farm back in the day. My folks left it to me, but with times changing, I decided to change as well. I started rescuing the odd stray cat, and it just grew. I rely on donations now, and we get some support locally. Tim never cared about this place.' She waved her arms around her, and April saw that she wasn't just a busybody. She was scared.

'You do all this – just you?'

Judith shrugged. 'Me and the animals. They keep me entertained. Come in.' She looked behind her, distracted. 'Elvis, stop licking Bowie!' Bowie was a very large white rabbit, who seemed to be enjoying the attention of the King of Graceland very much.

Walking through the gardens to the house, April couldn't help but gawp at the many different animals around her, all thriving. It looked idyllic.

The house had a large entrance hall with a porch, and Judith waved her away when she started to take off her footwear.

'Oh, with the dogs and everything, I just mop a lot. There's two robot hoovers doing shifts.'

As Judith spoke, a large black motorised circle rolled past, changing course to avoid a table leg.

'That one's Holly, she's a bit ditzy sometimes. Phil must be in the den.'

April grinned. Judith was quite funny.

'Your place is beautiful. Kids would love the animals,' *Orla might too.* 'Do you open to the public?'

Judith looked horrified. 'Oh no, I couldn't. I don't like begging for money, and around people I can be a bit … well …'

'Awkward?' April answered for her. 'I feel the same, trust me. Even back home, being an overweight woman who can't have kids was bad enough. When my husband left me for his office intern, well … it doesn't make for a yearning to be social. People are weird.'

Judith looked at April, her face expressionless for a moment. When she spoke, she spoke in hushed tones. 'I always thought it was me. I mean, I've always lived alone since my parents passed, and the time was just never right. Henry was around to help, and—'

'Henry?' she asked, wondering what type of animal he was, and in what way that would be helpful.

'The rider, from the first day you arrived?'

April scowled at the memory of the horse plop, and the long-faced man.

'Oh yes, Henry. He's yours then?' Judith flushed and April panicked. Social awkwardness, check. 'The horse, I meant.' Judith relaxed.

'No, that's Poldark.' She flushed again. 'Don't ask. Henry is my friend. He lives nearby.'

She looked a little sad at that, and April picked up on it.

'So, you never married then?'

Judith looked past her, to a frame on the wall. 'My parents, they needed a lot of care, so I stayed home a lot. It just never happened. I thought it might once, but then we got busy here again, and it just seems forgotten now.' She looked so sad, April couldn't bear it.

'I don't think that this place helps really. I still feel alone. I don't know what I was expecting. It's getting better though.' She thought of Cillian earlier, and shuddered. 'Small steps. You should open this place up though. I could even help you advertise at my place. It's so lovely here.'

Judith didn't commit there and then, but April could tell she was thinking about it. She wouldn't push it though. What would be the point?

'Come through,' Judith led her through to a large kitchen, once again stunningly cute and with a couple of animals dotted about. Two cats were sunning themselves on the long white windowsill, their ginger and white fur sparkling in the sun as the animals' bodies rose and fell in slumber. 'I wanted to show you this.'

She took April over to a table in the corner, on which sat a beautiful gift basket. Full of homemade items like jams, fresh eggs, and cute little bottles of bath salts and bath bombs. The local newspapers, little maps of the area.

'This was my idea.' Judith stood behind the basket, and April inspected it further, running her hand along the yellow ribbon that was expertly tied around the cellophane and tissue paper wrappings.

'It's all recyclable, and the jars can be used again or returned to us. I was thinking, seeing how you came here alone and want the park to get back onto its feet, maybe we could work together. I could help the animals more, and you could make a profit too.'

April didn't need to think about it. She wanted to do things like this, be part of something. Despite her clashes of late, she needed to be here.

'I think we have a deal, but think about opening up too, okay?'

Judith thought for a moment, and then held out her hand. 'I'll think about it, truly. Deal.'

April shook her hands, and the pair giggled.

'You're wrong too, you know. About this place.'

April doubted it. 'Why?'

'It might seem like a place full of lost souls, from the outside looking in. Hell, I devoted my life and my bank account to saving those souls out there, but that's not what this place is about. Not really. People come here over the years for more than holidays. They come to escape, or to start again.'

April thought of her mother, and for a second she was right there on that full back seat, looking around in wonder as her mum drove, crying silently half the way. The first half, from panic probably. *I don't know why I never recalled that detail before now.* Reliving it made April proud of her, hit by the wave of loss once more.

'It works too, sometimes.' Judith winked at April, the levity of the moment lifted by that simple gesture. 'I've seen it. This place feels like the end of the earth sometimes, I know that, but really, it's home for lost souls like us. We're all a little quirky in our own ways.' She looked back at the photos on the wall, faces of people obviously much loved. 'We just need to find our tribe in life, and humans are generally good at that. It just takes a nudge now and again.'

Her eyes were focused on one photo in particular, and April turned her head to look properly at it. It was Henry. She recognised the long face now. He was handsome though, his face smiling at the camera as he sat astride a large white horse. *Maybe Henry is the one needing the nudge.*

'Does Henry do lessons? I always wanted to horse ride. I used to dabble a bit.'

Weekends with Duncan were often a case of Duncan off working or golfing, while the wives and girlfriends indulged in spa days, riding days, or shopping trips. She would have much preferred his activities. The archery, the golfing even; she'd never been bothered about material things like the others were. That wasn't April. Sentimentality over designer labels. Funny how she could see now just how different she and Duncan were. It was so much clearer when the love goggles were off. Rose-tinted glasses did tend to blur out the glaring details till the very end.

'He does! He only does it part-time though, you know. He used to work much more but he helps me more now. I do owe him a lot.'

April looked at Judith, lost in a happy thought about Henry. Her face lit up when she spoke about him, and April couldn't resist.

'Well, if you could let him know I would love to be a new customer, maybe you could take me to meet him sometime?'

Judith blushed, lifting a jar of jam off the basket and offering it to April.

'Here you are, a prototype for the shop. See what your customers think.' April took it, and Judith clapped her hands together. 'Oooo I forgot! Why is your website not open?'

April groaned. 'I don't have a computer and my phone is … out of credit.'

Judith ran off suddenly to another room, a bark or two coming from behind the door as she disappeared out of sight. In her hands was a battered-looking laptop.

'It's not great, but I just upgraded. I needed better design software for the labels. You can take it; it's been wiped. Good as new really.' She gripped the edge of her sleeve and vigorously rubbed at a small black mark. 'The local pages online have been asking about when bookings will be open.'

'Really?' April gasped.

'Yes, well only a few, but that's how it starts! You should get it back up and running if you can.'

'Thank you, Judith, I … don't know what to say really.' She'd been threatened with a run, and then shown this lovely place, held together by this amazing woman. A woman strong and alone. Just like her. She couldn't help thinking that there might be something to the lost souls thing, but then she thought of Cillian again. His angry, closed-off demeanour. He flip-flopped between moods faster than even her hormones could keep up with.

'Nothing to say really, apart from bottoms up. Here.' Judith passed her another newspaper, matching the one in the basket. 'Give it to Martha, will you? She's waiting for it.'

'Is she now? Well, I had better get back then. She's not one to cross.'

Judith laughed. 'She's not so bad. You'll see.'

April was halfway to the gate when Judith called after her again. 'Do you really think that people would come, if I opened up the farm?'

April turned, her arms full of homemade Cornish love and care, and looked at her accidental new friend, surrounded by animals like a gloriously eccentric Miss Dolittle.

'I do, it's wonderful here. We could offer a discount or something, link the two businesses a bit. Help each other out.'

Judith beamed at her. 'Yes, that would be nice. If you ever want any chickens, you let me know!'

April laughed, heading to the gate and home.

You

I can't tell you where I am right now, but I know where I would wish to be. I was thinking about the last time we were together, on the beach. You snuck out to see me, and I knew I loved you then. Really loved you, as though my soul had turned and recognised its mate.

We lay on that sand for hours, and still I would give everything for just a little while longer. I still have the shell you gave me, I kept it safe at home. I didn't want to risk breaking it out here, but I have your photo to keep me company. Some of the lads asked if you were mine, and I said you were. I can say that for now at least. I may never stop saying it, even after you fulfil your family obligations.

I wish things could be different. I would change so many things. Meeting you isn't one of them though. Don't give up on your dreams, You. Please don't stop trying to feed your passion. Life is so bleak and cruel without joy and passion. You and you alone are my dream, and I shall never give up on mine. Take pity on a poor Navy man who loves you so, and go out there and fill your life with colour. You brought the colour to mine, and I love you for it.

Till we meet again, I shall remember the beach. Our beach.

Ever yours,

G

Chapter 8

The familiar smell of fresh-cut grass assaulted Martha's nostrils as she slowly walked up the well-maintained path. The smell of flowers hung in the air, and daffodils were growing wild all around her. Her lips pursed when her gaze fell on what she was looking for.

'I don't know why I'm here really,' she said out loud, already feeling foolish.

Martha pulled a small checked blanket from her bag, unrolling it and placing it over the wooden bench that she frequented most weeks. Sitting down, she looked at the row of headstones before her. She normally brought flowers, or a little sketch, but today, she had barely remembered the blanket to protect her from the splinters on the well-worn bench. Placing her bag next to her on the material, she sat back and wrapped one side of the flannel around herself. Since April had passed her that newspaper, she hadn't felt warm. Or herself.

Charlie's headstone was right in front of her, and she looked at it fondly. Charlie had been the best husband a woman could ask for. He loved her artistic side, put up with her temperamental moods, and was the best companion in life. They had a happy, quiet life, and she missed him still. Since he passed, she'd come to realise just how lucky she had been. Isn't it always the way? When things are gone, we realise just how huge a hole is left behind. The thing was, even with Charlie there, it had always felt like she had a huge hole in her life, one that she could never speak of, or fill. She had thought that art might bridge that gap, but even when she was working on her best pieces, she still couldn't help but feel her mind wander.

'He's coming back,' she said simply, wincing as she thought of the response Charlie might have had. Would he have been angry, or mad? Sad, probably. Which was why she'd never spoken of any of this when he was alive. Since he had passed, telling him certain things had been simpler. He was less likely to talk back, but deep down she knew that Charlie would have been calm, reasoned. Had he been standing in front of her today, he wouldn't have raged or shouted. He would have been as calm as a duck on the water, despite the paddling feet beneath. She loved him for that, as she did now. Her secret confidant in death.

A bird tweeted from the trees above her and she looked up to the sky, surprised to see how bright it was, even at this hour. The sun was just starting to rise, the birds were waking, the boats were out working nearby. Life went on, as it does, but today Martha felt like she was stuck in time. A time that she had never embraced.

'Morning!' April trilled as brightly as she could. Cillian, sitting on a swivel chair in the middle of the games room, didn't turn around, or acknowledge her presence. 'Morning!' she tried again. Nothing. Great. April, carrying a huge box of brushes and rollers in one hand, and two large tins of paint in the other, sagged. Blowing a piece of overhanging fringe that had escaped from her scarf headband, she dumped the stuff on the pool table and looked around the room. The flooring was sound; the walls needed minimum patching. A fresh coat of paint, some new games, and a bit of money on tech would make the place great.

She had been looking online last night at design ideas and something had sparked in her. For the first time, she hadn't groaned and moaned before getting out of bed. For once, she didn't feel quite so lost. This was what she needed to do: focus on the challenge.

Cillian turned a one-eighty in his chair, stopping with a jolt when he saw her. He jumped up in surprise.

'Holy moly, where the hell did you come from?' He pulled a pair of ear buds out of his ears, and April could hear the tinny sound of The Beatles in his ear. 'You scared the bejesus out of me!' He tried to get to his feet but ended up standing on one of the wheel-clad legs and flipping the chair arm straight into his private parts.

'Holy fecking hell,' he whimpered, dropping to his knees and cupping his manhood as he melted to the floor like a water-sodden witch.

April stared at Cillian, his face fading from a bright red to a sickly pale greenish hue, and she burst in laughter.

'Oh, I'm so … ha ha … oh no … sorry … I …' was all she could get out before she collapsed into fits of laughter once more. 'I just, the chair … and your … your …' She pointed at his groin, holding her side as a stitch took hold. 'Oh mercy, oh …'

He looked at her for a long moment, his piercing gaze fixed on hers, and then his eyes started to crinkle, just a little at the corners. She tried again to stop laughing, but one look at him trying not to laugh, still clutching his now probably very bruised crown jewels, was just too much. This time she took him with her, and the sound of them laughing together filled the room.

'Well, glad I made someone laugh anyway,' Cillian said eventually. April gained just enough composure to speak. He wiped a tear away from his eyes, and she wasn't sure it was laughter or real sorrow for his man parts.

'You certainly did. I needed that. I thought you were ignoring me,' she admitted before she could stop herself. She bit her lip.

She always had to go one more, make the awkward additional comment. That one that equated to farting loudly in a full lift. 'You know, because of yesterday? Your wife?'

He took the headphones and showed them to her before putting them in his jeans pocket. He had on a lumberjack-type checked shirt, red and black squares open over a white T-shirt. His jeans were ironed, a light blue faded wash. April noticed for the first time that he seemed a little less unkempt than usual. Cuter even.

'I was just listening to music, that's all. Orla is on a full day today at nursery, so I have till four. And I don't have a wife.' He looked at her hand and she felt her fingers flicker in reflex. No ring there. Just snot-coloured paint. 'Nice paint colour. Martha hates it too, which is hilarious.'

She nodded, moving her hand out of sight. No more mention of yesterday then. April mentally picked up the rug and brushed the matter under it. If he wanted to talk about it, he'd talk about it. She had a business to run, and the bookings were going to be coming in soon. It had to be right.

'That's fine, I have a lot to get through today too. First full day of working together.' She looked across the park to Martha's chalet, but she wasn't sitting on her porch as usual.

'She's gone out; she left this morning. I dropped her in town when I took Orla to nursery.' April looked at Cillian, but his expression was closed off as usual. 'She'll be back.'

'Do you know where she went?'

Cillian didn't even look at her now, busying himself by sweeping the floor clean. 'Yes, I do.' He turned away, grabbing one of the new dustpans she'd bought in town, and sweeping up all the dust and debris from the floor. The flooring itself was in pretty good nick. A good scrub and a new carpet in places and they would be in business. She'd spent half of last night researching arcade machines online on Judith's old laptop, and was delighted to find a small local firm who refurbished them and rented them out to businesses and chalet parks. A perfect way of saving money. Once she had things turned around and some money back in the bank, she could buy some machines instead, keep more of the profits. She didn't want her park to be all pay pay pay, but the machines would be a nice cheap crowd-pleaser for the kids and teens who would come here.

'And …' she tried, realising that he hadn't answered her question.

'And what?'

'Where did Martha go?'

'I said, into town.'

April rolled her eyes at him. 'I know that, but where? She hasn't left here since I arrived. Why today?'

Cillian sighed, and she could see from his body language that he didn't want to talk.

'Okay, sorry. You know, sometimes, it would be nice if I could go a day without feeling like I'm not in the way. It's only a question. Just forget it. I thought we could actually get along. Elvis has better crack than you.'

'What—' Cillian ran his fingers through his hair '—are you bleating about now?'

'Bleating!?'

'Yeah, bleating.' Cillian dropped the broom to the floor with a clatter. 'That's all you women do. Drop me here, fix this, do that, give me this, take me there. I'm here to work, not be a bloody cruise director. I like you, but I can't take your crap on top of my crap, okay?'

'Crap? I don't have any crap and I do not bleat! Bloody Elvis bleats, you stupid Irish windbag. I was only asking why—'

'I have no fecking idea why you care about what Martha does. The woman can't stand you anyway.'

'Oh really, well the feeling is "fecking" mutual!' She did air quotes here, but turned her hands around to add a two-fingered salute.

74

'Don't take the mick out of me, missy. I don't mock you for your weird talking.'

'Weird talking? What weird talking?'

'Oh you know, with your nowts and sommat's – fecking well speak the Queen's, will ya?'

'What the hell is your problem, Cillian!' She said his name as though it was the most ridiculous name in the world, like River Rainbow Bean the Third or something.

'Oh, nothing's wrong with me, Ape-ril.' Her eyes flashed as he touched on her old nickname. She thought of Duncan, and her jaw flexed. Any jokes equating her to a hairy primate never raised a laugh from her. They were mean, old and tired little digs. Not that Cillian knew that. 'I'm just wanting to work, and raise my daughter, and not answer to any mentally deranged bloody women!'

'Oooohhh!' April gasped, grabbing a paintbrush from the pool table and jabbing it in his direction. He glared at her, the two getting closer to each other as their words heated up. 'The reason us women are like we are is because of you and your type! Flashing your bloody manhoods around, marrying and impregnating anything that moves, moving on with your lives and not giving a fig to how anyone else feels!'

'Huh!' Cillian barked crossly, flicking the paintbrush away with the back of his hand. 'I do not impregnate anything that moves. I'm a good dad! It's her mother that's the problem, not me! I didn't move on with my life. I'm a huge mess! I can't even get my daughter to talk to me!'

A single hot and salty tear escaped from him and he brushed it away angrily, clearing his throat a half dozen times to try to calm himself.

Shit. She'd done it again. Open mouth, insert size-nine foot. Yes, she had big feet too. Another common source of fun for dear ex-hubby. April put the brush down on the table and started to leave.

'Come on,' she said, one hand on the open door. 'We need a coffee. We have time.'

Fifteen minutes later, Cillian was in the bathroom while April made the coffee. She'd invested in a posh one for the reception area, but at home she still drank the instant coffee her mum had loved. Duncan had always hated it, which made it taste all the sweeter now. Sod him and his bloody fancy gadgets. May he be impaled on one of them in a very unfortunate place.

Cillian shuffled into the room and April saw him put some tissues in his pockets.

'Sorry about that, I didn't mean to act that way.'

She waved him away, putting the coffees and a pack of biscuits onto a small round tray and leading him through to the lounge. She moved a paperback she was reading from the chair arm and motioned for him to make himself at home.

'It sounded like you needed to get it off your chest.' She met his eyes and saw such sadness there. It looked comfortingly familiar to her, like looking in a mirror. 'I was weird yesterday, because I don't do well around families. Children in particular.'

'Well, don't take this the wrong way, but why buy a chalet park in the heart of the Cornish tourist trade?' He laughed as he spoke, but his eyes focused on her.

Finally. Someone had actually asked her the question. No one ever had before. Work colleagues, friends, they had all just declared her mad. Warned her against it, asked questions about how she could afford it. It was all the logistics, never the reasoning.

'My mum brought me here one summer, when we were leaving my dad.' She'd never told anyone that before. Not even Duncan. Oh, he knew that she'd been here before, as a girl, but he never knew why. Why a single mum from Yorkshire had driven halfway across the country to take her daughter on holiday. 'I always liked it. It came up for sale, and I bought it.' She looked around her new home and Cillian followed her gaze.

'Well, it's starting to look better in here, I must admit. Why don't you like children?'

'Wow, you don't pull any punches, do you?'

He looked straight at her with those green eyes, making her suddenly want to be seen. By him. The look he gave her was a puzzle that she hadn't quite cracked yet.

'I'll answer, if you tell me why you hate women.'

'I don't hate women.'

'I don't hate children.'

'Glad to hear it. You hate men?'

'No.' *Just one or two.* 'Why doesn't Orla speak to you?'

'I asked first. Come on, answer me properly.'

April sighed, sitting back on her newly cleaned fabric sofa and buying herself time by taking a deep slug of her coffee.

'I can't have kids. We tried for a long time, but it just wasn't meant to be.' She didn't bore him with the details of her PCOS. The mood swings, weight gain, hair loss. Periods that came infrequently, if at all. When they did come she raged one moment, and cried the next. She was always so tired, so lacking in iron in the beginning that she never realised how much her condition had been affecting her life unseen. She wasn't about to discuss her heavy flow with a relative stranger, an employee at that. A rather hot employee. She felt herself flush, and she met his eyes again. He smiled. 'I have issues, and I guess over time, I just felt awkward around them. I love children, I just don't really have that gene, I guess.'

Cillian shook his head. 'I'm sorry to hear that. It must be hard. I don't think that there is a gene though. People are people – they don't often differ from who they tell you they are. You just have to learn to listen to what's not being said.' He looked stricken for a moment. April didn't ask why.

'It is hard,' she agreed. She felt like she didn't have to sugar-coat it with him, which was novel. Maybe it was because she had just had a fight with him. She felt like the air had been cleared somehow. 'My marriage ended, and I needed to get away, do something with my life.'

'Knitting might have been less hassle, or skydiving?'

She laughed at his joke. 'I can knit actually, but I draw the line at skydiving. Your turn!' She pushed the biscuits closer to him and he took one, dunking it straight into his coffee. She smiled inwardly. She'd been resisting the urge to do that herself.

'Turn?' he asked, suddenly focused on the book jacket sitting spread eagle on the table. 'Good book?'

'Yes, and your turn to answer the question.'

For a long moment, Cillian looked at her thoughtfully. She found herself blushing again as she tried to meet his eyes, but she could feel the flush of her cheeks spreading to her face and neck. 'You don't have to tell me, if you don't want to.'

'I don't hate women. I don't hate any woman, never have. Orla's mum is … It's difficult. She's not on the scene anymore and it's difficult for Orla. When she drops in and kicks off, I have to pick up the pieces.'

From his face, April could tell it was difficult for him, too. He looked wretched today, as nice as he looked in his sexy work clothes. He looked different. His usual alpha male gruffness was muted, and her heart went out to him.

'Will she come here, her mother?'

'Tina,' Cillian offered. 'No, I don't think so, and to be honest, if she does show up, it won't be good.' He got his mobile phone out of his pocket, and she noticed that it had a Hello Kitty sticker on the back of the plain black case. *Cute.* 'Can I have your number?'

Wait, what? 'Er … my number?'

'Yeah, your mobile? I only have the park number. I can send you her photo, in case she shows up.'

'Oh, of course!' *Of course, why else would he want it? You are his boss, he has a daughter, and he thinks you're a madwoman who is scared of tiny humans. Not exactly first date heaven, is it?* She pushed down the feelings of disappointment that rose up unannounced. She reeled the number off, and Cillian tapped a few keys, looking at her expectantly.

'Er, you not got your phone? I just sent you a text.' *Fudge nuggets. He's expecting me to look at it now.*

'Err, no. Sorry, I'll … just go get it.' She dashed into the kitchen, doing her best 'breezy, not in a panic at all' slow walk that looked as though she was power walking through the chalet. In the kitchen, she rifled through some drawers and found her smartphone. Just looking at it gave her a ton of anxiety. Turning it on, she prayed that the god of depleted batteries had decided to strike, but no luck. The thing sprang into life, the jaunty little bip bip bip bip mocking her as the home screen came up. The wallpaper was her and her mother, sitting on the beach together that summer. It was one of her favourite photos, and the original was still sitting in a frame somewhere in the boxes she hadn't been able to bear opening quite yet. Let alone had the time.

Heading back into the room, her notifications started going off and she switched it to silent quickly. Scanning through the text messages to the most recent, she saw a number she didn't recognise and clicked on it, hoping to God that it was Cillian's. She couldn't deal with anything else right now, especially in front of company. She could feel her palms sweating, and she left a little watermark when her finger touched the screen. She rubbed her hand down her jeans and opened up the text.

'She's pretty,' April said. *Oh, no. Open mouth, insert foot. Again.* 'Sorry, but she is. I haven't seen her here, but I'll keep a lookout of course.'

'Thanks.' He stood up, draining the rest of his coffee cup. 'Shall we get on? I have to get done on time to pick Orla up.'

They were just headed back to the games room, when he looked across at her again. 'You know, turning your phone off is all well and good, but you will have to deal with it eventually, right?'

He had a look of concern about him that seemed to soften his normally rugged and hard-set features. They walked into the games room, letting the door shut behind them.

'That obvious, eh?' Buoyed by the coffee and conversation, she didn't feel the usual pang of panic when she thought of back home. She lifted her screen to show him piles on piles of notifications. She hadn't even checked her email. Once the sale was done and she was on her way out of Yorkshire, she'd just dropped out of life.

'That's a lot. Won't people be worried?'

She winced. 'Probably, a little. I told those I needed to that I was going, but I did leave a little earlier than planned.' Truth be told, it was a fair bit earlier than planned, and not quite as dignified either, but that was a story with a two-drink minimum required. 'You think I'm a wimp now, right?'

Cillian was standing right in front of her. He looked her straight in the eye, pressing his lips together for a second before he spoke.

'I think that anybody who has the guts to go out there and change their life doesn't know the meaning of the word wimp.' He looked around at the space and nodded slowly. 'This place will be grand again, you'll see.' He picked up the broom and passed her the dustpan. 'Let's get this place back on the map, eh? The rest of it we can sort out later.'

Looking at her phone again, with its messy long list of things to click on, to drag her into the real world, she nodded. Turning it off and shoving it onto the table, they touched broom to dustpan with a determined knock of plastic and wood, and got to work.

'She's been a little unsettled today, Mr O'Leary. She didn't eat lunch and went to sit on her own a lot. I'm afraid she's only had a little drink too.'

Mrs Toon was sitting on a tiny red chair, one of six around a tiny round table in a corner of the nursery. The rest of the children had all left, only Orla and a couple of stragglers were left.

Orla was sitting on her own in the reading corner, her thumb poking out of her mouth and her index finger rubbing along the length of her nose, like a tiny little pink hook. She was engrossed in the book that was spread across her lap, one finger following the words as she read.

Cillian's heart squeezed when he looked at her, and he felt the prick of tears threatening to escape from his normally manly tear ducts. He knew he had to keep it together for Orla, but he hated that his own parents had taught him to be quite so tough. He decided then and there that once they got through all this, he wouldn't be that father. He would teach Orla to love, and be open and caring, and never bottle up her feelings. Which would be rather hard, since he was essentially Victor Meldrew these days, on a bad day at that.

Mrs Toon craned her neck to look up at him and pulled out the chair across from her.

'Please, Mr O'Leary, take a seat.'

He lowered himself gingerly onto the seat, his muscular thighs feeling like they were on either side of his head now, no thanks to his rather scrunched-up position. It was hard to keep a straight face, given that they were essentially in a meeting using furniture that the Borrowers would be glad of.

'Yesterday won't happen again, Mrs Toon. I have taken steps already to secure Orla, and to stop this happening. I don't want this any more than you do, but Orla is happy here. Making her leave will only upset her more. We've moved now. We live at Shady Pines and I work there too. It's safe there. I am there for her out of school, and my boss is understanding of the situation.'

Thinking of April, he realised that he was lucky. Basically he'd just hoodwinked himself a home, and she'd gone along with it, and put up with his moods to boot. He felt a wave of shame and brushed it away. It confused him further, because he'd enjoyed that coffee with her more than he'd wanted to.

'Mr O'Leary, you—'

'Cillian, please. You make me sound like me Da.'

Mrs Toon smiled at that, nodding her agreement. 'Fine, Cillian. You misunderstood my reasons for wanting to speak to you. We want Orla to stay here. We know how settled she is here, and we have no intention of uprooting her. Your daughter is a lovely, bright, and very sweet girl, and we love her, all of us. We just want to offer you support, to find out the situation as it changes, and to tell you that we are here to help, both of you. We do feel that Orla might benefit from counselling of some sort, but we would never overstep. We just want you to know that when Orla is in our care, she's safe and protected. The food issues are a huge concern though, so we do want to communicate daily, if that's okay with you.'

Cillian was so relieved he could have snogged Mrs Toon, let alone agree with her kind concern. It took him over a minute to formulate any words.

'Mrs Toon, thanks so much. I will of course keep you updated.'

She seemed to relax then, and he realised that she'd been nervous about the meeting. Was it Tina that had scared her, or the situation yesterday? Having a half-cut angry woman braying on the nursery doors, trying to take a child, must have been hard to deal with. They said Orla had been in the back, away from the noise, but Cillian knew just how bright Orla was. How sadly tuned she was into the moods and unpredictability of her mother. Standing up from the tiny chair, his legs and lower back protesting with pain, he knelt down by Mrs Toon's chair and held out an open hand.

'Mrs Toon, thank you. For looking after my daughter. I can't tell you how much I appreciate it.' He tried his best to give her one of his disarming smiles, and she shook his hand. Instead of letting it go, however, she turned it around, placing her hands around his.

'Cillian, we want to help. This is not exactly professional but, we do think that Orla is better with you.' They both looked across

82

at the little girl, who hadn't moved an inch other than to turn the page of the book she was reading. 'You can do this – we all have faith.'

Cillian squeezed the woman's hand and muttered something that hopefully sounded like a thank you. Her eyes crinkled at the corners as she patted his hand a final time.

'Come on, let's get Orla off home.'

'Daddy, you need to shave!' Orla twitched him away with her little hands, making him laugh. He swooped in again, wrapping the duvet around her and nuzzling his cheek gently against hers. She squeaked again, and his heart sang with the sound of it.

'I know, but how else can I get you to talk? My beard is the only thing that makes you speak to me.'

Orla snuggled down into the bed, her head sinking into the plush pillows that April had bought for all the chalets. Things had been arriving in parcels, every time April coming running out, taking the deliveries, marking things off in a big notebook she seemed to have glued to her. Today the games room had opened his eyes a little to the woman, and he found himself intrigued about what the following day would bring.

'Do you like it here?' he asked Orla, wrapping her in the duvet like a burrito, just how she liked it. She always had her arms out though, forever holding a book or sucking her thumb. She never used to suck her thumb, not when she was teeny tiny. That started after Tina had left her alone for an entire day and night while she went on a bender. Leaving her in the dark, because the meters hadn't been fed, and wondering why the hell she had been left alone at home, when she hadn't done a thing wrong but be born.

Cillian let her suck her thumb, hell, it was the least that he could do. The look on her face when he walked through the door that morning from work would haunt him for the rest of his days. He vowed then and there to never work away from home again, and he was damn well going to stick to it. Thanks to Martha and that panicked phone call, he felt like maybe, if he could just shake off this anger, things might be starting to turn around.

Orla looked around the room, taking in the clean warm space, the fresh sheets that smelled of fabric softener, the pink teddy that now snuggled next to her in bed.

'Yes, I do like it here.' She nodded, giving her dad a little fraction of a smile. He welcomed it and was saddened by it in equal measure. A chink of hope is still just a chink, after all. It doesn't mean that you are suddenly free to walk into the light. Not yet.

He picked up the pink teddy, moving the mouth to his ear and listening in. 'And you, pink bear?'

'Pinky,' Orla corrected.

'Sorry, Pinky. Pinky, do you like it here?'

He moved the bear's head, making it talk into his ear, his attention focused on what the toy was saying.

'He says he's glad you brought him here. He likes it. He likes the beach too.'

Cillian passed the bear to Orla, who reached out with both arms and hugged him to her.

'I didn't bring him here, silly, he was already here waiting on the bed. He belongs here. It's his home.' She looked at her dad, eyes so like his own staring at him with so much uncertainty in them. 'Are we staying here too with Pinky? He might get very lonely if we have to leave.' She hugged the bear that bit tighter.

'Yes, honey,' Cillian promised blindly, 'Pinky is home here, with us now.'

The little girl grinned and turned to pull a book off the shelf. '*Rapunzel* tonight, Daddy.'

'Again?' Cillian pretended to groan and fall to the floor. 'Please no, not *Rapunzel*!'

Orla squealed. 'Yes, Daddy! We have to get her out of the tower. If we don't finish the book, she'll never get out!'

The irony was not lost on him as he snuggled next to her on the bed, her little head resting on his chest. He saved his princess from the tower, and now they needed to get their happy ending. Which meant first thing tomorrow, he had to get to that appointment and fight for his only child's rights, even though it went against the woman who bore her. He lost himself in the story, ignoring the prick of tears in his eyes once more. It was quite a week.

It was pitch black outside by the time he'd got Orla settled and cleaned up the dinner things. The chalet was far better than the flat, and every night he'd look around and feel so grateful for the space. The thought of Tina turning up here was enough to keep him off the sofa, and he knew he wouldn't sleep even if he tried. It was too early anyway. Stepping outside, he surveyed the chalet park. Martha's chalet was still in darkness, and it did make him wonder where she was. He knew she was capable of getting around on her own – she was more than capable in fact – but the truth was that lately, since the park was due to change hands, she hadn't left. She'd been staging a very quiet, very dignified one-woman sit-in. Which made him think that either something was wrong, or she had just decided that the new owner wouldn't burn the place down if she had a day out.

The night was dark and full of stars. They lit the night sky over Lizard Point, making the waves in the distance sound like a lullaby, a mother rocking her baby. Side to side, side to side. Orla was flat-out asleep, exhausted after her busy full day. Cillian was about to head back indoors, to flick through the TV channels pointlessly for an hour before turning in, when he saw that the games room door was open. Looking back at his chalet, he decided to risk the short walk.

As he got closer, he heard a voice, low but sweet, and he ventured closer. The lights were still on to half the room, and as he pushed open the door, he heard singing. April was crouched down in the far corner, brushing and daubing pink paint over a large stencil on the back wall. She was singing to herself, to the

85

radio that sat next to her on the now swept and covered in dust-sheets floor. She was wearing a pair of tiny shorts, blue faded denim, and Cillian couldn't help but notice her long legs, spread out to one side, her paint-splattered top hanging loosely from one shoulder, exposing bare skin.

'Hey,' he said softly. 'Working late?'

She jumped a little, her cheeks flushing as she looked at him. She rested her paintbrush on the paint can, smoothing her hair down. It did nothing to the thick, loose bun but streak wet slivers of bright pink paint through the top of it, making her look a little punk-like. Cillian pressed his lips together to quell the surge of laughter threatening to bubble up.

'Sorry, could you hear the radio?' She looked behind him to the open door. 'Martha complaining?'

Cillian's face dropped to a frown. 'She's not here, hasn't been all day. I thought you might know where she was.'

April shook her head. 'Nope, same here. Orla okay?'

Cillian instinctively looked back towards his chalet, where everything looked calm and peaceful. 'She's asleep. I'd better get back. I just wanted to check everything was locked up.'

April nodded, awkwardly trying to get to her feet without putting paint anywhere. She was halfway to her feet when her elbow knocked into a roller tray with the remnants of cream paint flicking over her arm. She yipped and jumped away, catching her heel in a crease of the dustsheet and tripping herself up.

'Arrghh!' she shouted, her hands windmilling for purchase. A second later, she was suddenly flung forward, bashing her eye on a metal paint can, the breath knocked out of her as she landed on her front. On Cillian's front. Palms down, so now his black fitted T-shirt had two handprints of pink and cream paint, right across his pecs.

'You okay? April?' She could hear what he was saying, but her brain couldn't seem to crack the code in that instant. The response just didn't come. She was aware that Cillian's arms were around her. He had grabbed her and pulled her to his chest, taking the full weight of her 'always carrying a few extra pounds' body without a groin strain or a yelp of pain. His arms were still around her, tight, and she found that she didn't want to struggle against them. She felt a trickle of something down her cheek, and she prayed to the god of hot Irish handymen that she wasn't crying spontaneously at the touch of a man.

Cillian moved his arms, and she made a weak little sound of protest in her throat. He moved his hands to touch her face, his palms sliding up her cheeks slowly, delicately …

'You banged your eye on the way down there,' he said abruptly, turning her head quickly and peering at the side of her face. She tried to look demure, but a blob of something wet went into her eye and caused her to blink rapidly like a lunatic. 'Here, hold still.'

Reaching down between their bodies, their legs still entwined, one hand still cradling her face, he reached into his jeans pocket. The movement jiggled them both, and April felt her cheeks burning yet again.

'I can get up,' she said, awkwardly trying to get to her feet. His left arm shot around her again, and he turned her face to look to his.

'Stay still, you're bleeding pretty bad. I don't want you to keel over.' April nodded reluctantly, his breath hot and sweet on her face as she held her own in. She managed another nod, wincing when a flash of pain exploded behind her eyes. Cillian caught her wince and his eyes narrowed, concern flooding his rugged features. In this light, with the sounds of the night filtering through behind him, he looked …

'Breathtaking,' she murmured dreamily.

'What?' he said, his eyes locked on hers intently as he brought a cotton handkerchief to her eye socket. 'What's wrong? You're not going to pass out on me, are you?'

She shook her head, a tiny little movement, and Cillian's features relaxed a little. He was still holding her, his hand resting in the small of her back. After a moment, she tried to move again, just a little, but his arm tightened around her.

'Just … wait …' he said, and she stopped moving. She turned her head to her good side slowly, his hand still holding the handkerchief moving with it. She lowered her head, avoiding the worst of the paint smears, and rested her cheek on his chest. He dabbed at her injury again, and after a moment, his hand stilled. She felt fingers walking up her spine slowly. One finger, then another, brushing against her loose Bardot-neck top. He walked his fingers all the way up to the bare skin at the back of her neck, making her shiver. In turn, she heard his breath catch, and she slowly, gently, lifted her head to look at him.

'You're quite good-looking when you're not so cross,' she ventured, trying to break the atmosphere. And the sexual tension, which she could have grabbed to pull herself up on.

'You're not so bad yourself,' he rumbled, a cute smile lighting up his handsome face. He looked at her wound again, and his brows knitted together. 'Concussion?'

'No, I meant it.'

Cillian's eyebrows rose to his hairline. He looked at her lips just a beat too long before dragging his gaze back to hers.

'Funnily enough, so did I. I hope you're not usually this clumsy though, or I'll have to up my catching game.'

'Yeah,' she mumbled. 'Sorry about that. You make me nervous.'

Cillian's smile deepened. 'How so?'

'If I knew how so, I'd be able to tell you.'

'I don't doubt that – you speak your mind well enough.'

'About time too,' April countered, half to herself.

'Agreed.' Cillian laughed. 'Carefully now, let's sort that head. You get up first, I'll follow.' She slowly pulled herself up, Cillian moving with her like a magnet, stemming the flow of blood with the scrap of fabric still pushed against her head. They stood toe to toe, breathing hard. 'It's not too bad now,' he said, pulling the handkerchief away just enough to check whether the wound was knitting together. 'How many fingers am I holding up?' He held up a closed fist, the hankie hanging from it.

'Three and a half?' she joked. 'I'm fine, honestly. You should get back. Orla.'

He glanced back at the chalets, where the night sky made the line of buildings look all the prettier, like ornate treasure chests left on a moonlit beach.

'I do need to check on her.' He still had his arm around April's back, and he moved back, his hand trailing till the last moment. 'There's nothing else for it.'

April, feeling woozy now, looked at him warily.

'Nothing else for what?'

He strode over to the open paint tins, clicking on their lids and chucking the brushes into a nearby pot full of turpentine.

'Given the events of the night, I think it's best if you stay over at mine.'

You,

Your letter never arrived, and it wasn't the infernal mail system this time. The lads were all brimming with good news and perfumed kisses. I hate them today. Being stuck on a ship here makes me feel ever more alone. Missing you. I knew the date was coming, but I never asked you when. I didn't want to know. Is it over now? Am I too late? Write to me, please. If you can't bear to speak, I will understand your silence.

I saw a beach today, much like our little patch of English heaven. The sky was blue, and the sea looked almost emerald-green. I thought of all the things you would say if you saw it, how excited you would have been. I hate all the never wills – they choke me in my sleep at night. Write to me, I beg you. If only to say goodbye.

G

Chapter 9

It was cold now, the spring air having a little nip to it as Wednesday turned to night, and the sun went off to warm some other part of the earth. Martha regretted not wrapping up, but she'd been in such a dash that morning, she hadn't thought to pack. Even her Mary-Poppins-style handbag hadn't offered anything from his depths more useful than a plastic rain hood to protect her hair. She couldn't bring herself to put it on, even though the tips of her ears were starting to protest. She was nearly there anyway, and then that would be that. She would know she was being silly, and then things could go back to normal. She could go back to her chalet, and paint, and …

What? What did come next? Most of her friends had moved on now, to other parts of England, to sun-kissed terraces in Marbella, or Benidorm, or Italy. Some were donning Mickey Mouse ears and TENA Lady to attempt the big thrill rides of Florida with their children, and grandchildren. Some were gone too soon, and that made her think of Charlie again. She'd bared her soul to him that afternoon, even more than usual, and the guilt had lain heavy ever since. She hoped that when she saw him next, he would be as understanding as she thought he was in her own head. She'd washed the man's pants for over forty years. She knew the beat of his heart as well as her own, but she wasn't naive enough to think that a man, even a dead one, couldn't still throw a mood swing or two.

Her feet kept moving, one in front of the other, till she reached the main street. The shops were all closed up, shutters down, a few muted display lights lighting up the different wares. Fat Willy's Surf Shack, a family-run bakery, a charity shop showcasing clothes worn once and discarded like holey socks, and the art gallery. The walls of the gallery were all glass, giving it a goldfish bowl look compared to the rest of the shops with their neat, bare windows. It looked like it belonged there though, the floor of the shop display covered with sand, shells, and props sticking out as a kind of real-life beach backdrop to the art. In the main window, one white easel stood, with a plain white canvas sitting on top of it. It read:

Coming soon
Local artists welcome to submit

She used to sell her work here, before the owner moved on to the next challenge, and the shop stood empty. Another business she loved left to dwindle and die before her eyes. Another piece of her past altered, destroyed, and removed. She pressed her face to the window, but couldn't see anything else. The space had been cleaned out till it was a blank canvas, ready for the new owner to make their mark. She'd have to come back when it was open, but she didn't know when that would be. Her nerves were shot already.

She huffed to herself, pulling her thin jacket around her that bit tighter and stamping her feet on the pavement. From annoyance as well as to get the blood flowing back through her half-frozen toes.

'Hello, can I help?' a voice said at her side. A voice that she knew. One that she thought she'd never hear again. She wanted so much to turn, to look, but she found herself turning away instead, back up the street, towards home. Away from the gallery and the ghosts.

'No thank you,' she said in as posh a voice as she could muster and she kept walking, as fast as she could without breaking into a petrified bolt. 'Tourist,' she threw at them by way of explanation. She didn't draw breath till she reached the taxi rank on the corner.

'Taxi please, Shady Pines.' She fell into one of the plastic chairs in the waiting area, suddenly exhausted and depleted. 'Please hurry, if you can.'

It felt like forever before the man behind the glass motioned that the taxi had pulled up outside. She smiled weakly at him, gathering her things around her and heading back out into the night. Just outside, a car's headlights framed a shadow set back against the buildings on the corner. Martha kept her head down, not wanting any light to show her face. She practically threw herself into the back seat, hunkering down. She ignored the twinge in her knees as she bent herself double to stay out of sight. The startled driver looked at her, shrugged and started to drive.

Martha hugged herself tight, trying to stop the shakes that were rippling through her body. She was already denying to herself what had just happened. She'd felt sure when the voice spoke that she knew just who it was, but what were the chances? Playing it back in her head, she wasn't so sure now. Unlikely, wasn't it? It was just her, making things up in her head. It was stress, she was sure of it. All the upheaval at the chalet park, and now the gallery having a new owner, new possibilities. She should just get over herself, she knew, but the more things changed, the harder it was to ignore the fear.

Since Charlie passed, and she'd sold up and moved to Shady Pines, she'd felt a little lost. Blocked. She wasn't even able to paint anymore. Not like she used to. Her gift was diminishing, and she felt the loss acutely. She had just started to sketch again, but now what? After this, would that be shed from her psyche too? She felt wretched. More than a little nostalgic too.

'Love, you all right?' The taxi driver brought her back to the present. She nodded slowly, offering him a weak smile to reassure the pair of worried eyes in the rear-view mirror.

'I'm fine thanks, it's been a little bit of a day,' she said honestly. He nodded, turning the radio up just a touch and focusing back on the street-lamp-lit road.

'Tell me about it. Soon be feet-up time.'

She nodded again, but couldn't muster an answer. She knew what her night would offer. Whispering ghosts and shadows of the past would be her bedfellows tonight, if they let her sleep at all. Since she'd seen that article, she just couldn't settle. She wondered whether the huge slab of dread she felt in the pit of her stomach was fear alone. As she thought again of the voice, the shadow watching her depart, she knew it was far more complicated than that. The truth was, Martha didn't know quite what to hope for.

Chapter 10

'I'm still not convinced that this is strictly necessary,' April protested as they locked up the games room and started to walk across the park towards their homes. 'I'm fine. I have a headache, but I'll just take something and go to bed.'

'That's the perfect way to slip into a coma.' He chuckled. 'You're stubborn – I get it.'

April narrowed her eyes at him, but his face was lit up with mischievous humour.

'Just indulge me, okay? No boss, no home, no job. Besides, you need the cut washing out and covering over. You've been painting and rolling around here all day.'

April felt her lips tighten together. It made sense, but the thought of the close proximity was still making her panic. The way he'd held her to him on the games room floor had her head spinning. She'd felt completely safe and protected, the opposite to how Duncan had made her feel in those last weeks. She'd not even been here a week yet, and she was snuggling up to a man who was fascinating the hell out of her. He made her so nervous, so awkward. More socially awkward than normal, and yet he made her feel safe too. She realised to her horror that she missed it, and the thought kept her quiet the rest of the way. It was one night, and then everything would go back to normal. Normal as things were for her, anyway.

Cillian opened his front door and stretched his arm out theatrically.

'After you, Bambi.' He knocked his knees together, pretending to wobble and she rolled her eyes at him. A flash of pain shot through her head, and she winced. Cillian was at her side in an instant, one hand on the small of her back, the other cupping her cheek. 'Hey, hey. Shit,' he muttered under his breath. 'Listen, shall I phone the doctor?'

April was already shaking her head, gingerly due to the wave of pain that still shot through her skull.

'No, it's okay. I didn't get knocked out. I'm really okay, I can ...'

She made a move from the porch area to her own chalet, and Cillian's hand tightened around her back, the other moving to her side as he softly blocked her exit with his own body. She caught a waft of aftershave and what smelled like baby powder. A clean, fresh smell that fitted him perfectly. As soon as she caught a whiff, her nerve endings felt like they were on fire.

'I don't think so, April, come on. You can have my bed, I'll take the couch.' He was inches away from her now, leaning in so close she could have counted the bristles on his thickening five-o'clock shadow. His eyes were full of concern and she felt her stomach flip. She licked her lips without thinking, and his pupils dilated as his gaze followed the tip of her pink tongue.

'April, I—'

The crunch of gravel made them both freeze as the lights from a vehicle lit up the main road into the park. A taxi, pulling up outside Martha's chalet. Cillian frowned, muttering something under his breath before releasing April a little. He didn't completely let go of her and she found that she was glad of it. They both turned, their shocked expressions mirroring Martha's as she got out of the car. Cillian stepped forward towards her, but she raised a gloved hand and stopped him.

'I'm fine thank you, dear. Just fine.' The tone of her voice sounded off, even to April. It was weaker than usual, the usual sting in the tail of her words absent. 'April, I wouldn't mind a word if you have a moment.' April's shoulders went up over her ears at her request. Why did she always feel like a prize idiot around people here, like she dare not say no? It was bad enough that she was hot for her handyman, or was after he had practically dry humped her with concern after her fall. She could still feel his touch on her back, and she relished the feelings it evoked. Or she did when they were happening. Now she was just a bumbling tit with a head wound and a feeling that she was about to get the second sermon of the day from one of the Lizard Point matriarchs.

'Does it have to be tonight?' Cillian asked softly, his head constantly flicking back to his own chalet, distracted by his daughter sleeping alone just feet away. April's heart squeezed with something, but she didn't try to identify it or assess the feeling. She couldn't. What would be the point? 'We have a bit of paperwork to do.'

It was a week off the planned opening, rushed due to finances, but they were still a way off before they could get open properly. She played along, wondering why Cillian hadn't outed her as a doomed damsel in distress or used the opportunity to run back to his chalet away from them both.

Martha pursed her lips together, and then nodded slowly. She reached for a set of keys from one of her bags and waved them both goodnight.

'I'll come tomorrow morning, Martha,' April called after her. Martha just waggled her fingers over her shoulder, and she didn't stop till she was at the other side of the door. Within moments, Martha's chalet filled with warm lights, and she was pulling her curtains as she went from room to room. The pair of them found themselves standing and staring for a moment.

'Do you think she's okay?' April asked. She turned to look at

Cillian, but he was already looking at her. He flicked his eyes to Martha's place as though he had never glanced her way.

'I'm not sure, but this place is not the same without her here, so I hope it gets sorted.'

'I do too. It was strange without her today. Even with her sharp tongue.'

Cillian chuckled softly. 'Ah, she's not so bad once you get to know her. When Charlie, her husband, was here, she was a bit happier maybe.' His eyebrows pulled together, a faint hint of realisation crossing his features. 'To be honest though, even then she had an edge to her. Let me know if I can help tomorrow, okay?'

He headed to his front door and turned as he reached for the doorknob.

'Come on, you'll catch your death out here.'

She looked at her chalet, and back at Cillian. He gave her a little smile, showing off the dimples in his cheeks, and she found her feet moving towards him. She went along too, ignoring all the tiny little niggling voices in her head that told her that this was a bad idea. It was one night. She could get through one awkward night. Back during her marriage, she'd had plenty of practice.

Cillian reached for her arm, gently pulling her into the chalet and locking the door behind them. He put the keys on a little hook she hadn't seen before, holding a picture of Cillian and Orla beaming into the camera as they sat on the sand. Cillian was holding his daughter so protectively it made her think of how he had reached for her when she fell. How his arms had felt around her. She pushed the thought away before her red cheeks gave her away. She didn't have a poker face, and she could feel the heat shivering up her neck. It was her hormones, she mused. Nothing a little oil of evening primrose and a cold shower or three wouldn't fix. She was still looking at the picture when he walked back towards her, pulling Orla's door closed behind him.

'She's fast asleep. Her nightlight's on,' he said, the relief at being back in the chalet with her palpable. April swallowed down a bunch of questions she wanted to ask, and smiled back.

'She's adorable,' she said truthfully, pointing to the key frame. His face lit up, and April marvelled at how just thinking about one person could literally change a person's whole demeanour. She didn't have anyone like that now. Her mum always looked at her that way, so maybe that was enough. Maybe the 'one love' thing wasn't all romance, or wasn't for everyone. Maybe it was just love for another person who smiled at the mere thought of the other. 'Does she like it here, so far?'

'She's doing better at nursery, and being here seems to be helping too. It's early days, but I'm thankful to you.'

She pushed out a soft laugh.

'Oh no, thank you. Judging by my DIY skills, I would have probably lit myself on fire or worse if you weren't here to pick me up.' *Eeep, awkward wording.* 'Not that you are picking me up, of course. I mean, I'm your boss and …' She was full-on babbling now, something about employer rules and other incoherent bumbling. He saved her, thankfully. Yet again. *This is becoming a habit, April. Stop it.*

'I knew what you meant. Have you eaten?'

He led her through by the arm to the sitting room, his hand half in hers. If she just stretched out her fingers, just a little, she could interlock them with his. She felt them tingle with missed opportunity when he showed her to the sofa and pulled a take-away menu from a drawer in the side table.

The sitting room was lamp-lit, the TV off in the corner. A paperback lay over the arm of the armchair. April went over and picked it up, glancing at the open pages.

'Good book?' she asked. It was the same book she had been reading. When she'd finished, she'd decided to put it into a basket in the reception. She'd marked it 'take one leave one' and popped it in there.

'Not bad.' He shrugged. It was a love story, not one that she would think Cillian would be into reading. She was happy to be proved wrong this time. 'I put one in the basket, see what you think.' He disappeared into the kitchen and came back with dressings, cotton wool pads, and a bowl of warm water. She sat still as he got to work, his face paling with concern when she winced a time or two.

'Ah, the blood made it look a lot worse than it is,' he said, gently washing and drying the cut. 'It's not deep.' He took his time, his little pink tongue peeking out at one point when he was concentrating. It was adorable, and April had to tense her whole face to stop herself from touching him. 'All done,' he said softly. He stroked the back of his hand down her cheek. 'No scars on this face.'

'Thanks. How bad does it look?'

Cillian stood with the bowl in his hand and looked straight down into her eyes.

'You look good.' His eyes widened. 'Bit bruised like.' He cleared his throat loudly, passing her his mobile phone from his pocket.

April prayed to God she didn't erupt like a tomato. *You look good.*

'It doesn't have a lock on it. I wanted Orla to be able to use it if she needed it. Will you order, while I go make the bed up?'

She took the menus, scanning through the appetising dishes listed till her stomach grumbled.

'What do you fancy?'

He shrugged again, his manner relaxed now, open even. It was nice to see, and she found herself sinking further back into the sofa, her muscles slowly unclenching as time went on and the awkwardness subsided to a more acceptable level.

'I'm easy, just order me what you get. I won't be a minute.'

She focused on the menu, as Cillian left the room and came back with two little white tablets and a glass of cold water.

'Just paracetamol, take the edge off that headache. Shan't be long.' He raised one brow. 'Don't forget the prawn crackers.'

She looked up at him, being so nice to her when she needed it the most. He didn't even realise how much he'd helped her just now. Seeing how much he loved his child, how he'd bared his concerns to her earlier. She admitted to herself that it was there, the attraction, but it was more than that. She actually liked him as a person.

'I wouldn't dream of it.' She laughed, waving him off. He looked pointedly at the tablets again, and back at her.

'Take those tablets.'

She did as she was asked, swallowing the chalky little capsules and washing the lot down with a huge glug of water. Touching her injury gently, she winced at the swelling she felt. It was sore, but not serious. She felt fine, if a little sheepish. Sheepish, confused, and blinking starving.

Selecting a few things from the menu, she went to dial the number. The phone sprang into life when she touched it, and a photo of Orla came up. She was in nursery this time, beaming over the top of a handmade volcano, foam squirting out from the top. April found herself grinning back at the photo. It was a happy little moment, captured forever. She didn't for once feel the urge to pet Orla like a Labrador, or the squeeze of her ovaries as she felt the loss once more. Progress. Or maybe hunger just trumped heartbreak. She was just dialling the takeaway number when a text popped up on the screen. April jumped, and accidentally speed-read the words *The nursery called the police, Cillian. I wonder whose idea that was!* before she put it face down on the table. Cillian came back in, a throw and a pillow under one arm.

'You not ordered yet?'

Her expression turned his easy smile upside down.

'What's wrong? Your head?'

He was kneeling at her feet now, the contents of his arms

tossed onto the sofa nearby. She picked up the phone, showing him the screen.

'It popped up while I was dialling. Sorry. I didn't mean to read it. Bit of a fast reader – it's a thing I've always been able to do. I am sorry. I can go.'

She watched his eyes move across the screen, his beautiful sea-glass-green eyes darkening as his expression turned almost murderous. His jaw clenched and she heard his intake of breath as he processed the words. Taking the phone from her gently, he dialled the number from the menu and passed the handset back to her wordlessly.

'Hello, Golden Dragon?'

He left the room, half stomping, half shuffling to the kitchen.

'Hi, yes … sorry …' She realised the person was waiting for her to answer, but she was too busy watching Cillian. He was leaning against the kitchen counter, his head in his hands for a moment. She turned her attention to ordering their food, and by the time she had rung off, he wasn't in the kitchen anymore. Frowning, she looked out of the back windows and saw a little red orb of light outside. Pushing open the back doors, she wrapped her arms around herself and slipped out into the night.

It was beautiful outside, especially after dark. Each chalet had their own little front and back areas, but the two Cillian and April lived in were nearest the beach path, backing right onto it. Right out of those back doors, you could smell the salty spray coming off the waves, see for miles and miles. She loved this view, and once more she found herself in awe of her new quirky home.

'I'll be back in a minute,' Cillian said from the shadows, gruff. A plume of white smoke came from his direction. The little red orb.

'Bad habit that, you know.' She shivered when a gust of wind billowed past, pulling her arms closer over her chest.

'I know. I stopped before Orla came along, but sometimes I just need to have one to take the edge off.'

April moved through the dark, their porch lights lighting just enough to see her way to him.

'I'll eat and then go back to mine. I'm fine, really, and I think you need some peace.'

He huffed deep in his chest and took another deep drag, the red embers glowing bright.

'I'll never get that – you saw the text. I don't want you to leave. Stay.'

'Okay,' she agreed, finding herself thrilled that he didn't want her out. 'Does Orla want her mum in her life?' She felt cheeky even asking, but she couldn't silence the question in her head. She needed to know what she was getting into. Not that she was thinking like that. Not much anyway. God, he looked gorgeous tonight.

He narrowed his eyes at her impertinence, missing her semi-lustful gaze entirely with his pig-headedness, but she stood her ground. As well as she could while covering her rather cold chest. She only had her painting clothes on, and she was aware that her nipples were proudly displaying their aversion to the chill in the air. 'I only ask because, well, I lost a mum. I'd give anything to have her back.'

She choked a little on the words, but got them out. Somehow, she felt like she needed to say it. To advocate for Orla, which was a first for her. It felt rather odd. Maternal. Cillian didn't say anything for a beat, just pulling once more on the cigarette before pinching off the cherry and holding the tab end in his hand.

'She's scared of her.' The smoke came out of his mouth and floated off into the night, curling around the four words. 'Were you scared of yours?'

April shook her head sadly. 'No, of course not.' She felt scared now, not to have that feeling of knowing her mum was out there somewhere. Tending to her garden, cackling with her friends, living her life. She was just gone, and April felt the loss every day. She wondered what Orla felt. 'Is it bad?'

He sighed heavily, and she was suddenly moving forward, stroking his arm with her hand. He reached up after a moment and wrapped his hand around hers, pulling it away. April was just beginning to feel foolish when he linked his fingers through hers, and pulled them to his mouth. Dropping a warm kiss on the back of her hand, he looked up at her.

'We seem to be a pair of right miserable buggers tonight, don't we?' she quipped, trying to cut through the tension in her usual ham-fisted way. What she really wanted to know was what that cigarette would taste like on his lips. She'd been jealous of it, watching him smoke, and it wasn't the nicotine she craved.

He chuckled, rubbing the scruff of his beard along her skin and kissing it again. Just once, a little peck that felt like a fireball to her nerves. He looked her over, and she felt his eyes wander from curve to curve. She shivered.

'Ah, look at me would you, keeping you out in the cold.' He walked them both back inside, not letting go of her hand as he passed her a bottle of white wine from the fridge and grabbed two glasses with his free hand. Going into the living room, he put the glasses down, taking her wine to sit with it, and didn't let go of her till they were both sitting under the throw on the sofa.

'Do you think I'll be okay drinking that, given my alleged concussion?' she said sarcastically as he passed her a full glass.

He shrugged. 'You're staying here anyway, right? It'll be grand, I'm sure.' He winked at her. 'Just the one.'

'Cillian, I don't think I should be here to be honest. You have enough on, and I'm fine. Calamity Jane, that's me.'

'Humour me then,' he said. 'Stay over so I can be sure.' His easy smile faded a little as he sat back, taking his glass with him. 'I could do with the company to be honest. Orla won't bother you in the morning, don't worry.'

She sat back against the back of the sofa, taking a tentative sip. One little glass wouldn't do her any harm, and to be honest, as odd as the arrangement was, she found that she didn't really want to leave either. It felt homely here, and Cillian was different every time she saw him. She never knew which man she was going to get each time they met, but that was only serving to intrigue her more. She wanted to see how the pieces of him fit together, and which parts were missing. Like the parts missing of her. And Martha, it seemed. Maybe this place was a last chance saloon for the lonely-hearted, like Judith had said.

'Orla wouldn't bother me at all,' she assured him. 'I like her.'

Cillian's eyes crinkled in the corners as he smiled at the thought of his daughter, but it faded before her eyes. The room seemed to darken as a result.

'I have a lunchtime appointment tomorrow with a solicitor. I'm going for sole custody, properly, and they are going to keep her away from her mum. For now, at least. She can't be around her; it's not good for Orla. She came to nursery, made her cry. You hear about that?'

'No, I didn't.' She wouldn't have breathed a word of it if she did know. The thought of sweet little Orla and her pals being scared at nursery chilled her to the bone. 'Is she okay?'

'I don't know in all honesty. She barely speaks when she's out in public. She doesn't eat well. Since she came here, she's slept better though.' His expression changed as something crossed his mind. 'Did you leave the pink bear, in her room?'

April nodded sheepishly. 'It was mine, from when I was younger. Albie will look after her.'

'Albie?' Cillian checked. 'He's called Pinky now. What kind of kid were you?'

April laughed, taking a deep pull on her wine as she felt herself relaxing.

'I was the slightly pudgy kid who blended in as best she could,' she admitted. 'Albie was a great confidant to me over the years.'

'Kids are horrible aren't they sometimes. Orla had a bit of aggro from one of the other kids about her mum. Broke my

105

heart in two.' He held his hand over where his heart was on his chest.

'They have their moments. Does Orla's mum ask about her?'

'No, she doesn't, and that's what makes it worse. She wants to come off as the injured party, but it's not about her or me, or our car crash of a relationship. It's about who came of it, but she's never really understood that. She's angry I suppose, maybe a little bit embarrassed.'

April could see that he was in turmoil, and she felt unqualified to comment. She didn't know the toll of motherhood, and how it affected people differently. She had wanted to block out anyone pregnant within a five-mile radius at one point back in Yorkshire. She'd avoided events just in case the small talk descended to babies and school districts.

'Maybe,' she offered in response instead. She didn't feel like she could comment on anyone's past. She was still hiding from hers, even now. 'It must be hard.'

Cillian was saved from answering by a knock on the door.

'Food's here,' he said softly, looking at her intently before getting up. 'Get the plates?'

The sounds of the sea could be heard faintly in the chalet as Cillian lay on the sofa, trying and failing to get some sleep. He was keeping an ear open for Orla, but she hadn't so much as stirred the whole night. She was more settled here, the best she'd been for a while, and Cillian was encouraged by the thought. When he used to work here before, he'd always loved the place. Tim notwithstanding. To see a glimpse of how it used to be come back to life was amazing, and he knew it had a lot to do with the woman who was currently sleeping in his bed. She had something she was working through, he knew, but what with her, his issues, and Martha flitting off and being so secretive, he was beginning to think that the place was more of a therapy centre than a holiday park.

It would be opening soon, with bookings coming in steadily through the website and repeat customers building up. The photos on the site were all out of date, but to be honest Tim hadn't really kept up to it anyway, so the guests wouldn't be disappointed at least. The shop and reception area were getting done, with new stock arriving all the time. It would be busier from now on, and he was looking forward to seeing people using the place again. Maybe Orla would come out of her shell more with the children that would be hanging around. Maybe it would do them all good to have a bit more life around here.

April had listened over their takeaway as he'd spilled his guts. About him and Tina meeting while he was working in Cornwall, how they'd gotten pregnant after just a short space of time, unplanned. He'd never regretted it. It was a shock of course, and they were not a lot more than friends with benefits, but the baby didn't care about any of that. She was coming anyway, and Cillian had stepped up.

'So you left here, to get better work?' April popped a piece of prawn cracker in her mouth, leaning forward to pick up her wine glass from the coffee table. They'd finished all the food before his tale was done.

'I worked away, short-term agency contracts. Tim was running this place poorly, and things were beginning to feel different. No stock being bought in, my hours getting less and less. He was winding down – I could see it. I went to London, laboured where I could. I'm a carpenter by trade, but I did pretty much anything I could to get the cash in. I guess that's where it went wrong.'

It had been while he was away that Tina's true struggles came to light. Struggling alone with a newborn unplanned baby, her boyfriend away in the week, the cracks soon became huge fissures. She blamed him for leaving her with Orla; he couldn't get through to her that he was doing it for them. To give them the best start as a new family. They were laying the foundations, making the best of it. He had hoped that if they raised enough for a house

107

deposit, things would settle down. It just hadn't quite worked that way. Tina was a total stranger to him by then, and when she started drinking of a night, it was already over. No one had spoken the words out loud, but they both knew. What came after, leaving Orla on her own, had finally smashed them apart. He did get it, he wasn't oblivious to what she had to do daily. Since raising Orla on his own, he'd realised how hard it was, how isolating. If he could calm down enough, he would tell her that. If she'd listen. Just to clear the air, to try to move on. For all their sakes, least of all the legal bills.

'There's no chance then, for you two?'

Cillian shook his head, clenching his jaw at the thought. They'd never been right together. He'd told April more than he ever had Tina. Maybe that was part of the problem.

'Not a chance. I can never forgive her, even though I get it more now, and she doesn't want to listen. For her, it's about saving face, nothing else. She has things to lose now, her new life.'

April smiled at him, as if she wanted him to know she was listening. 'So you came home.'

'So I came home. I worked when I could, around Orla, but it's been hard. She's just started to settle into nursery now, and come September she'll be full-time.' Cillian explained how the nursery teachers had just begun to draw Orla out of her shell.

'Do you think she'll settle?'

He smiled back then. 'Early days, but yes, I think so, and it means I can do more hours around here and not get choked with childcare.'

'More time for me then,' April said, grinning. Cillian's eyes locked with hers. 'Sounds great all round.'

'More time for you, yes. I had thought of that, too. A lot.' He didn't look away, and April's cheeks flushed. It made his stomach flip. She sure was something.

'I meant the Pines, of course,' she clarified, eyeing him over her wine glass. God, the woman was attractive. He'd started noticing little things about her. The way she blushed with any kind of compliment, the way she always covered her body. Loose-fitting clothes that didn't so much hang off her curves as dwarf them. He couldn't help wondering what her husband had looked like, how he had treated her. Did this lack of confidence stem from him, or somewhere else? He liked every inch of what he'd seen. His eyes couldn't get enough of her.

'Of course.' He'd chuckled, draining his glass.

He heard a door creak open, his daddy ears springing to attention like a guard dog.

'Orla?' he whispered, fearful that she would sleepily head straight for his bedroom.

'No,' a whisper came back. 'It's me.'

April padded into the living room doorway. She was wearing a pair of his shorts and an old T-shirt that had never looked better than it did right now. He tried not to stare, but he couldn't help taking in her long legs, her curves, now released from the confines of her baggy clothing.

'My clothes fit you well,' he called to her. 'You okay?'

He went to stand up, but she held up her hand.

'Yes, I'm sorry. I was a bit thirsty that's all.'

He pulled the throw back, his tracksuit bottoms still on and hanging low on his waist.

'Tea?' he offered, and she relaxed, nodding gratefully. 'I can't sleep either.'

She followed Cillian into the kitchen, him clicking on the kettle and her getting the cups out on auto pilot. They moved around each other in the space, tiptoeing and moving slowly. As she went to grab the milk, he reached for a spoon from the drawer, putting his hands on her hips as he gently navigated around her. She drew in a sharp, audible breath and felt herself tense. His hands were warm, but they stilled the second she gasped.

'Sorry,' he whispered dramatically, putting his hands up in the air. 'I didn't mean to …'

'It's fine.' She waved him away, embarrassed. Reaching for the milk, she gave herself a second to pull her face into a less panicked expression. Duncan hadn't touched her for such a long time, she'd quite forgotten how it felt. 'You just surprised me.'

Cillian looked at her like he wanted to say something, but he closed his lips tight together.

'Can I ask you something?' he asked after a tense moment, his head turning to one side. 'Without getting too personal?'

The kettle clicked off, and she focused on finishing her task. 'Go ahead.' She dared not look at him. *Anything but the weight, please. Don't talk about my weight.*

He looked at her once more, his gaze dipping just for a second before he opened his mouth.

'What did you really come here for?'

Chapter 11

On Judith's farm a short distance away, Kenneth the cockerel opened his little birdy eyes and cleared his throat. Surveying all his sleeping hens, tucked away safe and sound in their straw-filled huts, he gave a little shake of his head to fluff out his feathers, and went to his usual place to do his alpha poultry duty and wake up the residents of Lizard Point. Standing up, tall and proud on the little blue gate, he steeled himself for the dawn call.

'Cock-a doodle-doooo!'

April's eyes sprang open, and she jerked up, regretting it when a dull ache reverberated around her head. A mixture of her injury and the wine she and Cillian had put away between them. She went to sit up, but found that she was pinned by something. A muscular arm around her middle. Looking around her, she saw that Cillian was fast asleep, his dark lashes fluttering as he leaned into her side.

'Shit,' she said, a little too loudly for the hour. Cillian's eyes fluttered again, but she managed to get out from under him without waking him. She laid his head on one of the cushions, and covered him over with the throw. Looking at the clock, she knew Orla could wake at any minute. She needed to get away, and quick. Gathering her things from the bedroom, she made a quick exit out of the front door, still wearing Cillian's clothes.

Closing it behind her, she sighed heavily. She'd enjoyed last night far too much, and this morning was a rude wake-up call. She didn't have time for fantasies about the handyman, complicated ones at that. She needed him to help her with this place, not to file a sexual harassment charge against her and clean out what was left of her fast-dwindling bank account. What with all the repairs, the painting, the games room being kitted out, the touches to the interior of the chalets, she was about broke. She'd sunk just about every penny she'd ever had or inherited into the place, and it wasn't officially open till the following week. She only had Martha's income, and with Cillian's wages and everything else, she was starting to panic.

Which was just how her mother must have felt, driving down here all those years ago. Without a plan and adrift. Free, but adrift just the same. April hadn't even turned her phone on, relying on the office phone to make any business calls she needed. She'd been using the park's email to correspond with customers and the like, so she was technically dead. Dead as far as social media went, anyway. Were you even a real person if you didn't document your daily life for all to see? She used to love being social, but that was before Duncan, and before the baby elephant in the room grew too large for even her to ignore.

She walked down Cillian's porch, turning left to go into her chalet and start the day. The early morning dew on the grass tickled her bare feet as she moved, and she wiggled her toes in among the blades. Looking across at Martha's, she was startled to see her sitting on her porch, sketchbook in hand. Her glasses were halfway down the bridge of her nose, her keen eyes looking right at her.

'Morning,' she ventured, shuffling her bundle of clothing from one arm to the other. 'You're up early.'

'Catches the worm, and all that,' Martha replied briskly, tapping the sketchbook. 'You?'

April's eyes narrowed. How much had Martha seen? She tried to gauge it from her expression, but failed. Martha was a master of subterfuge, and April needed a bucket of coffee first to shake her brain into life. And a cold shower, because she couldn't quite bring herself to block out how nice Cillian had felt wrapped around her on that couch. She regretted waking up early. Bloody cockerel.

'Depends.'

Martha's lip twitched. 'On what?'

'How much you saw.'

Martha smiled, pushing her glasses up her nose. 'Come sit, please. I need to speak to you.'

April shot a glance back towards Cillian's, before padding over barefoot. Martha pulled herself up, closing her sketchbook and motioning for her to follow her inside. April did as she was asked, wiping her bare feet as best she could.

In the lounge, on the coffee table, there was a large wooden box in the centre that hadn't been there before. Martha eyed it like it belonged to Pandora, and April followed her gaze. She could feel the unease coming off Martha in waves.

'Sit.' Martha sat down herself in her easy chair. 'Please.'

Putting her bundle to one side on the floor, April sat down and waited.

'The favour I spoke of yesterday? I need you to go into town, if you like. Cillian too, if you don't mind. He has an eye for these things. Art things.'

April ignored the fact that Martha obviously didn't rate her artistic side, given that she struggled to draw a stick man on her best days. She'd already disappointed her only tenant with the Lizard-themed hut, for families of little ones. April had been thrilled, but Martha had dubbed it the 'snot box' in the reservations book, complete with a tiny drawing of April, one cartoonish finger delving up her rather disproportionate nostril. *Wait till she sees the lizard stencils, and the colour scheme inside.*

'He's a carpenter,' she spat back a little childishly. Maybe she should show her the farm animals she'd stencilled in the games room, or the painting she had planned in the shell-themed hut.

'Carpentry is a form of art, don't you think?'

She had her there. And April knew carpenters were talented. She was just being catty. 'I do, I suppose.' Cillian was talented – there was no doubt about that. Which made her think of his hands again. Working with the wood, helping her to make the place what she had pictured in her head. The feel of them across her body. 'Yes, I do.' She fanned herself with one hand, and Martha smirked at her. 'What do you need us to do?'

'I need you to go to the local art gallery. It's not quite open yet, but I want to see what they are planning. Will you do that for me, and ask Cillian too?'

April looked at Martha, so anxious, and found herself agreeing. 'Do you want us to mention your work?'

Martha boomed, 'No!' startling them both. 'No,' she tried again, a little less panic-stricken. 'No, please don't. In fact, it's probably not a good idea. I …'

Sitting forward, April stopped her. 'Martha, that's fine. We'll go and have a look. We won't mention you.'

'Or this place?' she checked, her hands twirling a dry paintbrush and rolling it between her twitchy fingers. 'Don't go yet.' She nibbled at her bottom lip. 'Leave it a few days, let the dust settle.'

'Okay, and we won't mention you. Or this place,' April agreed. 'We won't say anything, I promise.'

Martha breathed out slowly, and the tension that had shadowed her face seemed to lift. She looked lighter, right before April's eyes.

'Thank you, April,' she said earnestly. 'Thank you.'

'Happy to help.' April beamed back at her. Today was pretty awesome so far.

'This doesn't make us friends you know,' Martha added, deflating the image of harmony in April's mind. 'You've not done a week yet. Cillian tells me you are planning to open next week? We can revisit the idea then perhaps.'

April rolled her eyes. 'That would be lovely. Thank you for considering liking me.'

'You're welcome,' Martha replied. 'And I know about the stencils. Orla ratted you out. I'll do the lizards, if you must have the wretched things on that giant pea. I'll paint them.'

'Er—'

'Thank you is customary in these situations, dear, and you're welcome.'

Chapter 12

April was signing a delivery note for the last of the machines and pool tables for the games room when a little voice behind her startled her.

'What's in the van?'

She turned, lowering her gaze till she saw Orla, holding Pinky and sucking her thumb. Cillian's eyes looked out from under her little lashes, and April had to ignore the squeeze of something in her chest. Something warm and fuzzy.

'Good morning, Orla. Pinky.' She gave the clipboard to the driver, showing him with a friendly point where the delivery should go, then kneeled before Orla. She gave the bear a little salute, and after a moment, Orla moved the bear's arm to give one back. 'This van is full of games for our new games room, so we shall have loads of fun when the other guests arrive.'

There had been a steady stream of bookings over the last few days, well, more of a trickle than a stream. Which was good, since everything was still coming together. The huts looked a lot better and they had started to finish some of them on the inside too. April was enjoying making the chalets look great on a budget, and the holiday homes were looking more welcoming and cosy than her old house with Duncan ever did, with their premium carpets and expensive trinkets. It was starting to feel like home, and she couldn't wait now to open.

'Orla, come and get your bag love, and put Pinky inside. He can stay here while you're at nursery.'

Orla looked at Pinky a little fearfully.

'We'll look after him, pinkie promise,' April said to placate her. She didn't like to see the little girl frown. She always looked like such an old soul, which broke her heart to watch. Orla lifted up the hand not clinging to the bear and raised her little finger. April laughed softly and wrapped her pinkie around the little girl's. 'High five for a good day at nursery!' Orla giggled, slapping her palm against April's. Hugging the bear in both hands, she turned and ran off past Cillian to their chalet.

'Morning,' April tried, but Cillian walked straight past her, van keys in hand. 'Cillian?'

Still nothing, and he was half in the van now. Looking back towards the chalet, with the door still ajar, she huffed. What was his deal lately? He'd been so weird after that night on the couch. Feeling more than a little irritated, she tapped on the passenger-side window. Cillian glared across at her, but after a heavy sigh, he wound down the window. She had a plan to get him talking to her again. Burying himself in work had meant that things were speeding along nicely, but the relaxed atmosphere was gone.

'Martha needs us to run that errand for her today. Could we go first thing?'

His green eyes were different too, as though the shine had been taken right out of their surface. He ran his hand roughly down his face and nodded.

'Your money, boss. What's the errand?'

April heard a door slam behind her and opening the van door, she leaned in quickly. She could hear Orla's little steps on the path, and she didn't want her to hear.

'Cillian, what's wrong with you lately? Is it because of the other night? I'm sorry if I overst—'

117

'Why did you leave?' he said simply, not even looking at her. 'I woke up and you were gone.'

April couldn't help but show the shock on her face, and Cillian's face closed down even further when he looked at her.

'It doesn't matter,' he practically growled, as Orla reached them. 'I shouldn't have said anything. I'll be back to pick you up.'

She didn't argue, turning to smile at Orla as she stepped aside for the little girl to get in.

'Have a good day, Orla. Pinky will be doing a bit of work with me, so he'll be fine.' Orla gave her the cutest little grin, and she melted. This kid was such a cutie. *Like her dad,* she couldn't help but think. 'See you soon, Cillian.'

She heard something that sounded like a grunt, and after closing the van doors she watched as they drove away. The curious excitement she had harboured about today was useless now. They had a million and one tiny little things to get sorted before they opened, and after the other night she had been excited about their ... whatever it was, too. But now? She just didn't get it. What was his problem?

She checked on reception, diverting the phones to answer machine for when they went out. She needed to get a tablet at some point, so that she could book people in even when she wasn't sat in the reception hut, but that was a moot point when she was too chicken to use her smartphone yet. She'd left it turned off since Cillian had sent her that picture. Another little thing on the huge towering pile of errands and tasks to wade through. She hadn't even been to the beach since the first day, and the thought depressed her. She knew things would get better, but when? The few people she knew around here were all acting pretty strangely, lost in their own inner struggles. It came to something when she was the only sane one around.

Heading to the games room, she checked in on the installation of the equipment and took a flask of tea down for the workers. She had been taught well to look after people she worked with,

118

and it came second nature to her now. It made her feel wanted, and special, and seen. Everything she hadn't felt since Duncan left, since Mum died and left her alone in the big bad world. Whatever Cillian's deal was, she felt sure that she hadn't done anything wrong. She'd been polite, grateful, and hadn't left a mess. She didn't understand how they could go from that night to talking like they did this morning. The more she replayed it in her head, the more it baffled and perplexed her.

She headed to chalet 9, which was still bare bones after being cleaned out and freshened up. In the centre of the dining room table was a pile of sheets and cushions, and on the floor were two boxes of freshly cleaned utensils, pans, et cetera. This was the fun part, putting the chalets together, but as she worked she just got mad. She just got madder and madder. Falling asleep together that night had surprised her, but that morning, when she woke it had felt so natural. The feel of his arm around her, protective and loving, made her want to weep now. She hadn't realised how much she had missed the feeling of being held, and it boiled her blood that he'd tainted it. He'd taken a precious little moment and ruined it with his sore bear head and petulant grunting.

She was onto her fourth kitchen cupboard when she heard his van come up the drive. She'd come to learn the noise of his engine, the path he took to his chalet. It felt comforting normally; hearing his van meant he was back. Another steady pair of hands, and Orla wasn't a bit of bother. Quiet, ever watching but no bother. Usually his little van noises made her smile. Her heartbeat quickened even to see Orla's little pieces of art, Martha ever praising as Cillian looked on. Every inch the bashful, proud dad.

Now hearing his wheels drive into Shady Pines, she felt something else. Anger. Rage. It was the time of month where she felt pretty crappy anyway, but this was anger now. She'd had enough of trying to gauge people's moods while hiding her own. It was time to stick to the plan and be the master of her own life. Cillian be damned. Putting some serving dishes onto one of the shelves, she locked up and went out to meet him.

Martha was standing next to him as he leaned against his van. He was shaking his head vigorously at her, but she wasn't having any of it.

'Everything okay?' April half shouted, feeling strangely jealous that they were as thick as thieves with each other. She swallowed down her anxiety and dusted off her anger at the grunting Neanderthal she had apparently employed.

'Yes,' Martha acknowledged her first. 'I was just filling Cillian here in on my little request.' Cillian looked at her but didn't say anything. Martha frowned at him, but thankfully let it go too. April couldn't help but blush when she thought of her failed early morning flit from Cillian's. 'Games room all done?'

'Yes, getting there. The lads are just putting it all together for us now. I have a delivery this afternoon too. Something for the play area. I should be back though.'

Martha waved her away.

'I shall be here. I can deal with it.' She reached out and placed a hand on Cillian's arm. 'Thank you, dear, both of you.' She sounded a little deflated, but she was soon off, heading to her chalet with a backward wave to them both.

'I hope she's okay. I feel like something's wrong.'

Cillian pushed out another reluctant grunt. 'Let's go. Quicker we go, quicker we can get back to work.'

Wow, Mr Sunshine – turn down that sparkling personality! She'd been looking forward to going into the town with Cillian, truth be told. She hadn't really ventured that far, not wanting to waste a moment with the park being such a task. She'd only seen snippets and peeks of what was around here, and she longed to explore her home. Just a little. She was a local business owner, after all, even if she lived in a panicked state half the time looking for a more adult-like adult to show the way. Which, she supposed today, was Martha, pushing them to go to town as Cornish spies.

'I need to get my bag, and a jacket. Two secs. We need to talk, so please stop being so moody.'

'Whatever,' she heard him growl at her retreating form. Opening her front door and grabbing her things, she spied her smartphone that was still switched off and sat on the side table in the hallway. She grabbed it, shoving it into her pocket and heading back out. She needed to start using it; she knew it. She might need it today, and it was pathetic now. The place would be fully open next week, and the bookings would only get busier, God willing. She needed to enter the real world at some point. It was almost April now. The first few days of her namesake were upon them, and she was ready to have a good summer, regardless of those around her. She'd already escaped the stares and the pointing; she wasn't about to feel awkward because her Man Friday was in a bit of a mood.

Giving herself a sideways glance in the mirror, she pulled on her little black jacket and headed out. Cillian had pulled up outside hers now, the passenger-side door left open. She hauled herself in, pulling the seatbelt around her. It was a little van, only three seats in the front cab. The middle seat was the only one unoccupied, the other being take up by Orla's pink and white car seat. Great. Now she was squashed between it and Cillian, and she felt self-conscious about him being so close again. It should have felt normal, natural even, but she just felt so awkward now.

'You in?' Cillian asked, glancing across. She saw him check her seatbelt, but that irked her further for some reason.

'Yes, I'm in,' she said curtly, turning towards the window. 'I learned clunk, click a while ago.' She was wearing a pair of black slacks, a simple white blouse under her jacket, and floral pumps on her feet. She'd made the effort today, she really had. It had been the first time for weeks that she hadn't been encrusted with dirt and grime, or splattered in paint. She'd even curled her hair. 'Do you know where we're going?'

'Martha told me.' He pulled away from Shady Pines, heading to the centre of town and the art gallery that they had been asked to check out. 'How do you want to play this?'

'Play what?'

Cillian turned and looked at her properly for the first time that day. 'I mean for the gallery. What's our story? A couple looking for art? Tourists?'

'A couple would make sense I suppose. They wouldn't think anything odd if we went with that, would they? It's believable, right?'

His features softened a little, but his focus was soon back on the road.

'Yeah, us together is believable.' His jaw flexed. 'I can see that. How long have we been together then?'

April drew in a shaky breath, playing his words over and over in her head.

'Three months?' she ventured. 'That's short enough to still like each other, and not long enough that we would be all over each other.'

He suppressed a smile. 'Depends on the people. Three months doesn't sound long enough to draw breath with the right one. Where did we meet? Why are we buying art?'

April thought for a moment. 'I moved here for work. We want to buy some art for my new place. We don't live together yet, but we hang around each other a lot.' Looking out of the window at Cornwall spread out before her, she remembered the car seat. 'What about Orla? I think three months is a little short to have bred a pre-schooler.'

Cillian laughed. 'People have kids when they meet people you know. We can stick to the truth on that one.'

'Okay, deal.' The van descended into silence again as they headed through the streets. 'Did Martha tell you what this was about?'

'Nope, but she's been a bit jumpy for a while now. She doesn't

122

like change at the park. I think the art gallery changing hands again is just a bit much for her at the moment.'

'Hmm, you're probably right,' April said noncommittally. She'd seen that box out on the coffee table. She recognised it. Her mother had had a similar little box, full of past memories and unspoken truths. She had a weird feeling that the two things were related somehow, but she couldn't quite piece everything together. Either way, Martha had chosen the pair of them, so for whatever reason, they were doing it.

Pulling into the pay and display car park nearby, Cillian ran out to get a ticket. His van was tidy, and neat. The car seat of Orla's was pristine, and in the passenger doorwell was a colouring book and a box of pencils. She could picture Orla sitting in here, colouring on the way to nursery, or the shops. Showing him her drawings and laughing at his funny faces. They were a little team, rock solid in their devotion to each other, and Cillian obviously adored her. His protective streak around her was so endearing. Insanely hot too. She hadn't been totally oblivious to that either. Playing princesses one minute, complete with tiny ribbons in his hair, the next, cutting wood on the park grounds, shirtless. She'd watered her windowsill plants four times that day. Two of them were plastic.

'Come on then, darling,' Cillian declared sarcastically, opening the passenger-side door and leaving the ticket on show on the dashboard. 'I got two hours. I figured we could have a little walk around too, grab some lunch to take back.'

'That sounds nice,' April agreed. He shrugged, dull and lifeless again to her. It was like a switch flipped in him. He only turned it on when he was forced to talk to her.

'Yeah, well we have a lot on. Better to stay fed.' He ruffled his hand through his hair and watched her try and fail to climb over the car seat and out of the van. She was almost there when he swooped in and pulled her out, setting her to her feet just in front of him.

'Thanks,' she breathed, trying to keep her lumps and bumps covered. He barely even nodded at her, but his hands were still wrapped around her arms. She brushed him off, angry now. 'For God's sake, Cillian, I don't know what I did to annoy you, but I can't cope with your mood swings on top of my own. What did I do?' They were standing in Lizard Point car park, toe to toe in more ways than one. 'I get you and Martha think I'm some hapless weirdo, but I don't deserve to be treated differently from one day to the next. Just what's your problem?'

'I-I …' he groaned. 'Just forget it. I was in a mood this morning. It's nothing.'

'It's not nothing, and it's not just this morning. It was after the night I hurt my head. That night was a good night. Today, I feel like I woke up with a stranger on that couch.'

'You didn't wake up with me,' he spat. 'You left before I woke up.'

'Yes, exactly!' She prodded him in the chest with a stern finger. 'I left bef …'

His feet shifted from side to side, and he let go of her arms.

'That's it, isn't it? Because I left?'

He went to leave, walking halfway across the car park before turning on his heel and striding back. She was just getting ready to roll up her sleeves and deck the moody git when he took her into his arms and kissed her. Hard. April, having been taken by surprise with her arms-folded, foot-tapping stance, couldn't move as he held her tight, kissing her with everything that he had. She opened her mouth. Not to protest, but to kiss him back properly. He felt rough to the touch, his bristle scraping deliciously against her cheek. She was just trying to get her arms loose so that she could run them through his hair, and he stopped, breaking the kiss. They both looked at each other, breathing hard.

Don't stop. Even the voice in her head was breathless. 'You didn't like it, waking up on your own.'

Cillian wiped at his mouth with his thumb, a smear of her lip gloss streaking his skin. Her own lips felt like they were on fire. After a moment, he shook his head.

'I'm sorry. I got woken up, and I didn't want Orla to be disrupted, so I went. Is that what all this morning was about? With Martha too?'

Another slow headshake. *No, so Martha didn't tell him she saw me. Fair play, Martha. Way to watch a girl's back. We're even on the bogey drawing.*

'So you kissed me because you were mad?'

Yet another headshake. He'd put his hands in his pockets now, and was trying to stare a hole in the asphalt beneath them.

'Give me something, Cill. I don't get it.'

A bloke in a blue Audi drove around the side of the van, tooting when they found that Cillian was standing in the empty space he wanted. He glared at the man till he wilted behind his steering wheel, then linked arms with April.

'Come on, let's get this over with. We have a lot on. Ready?' She waited for him to look at her again before she said anything. She wanted to see what was behind those green eyes. When he eventually looked at her, he slowed down and pulled her into a card shop doorway. She went with him, getting used to the feel of his hand in hers, the feeling of him around her. She wondered if the jolt she felt would always be there. It took her by surprise every time.

'I got mad when I woke up and you weren't there. Brought up a bad memory I suppose.'

'I can relate,' she said honestly. 'Back home, I never really saw Duncan. I felt like a widow half the time, chasing a ghost.' She reached up and touched his face, her thumb rubbing off a slick of lip gloss from his scruff. He closed his eyes when her skin touched his, and she felt it too. The connection between two people who were ultimately lost, fumbling in the dark and finding another lost soul to provide comfort. 'What *is* this?' she asked

125

him, curiosity overpowering her need for self-preservation. In a world of labels, she felt adrift once more.

He shook his head, moving closer till his forehead touched hers.

'I need actual words, Grunty,' she chided. Something devilish flashed in his eyes.

'Great kiss. That's two.' He waggled his eyebrows at her, laughing when he made her chortle out loud. 'I don't know, April. I just … don't know. Do we have to know, right now?' He was being friendly and chilled with his responses, but his body told her different. He was leaning in closer now, pressing the front of his body tight against hers, mere millimetres between their lips. She felt like the only woman in the world when he was around her. This was bizarre, and April was terrified, but when she thought of him with Orla, with her, and with Martha, she knew that she trusted him. Not with her whole Scotch-taped heart, but his was broken too, so what was the risk?

'No.' She brushed her lips against his, feeling him respond immediately. 'We don't need to know.'

He didn't answer her with words, and she sank into the kiss. Kissing a hot guy in a Cornish shop doorway was a first, and perhaps her favourite thing so far about her new life. No labels needed for that. She could almost hear her mother clapping from her cloud, and that was about all she could attempt to decipher right now. A pair of women chuckled as they brushed past them, and Cillian tucked her into his side, nodding at the ladies jovially.

'Good morning, ladies, and how are you this fine morning?'

One of them had a shock of red hair piled up in a beehive. It matched the tartan on her wheelie shopper. She nudged her friend, a mousy-haired woman wearing a rather loud floral coat.

'Not as good as she is,' the mousy woman quipped, winking at April, who developed a blush that would make a post box look a bit peaky. 'Eh, Jan?'

Jan laughed till her beehive wobbled.

'I know. Which shelf did you get him from love? I'll have two!' The two women burst into laughter as Cillian led her away, a smug smirk on April's face. The laughter erupted again as they told the woman behind the counter.

'Well.' He looked across at her, squeezing her hand as he wrapped his around it. 'The locals seem to be happy about it, anyway. Who needs a label?'

She elbowed him in the ribs, setting him off laughing again.

'Okay, Magic Mike, calm down. Let's just suss out the gallery and get back home.'

She wanted to bite her tongue off at how domesticated she sounded, but he just nodded and before they knew it, they were staring into the picture windows of the gallery. April clocked the sign looking for local artists, frowning.

'I thought Martha sold her pieces here already?'

Cillian pushed open the door. 'She does. Or did. To be honest, she hasn't shown me anything for a while. She's drawing – I know that – but something's up. She hasn't had many deliveries, has she? No art supplies, magazines? They dropped off before, she started working less, socialising less, once the park hit the skids. She still had *some* stuff going through though.'

April thought for a moment, then shook her head. 'Food – that's it. The prescription delivery service van came yesterday.'

The space was wide open and welcoming, the lights strategically placed to give a warmth to the space, softening the hard, white edges and surfaces that made up the gallery.

'Good morning.' A man wearing a crisp grey suit stood up from a large reception desk at the back of the room. 'Technically, we aren't open as yet, but I'm happy to help.'

Cillian shook the man's hand. 'Cillian, and this is my … April. We just wanted to come and check out the place really. This one here loves a bit of art.'

'Luke Beaumont. I run the gallery here, and a couple of other businesses in town. You lifers?'

Cillian nodded. 'Yep, came from Ireland a few years ago and never looked back. April's a newbie though.' He cupped his mouth with his free hand. 'Northerner. Flat-cap type, you know.'

Luke laughed, shaking April's hand. 'Well, my family lived here years ago, before my time. We just moved back into the area, still finding our feet.' He addressed April. 'How are you finding it?'

April had a flashback to annoying cockerels, stolen kisses, loud goats, and demanding neighbours.

'I like it,' she said. 'It's definitely growing on me.' She could see Cillian's smile from the corner of her eye and her stomach fluttered. 'So, tell us more about the gallery, Luke. This poster about local artists – have you had any interest?'

The waitress brought their food to the table outside, and April clapped her hands together with glee when she saw the gorgeous fresh food on her plate. They'd both ordered heartily, and Cillian had made no comment about how much she had ordered. The truth was, she often fasted at breakfast, and so by lunch she was starving. Carbs and sugar were the enemy of PCOS, but today she had thrown caution to the wind and ordered everything she fancied.

Taking a mouthful of her dish, she groaned with pleasure.

'Nice eh? This food is the best in Helston. I always thought that the Pines should have a restaurant of its own, a little pub maybe. There's the room, and peak season it would be packed.'

'A pub?' April replied in between huge bites. She was trying to be a little bit demure in front of him, but the call of the food was strong. If he wasn't here she would have inhaled it and started checking out the dessert menu. For now, she settled for tucking in with gusto. Her food intake had a direct correlation to her moods. If she ate well, she was happy. If she didn't, well, the word *hangry* had a whole new meaning. 'Ambitious, isn't it? We barely have a laundry room. Speaking of which, will you help me to get some new equipment?'

'Today?' Cillian frowned. 'I have the solicitor again after I've dropped you off, then we have loadsto do. I can't cancel again.' he said.. 'Tomorrow? It's going to be great though. I can fit the machines. Orla has a sleepover tomorrow night at her friend's house. I can work late.'

'That would be great. I'll pay you extra of course. And diesel. Small steps I know, but I can see it now.'

Cillian nodded as he ripped off a hunk of bread from his side plate and slathered it in butter. 'Nice little family place, good food and drink, nothing rowdy.'

'The pub idea again? I was thinking nice big dryers and decent washing machines. Been thinking about it a lot, have you? The whole shebang?' she teased, pleased that she had him on her side. She still shuddered to think what she would have been like without him. She had an image of her and Martha sitting in matching cardboard boxes, tethered to the rocks to avoid being blown off the end of the point as they slept, shivering and crying. She brushed the thought away, glancing down at the gallery pack she'd been given.

'Some. Tim really did a number on the place. It was sad to see it go downhill. I stayed on as long as I could, but the hours were dropping and I needed the money.'

She started looking for the salt pot, and he held it out to her in his hand.

'Here.'

'Thanks. Err—?'

He was already holding out the pepper to her.

'Yep, that too, thanks.'

'Welcome. So I left, but I always kept an eye on the place.'

She took the pot from him, seasoning her food and tucking back in with a delighted squeak.

'And by that particular set of eyes you mean Martha, right?' She leaned back in her chair, letting her stomach rest a second so that she could finish. The portions were lush and huge, which was great, but not for a woman who had been living off snacks and quick bites for weeks. The heartbreak diet. 'It's a great idea, for the future. I need the next few seasons to go well, to survive the winters, and get the place how I want it.'

He nodded, his mouth full.

'Luke was nice, wasn't he? Do you think she'll go and see him, show him some work?'

Cillian shrugged. 'I don't know, but I feel like we will soon enough. Martha's not one to mince her words, is she? She's been sketching loads, so that's a start. Losing Charlie hit her hard.'

April nodded. She knew the loss of a husband herself, although in her case she would happily have buried him under the patio to avoid what happened. She couldn't imagine being separated from a soul mate by death. It seemed like one of life's cruelties, and she had endured enough of them.

'Where did you go?' he asked, touching her hand with his across the table. 'You okay?'

She ran her thumb along the length of his, before pulling away and reaching for something in her bag. 'I haven't turned my phone on yet, not since you sent me that picture.' Cillian's brows shot up to his hairline, but he didn't say anything. 'I daren't really. I'm a chicken, I know.'

'I didn't tell my ex where her daughter was till I could get a court order in place to stop her from seeing her own child,' he said, monotone. 'I think chicken is a strong word for you. Do it now,' he suggested. 'Turn it on, put it on silent. Delete what you can't cope with. You need a phone. Once the park's open you won't want to be glued to the landlines. You'll be busy enough.'

It made perfect sense, and they both knew it. If they were to get Martha back painting, neither of them would have the time to be stuck to the reception desk all day. Maybe once she had guests coming in, paying good money, she could hire a receptionist. A local who loved the place and knew all the local highlights and must-see attractions. She put the handset on the table, pushing it into the centre with one finger as though it was a loaded trap.

'Maybe after lunch,' she lied feebly. Cillian arched a brow before shovelling a fork full of salad greens into his mouth, his eyes near crossing as they both ripped into their food. After their morning, they were both ravenous.

'Three,' he said, swallowing his food and placing his index finger on the power button of the phone.

'You wouldn't,' she teased, half terrified, half intrigued by his change in mood.

'Ah, never dare an O'Leary man. Two.' His eyes locked with hers, and she put down her knife and fork.

'Cillian?'

'Yeeeeeesss?'

'I'm scared,' she admitted. 'People might be mad. I did sort of leave in the middle of the night.'

'Without telling anyone?' he said, unable to keep the surprise in his voice. 'No one?'

'Yep.'

'Not one person?'

She thought for a moment. After she'd left the baby shower, she'd gone straight home, emailed the estate agent of her mother's house to tell him where she would leave the keys, and packed everything up. Hours later, she was on the road, everything she owned strapped to her mum's old car.

'Well, I told my mother, but I don't think talking to ashes counts.' She stabbed her fork a little bit too hard against her plate, and the noise set her teeth on edge. 'Press it.'

He bit the corner of his lip, and then pushed his finger down onto the button. The phone sprang to life, lighting up as it ran through the boot-up. The welcome screen came and then—

'Password.' Cillian nudged it towards her with his hand, turning back to his food while she entered the code. It was her wedding anniversary. She cringed as she typed it. Once she was truly back in the land of the living, that would be the first thing to go. The photo of her and her mother on the beach popped up, and then the phone went haywire. Some of the other diners looked up, irritated, and April gave them apologetic looks as she turned the sound off. She was just starting to look at it when she felt Cillian's hand on hers.

'Not now. Leave it for a bit. Have lunch first. If you get upset here, you'll make me cry, and no one here wants to see that. I have a very ugly crying face.' He winked at her and she relented. To be honest, she was grateful. She had already seen a couple of emails that had made her feet tingle with the urge to run.

'I don't know, people love a sensitive new-age man. You might pull.'

It was a joke, but his face fell and his cutlery clattered to the plate. 'I don't pull. You should know that about me at least.' His eyes were full of reproach as he looked at her, and to the phone. 'Eat up. The parking meter hasn't got long left.'

She opened her mouth to say sorry, but she could tell just by looking at him that he wasn't the man who kissed her in shop doorways; now, he was back to being Mr Grump.

'Bit of a Jeykll and Hyde, aren't you? Is that with everyone, or just me?'

His jaw flexed, and she could see he was trying not to bite back. The diners all had half an ear on them, enjoying the little sideshow with their lunches.

'Says you! I never know what sort of mood you'll be in. One minute you're all sunshine and rainbows, the next you're looking for the exit!'

'It was a joke! I didn't mean you were some kind of mega slut, did I? It was a joke. What's the problem?'

'Lower your voice,' he said, a little too loudly.

'Lower yours!' she shouted back, reaching into her purse and throwing a few notes on the table. 'I'll see you later. I'm going back to work.' She'd had enough of being shushed at lunches.

Duncan always chided her for laughing too loudly at jokes, or cracking bad ones of her own. Whenever she'd been tired, or moaned at being dragged along only to be left standing alone, being openly looked over by the other party guests, all she'd gotten was a shushing, a glass of Prosecco pushed into her hand. Pure sugar – cheers, darling. Screw the fertility testing and all the calorie counting. She didn't want to be shushed any blinking more.

'April, wait!' Cillian called after her, but she didn't give him the chance. She was out of the door and down the street running before she heard him call her again, and she didn't stop till she was well around the corner and out of his reach. She needed a minute to clear her head. One wrong comment and Cillian had turned again, back to the moody, closed-off wreck she'd first met. The worst thing was, she understood what he was saying. She was moody and contrary, but she couldn't help feeling that way. She was just so confused, and the biggest confusion was him. Over the last week, she felt like they'd been there together for a month. Everything was amplified. Working and living alongside each other, she'd gotten to know his little ways.

She knew that he thought men who ate sandwiches with the crusts cut off were not real men. She knew that he hummed Orla's favourite songs while he worked. She knew that he could kiss a woman so well she could forget her own name, let alone worry about the consequences. She knew that he, like her, had been so burned by love they still smelled scorched hair in their darkest moments. He infuriated her, yet she was fast realising that the time she spent with him, at the park, were the best times she'd had for a long time. It came so easy sometimes, till real life got in the way.

Then she was catapulted back to the chunky, nervous little wife she once was, always apologising for everything. Her circumstances, her job, her dress size. The fact that her body didn't work as others' did. Hell, at one dinner party she'd been dragged along to, she'd even apologised for having a novelty Hello Kitty bag as part of her outfit. The truth was, she was on a budget and didn't see the need to empty out her bank account just to buy a piece of fabric. The Hello Kitty logo she hadn't seen on the back led to a lot of questions. Duncan had been mortified about the whole evening. That night, he'd gone back to the office to work and didn't come home all night. She should have known then that their marriage was over, but her mum hadn't been feeling great, so between ferrying her to the hospital appointments and working shifts, she didn't have the time to sit and watch her home life crumble.

She turned around another corner and stopped. She didn't know quite where she was, and she was starting to panic. Her anxiety was getting the better of her, and she still felt so mad about Cillian. Where did he get off, trying to be all macho at the lunch table? She'd felt so foolish, people looking, and Cillian didn't seem to care. Well, she cared, and she wouldn't be made to feel ashamed in public again. She'd had her fill over the years, and the sting of it seemingly served to strike on old wounds still healing.

'You're there,' Cillian said from behind her. She didn't look, choosing to stomp off instead in the opposite direction. 'April, stop!'

She rounded on him then, the anger of past slights and humiliations bubbling up to the surface all at once.

'You should never do that to someone! What's your problem?'

Cillian looked like he wanted to bite back, but then the fight went out of him and he sagged before her.

'I'm sorry, okay? Past stuff. You hit a nerve. I'm still working through some anger. I can't help it.'

Wow, he's admitted that he overreacted. I can't back down, can I? 'Yeah, well you hit one of my bloody nerves too! This is pointless. We're both too screwed up to be kissing each other, as gorgeous as that was.' There she was again, blurting out the daft

134

comments. 'You have Orla, and I have the park to run, and work, and Martha. We were better off before. We shouldn't be doing this.'

'We don't even know what this is,' he said quietly. 'If you feel like that, it's fine. It's not what I want, but I get it. Just ...' He sagged further still, his beautiful shoulders low. 'I'm here. Come back to the van. We have to work together. For now at least.'

Her head whipped to look at him and he smiled sadly. 'Not a threat, I'm just saying as long as you want me, I'm here for ... work.'

Here for work. As soon as she'd said they shouldn't get together, she knew she didn't mean it, not really. She actually liked him, and she couldn't believe it was all over before she even had a chance to really sabotage it for herself. Which she probably would have done. It was her, after all.

'Thank you,' she said, trying for once to act like an aloof, very important and busy employer and business owner. 'I think we should get back.'

Sighing softly, Cillian pointed back the way she'd just come from.

'The van's over there,' he said. 'I think your bottom lip obscured your view before. You walked right past it.' He laughed softly, and she felt a glimmer of embarrassment once more. She whirled around, stamping down hard on his foot as she did.

'I'll give you a bottom lip!'

Cillian, who was laughing at his own lame attempt to break the tension and make her laugh, gasped. He didn't flinch though, and it didn't feel as satisfying as she expected. She actually thought, as she looked down in dismay at his steel-toe-cap boots, that she might have chipped a bone in her foot.

'Argggghh!' she screamed in his face, pointing at his shoes. 'Trust you to wear stupid shoes!'

'Well, they're not very stupid, are they? Giving that my tootsies are snug and warm, and you're bounding about like a mad thing.'

She was hopping on one foot now, holding the other cradled in her hands as she bobbed and weaved in front of him. People were actively walking around the pair of them now, and Cillian smiled at them distractedly.

'Don't mind us, hopping competition practice. Have a good day!' He bowed theatrically, and when he went to stand again, he swooped. Picking April up in an awkward fireman's carry, he hoicked her over one shoulder and strode off in the direction of his van.

'Cillian, let me down! Now!' She was trying to fight him, one leg hanging limp and bumping against his back. 'My bottom is hanging out!' It wasn't, but there was a hint of builder's bum. So much for dressing up for once. She might as well just buy seven sets of dungarees and have done with it all.

Cillian twirled her around in his arms as though she were a baton, till she lay in his arms like a sack of spuds. He turned and glanced behind him to see if anyone was checking out her posterior. She took in his broad neck, the stubble around his jawline. *Lickable.* She licked her lips instead.

'Anyone see your fine arse?' he asked, looking for the first time at her properly. She blushed in his arms, secretly getting a thrill that he might be mad someone had seen her wobbly bits. It was insanely cute, and the polar opposite of Duncan and his little 'chunky monkey' comments.

'No,' she said, the anger missing from her voice now. 'No one saw. Thank you.'

He nodded, just once, a curt little movement that made her want to wrap her arms tight around him. Instead, she settled for just gripping his back to hold herself steady. Her foot was throbbing, but she found it hard to concentrate on that while in her current position. They neared the van and Cillian opened the door, slotting her into the passenger seat carefully. They both reached for the seatbelt in the same instant.

'I can do it, Cillian, I didn't hurt my hands.' He pulled his hand away, closing her door and running around to his side, a lost little boy look in his eyes that April couldn't help but think she had put there. Why was everything under the Cornish sun so blurred and complicated? After a couple of attempts to start a conversation, to which Cillian just made noises from this throat, she gave up and they drove home in silence.

As soon as the van came to a stop outside Cillian's chalet, April jumped – or rather, hobbled – out, gingerly placing weight on her injured foot. It was bearable, probably just a bruise to come out. She reached into her bag for her keys and strode straight to her own front door. She had to get away for a moment.

'Er, April?' Martha called from across the way. 'Everything okay? I need to have a word with you.'

Grrr. Another one. She was only just done with the last favour she'd asked for, and look how that had turned out.

'Not now, Martha. I need to get on. I'll come see you later.' She didn't turn around. She'd heard Cillian's van drive away a second after she'd slammed her door, but she didn't want to look at him. She couldn't, not while feeling so embarrassed. She threw the key into the lock, and minutes later, she was standing in her bedroom, the tears flowing now, and April couldn't even really decipher what the reason was.

'Come on, pull it together.' She had a delivery coming that afternoon, and she needed to be ready to accept it. She'd been so excited when she'd ordered it, and she couldn't wait to see what the park guests would make of it. She didn't want it to be overshadowed by the horrible weird morning, where she had started off kissing Cillian and ended up showing half her bottom to the residents of Cornwall. She needed something good to happen. Sniffing loudly, she reached into her bag for the packet of tissues she kept there, but her phone was what her hand closed around. She paused for a moment, wiping her tears with her sleeve, and slowly pulled it from her bag.

Sitting down on the bed, she scrolled through her emails, realising with relief that other than a few friends asking where she was, and many emails from people obviously just snooping under the guise of mild concern, the emails were all general life stuff. No missed bills, no disaster from back home to deal with. She deleted the list of notifications, and looking out of her bedroom window at the beach, she took a simple snap. The sun was getting high in the sky now, casting off rays through the white clouds and lighting up her scene. It looked amazing. She posted it on her Instagram feed, deliberating over a caption for ages before finally clenching her teeth and hitting send.

The photo looked gorgeous, the epitome of Cornwall captured in her own bedroom window, a framed photograph of her mother sitting at one side of the windowsill. Smiling, she looked at the caption she had written. A bit cheesy, but it worked.

New life, new view #ShadyPines

Later, she would add an account for Shady Pines, when she was ready. She could document the park being changed, showing the before and after pictures. Engage with the guests and lovers of Cornwall. She clicked to add it direct to the other social media pages, and went to check Facebook. Immediately, she wished she hadn't. Her post was there, but scrolling down she could see people had messaged her, talking about her flit and asking if she was okay. She'd told no one at work, but since she had left her job when Mum got sick, she hadn't expected them to care. She scrolled down, horrified that she'd hidden for so long and made people worry. In all honesty, she didn't expect more than a couple of texts asking where she was. Not this. This was bad. The next name on the list made her blood run cold. Duncan Statham. Three days after she had left, he'd put a message of his own on.

Be happy, April.

Be happy? BE HAPPY?

'I can't believe I washed his underpants for so long.' She

scowled. 'I hope his new bloody fiancée shrinks them till his thingy drops off.'

She should have blocked him from the get-go, but with the divorce going through, she'd kept it open in case he tried any wrangling over money. Another thing about Duncan she didn't miss, along with his wonderful heartfelt messages on social media, was the fact that he could peel a satsuma in his pocket without spilling a drop of juice. For a man born into a better life, he sure was a tightwad. She could block him now though, and she found herself smiling as she thought of his face when he realised. *Up yours, Duncan.*

As his page loaded, she steeled herself for the inevitable vomit fest that would be the pair of them. His new wife to be was at least ten years April's junior, and she looked even younger. April, at thirty-five, had socks in her knickers drawer older than her. The profile picture was a photo of the two of them from the baby shower April had ran away from, standing against a flower wall, cardboard fake moustaches and wigs comically placed against their smug faces. She was just about to go to settings to block them both, when she noticed the grainy grey page header he had put on. It used to be of the two of them, a long time ago. Standing in the snowy entrance to their once-loved home, their matching Christmas jumpers and Santa hats making the scene look like a holiday card. Now, it was a blob of white, surrounded by greys and blacks. Sitting down on the bed before she collapsed, she clicked onto the image, bringing up the post.

Under the photo of the sonography scan, Duncan had written:

When one door closes, another one opens. Darling, I will love you forever. Can't wait to play mummy and daddy with you! A wedding, a new home, and a baby in one year. The Stathams really are #blessed #babystatham #sonandheir #finally

The #blessed was a shot to the heart, but the other hashtags sent her to the floor, her wet cheeks dripping onto the white wooden floor as she howled in pain, rocking back and forth. Her phone dropped to the floor, the hashtags silently mocking her as she broke down.

#finally

The pain felt as fresh as the day she'd found receipts in his suit jacket pockets, and knew what was coming down the road. If anything, it felt much, much worse. She hated an unborn, innocent child, simply for daring to exist, and that confused and angered her all the more. She sat and cried for a long time. Finally pulling herself up, she left the chalet. Walking down the path, her shaky legs working just enough to get her there. She took the phone to the beach, and bashing it over and over with a rock and shoving the bits into the nearby dog poop bin, she screamed at the water's edge, hoping her anguished cries would be enough to prevent her heart from stopping altogether.

Chapter 13

April lifted her head and squinted against the sun as she sat on the freshly dug and bark-chipped play area. It had been kitted out in a type of bouncy tarmac, a local play equipment firm undertaking the work with a nice discount for her advertising their services. She had business cards in the shop, and a little plaque off to one side had the business name on, right under the flowing words that Martha had drawn. *Shady Pines Play Area* looked simple, but perfect. She was hoping that Orla would be able to make friends here, and not just fictional book characters. If Cillian would let her play there now.

After this morning, she couldn't think of a way forward anymore. She was stuck, and numb. The thing that bothered her the most was that she couldn't even process the baby news properly because she was too hung up on Cillian. The little glimpses of them together had told her how right it felt, but there was just too much around them. Too much past in their present to even see the future. Any future.

The only thing she knew at this moment in time was that a delivery was coming, and she would sign for it. Right here. That was enough for now. It was all she could bear to focus on. She thought of her smartphone, sitting in tiny bits in among the banana peel and doggy poo bags in that bin, and felt a little better. Off the radar again somewhat. She felt horrified about her own post. She would never have posted it had she known. Would people think it was in response to Duncan's news? Probably. She might as well have thrown herself a divorce party online and had done with it. How could he do that? Why didn't he block her himself?

She knew why of course. Because he was Duncan. Big old Dunc with his army of yes men and simpering women. Now he could prove he could fill a pram, it was happy days for Mr Diamond Shoes. The truth was, he was that thick and shallow-minded that he wouldn't have even thought about it. #finally said it all. He might as well have loaded that hashtag into a gun and taken aim. Typical 'have to have it all right now' Duncan. Screw anyone the posts upset. The opposite of Cillian, who grafted every day for his daughter and thought nothing of himself. He took far more pleasure in the simple things. . His patience around the park, around Orla, it was calming just to watch. A contrast to his Irish temper, and his stubborn, arsey ways. Orla had him in the palm of her hand, and he loved every minute. Cillian loved being a dad, but to Duncan, it was another achievement to hang from his belt. Father, check. It's not like he'd even be there much to raise the poor mite. She felt the sting of tears again, and she punched down hard into the tree bark.

'April? Are you okay?'

Martha was standing there, like some kind of Royal-Jelly-scented ninja. April could see the box from Martha's coffee table tight in her hands. She was in a pair of loose white cotton trousers, a paint-splattered red blouse, and a pair of sneakers, also spotted at the toes with different drips and flashes of colour.

'Not even a little bit,' April replied truthfully. She looked again at the box in Martha's hands, and then in the woman's eyes. 'Are you?'

Martha shook her head. 'Not great, no. I might punch a bit of bark too, if it helps.' Both women smiled feebly at each other, equally depressed but thankful for the other's concern. 'I saw Cillian took off in a hurry. Orla okay?'

She looked up the long path, as though his van was still there, making its obvious getaway.

'Orla's fine. He's mad with me, I think. He … I … It's complicated.'

Martha went and sat on one of the tree stumps that sat off to the side of the bark, placing the box on another nearby and patting the lid.

'Most things are, in this life,' she said softly. 'Did you go, to the gallery?'

'We did, a man called Luke gave me a pack.' She went to reach for her handbag, but then she realised she'd run off to work with nothing but the keys in her hand. 'Sorry, it's in the chalet. They are definitely looking for new talent; apparently they bought out all the art that was there before. A hot local artist, apparently.' Something occurred to her then. 'Was that your work? Is that why you're upset?'

Martha shook her head. 'No, the old buyers sold all that.' She looked a little confused herself now. 'I never thought about it that way. I just assumed that they had paid the whole amount in one because they were closing. Maybe I should give them a call.' She looked at the box, an odd expression crossing her features. 'I've been trying to paint new pieces, but I haven't been able to yet. Nothing good anyway. I'm hoping that today's the day.' She ran her tired eyes over April, frown lines pushing her glasses halfway down her nose. 'Why are you sitting here?'

'Delivery,' she replied dully, picking up a handful of bark chips and letting them fall through her fingers. 'My ex-husband is getting married to the woman he left me for, and having a baby. I just found out. About the baby, I mean. He already dropped the other bombshell in person before I left.'

Martha's lips pursed together tightly, and April's eyes fell onto the box once more.

'I am sorry. It's the cruellest thing sometimes, to be a woman in this world. I never had children myself. My Charlie couldn't, and I was fine with that in the end. Couldn't be helped much in those days, and I had him, and my art, and the love of my life.'

April wrapped her brains around Martha's words, blinking rapidly as she began to understand, and Martha laughed.

'You heard right. It sounds so simple, when you say it out loud. To someone alive, I mean.'

April's brows knitted together again, and Martha patted the top of the box. 'You know, I think you might like to have a look at this. I'll leave it with you, but please know, it's precious.' Her face changed back to its severe default mode and April found herself agreeing rather solemnly.

'I will, I promise.'

Martha relaxed a little, stretching her legs out in front of her and rolling her feet around in alternate circles.

'I trust you.' After a moment, she spoke again. 'He does too, believe it or not. Where did he run off to?'

'Solicitor's,' she replied before she could censor her answer. Martha didn't look surprised; in fact, she looked rather happy about it.

'About time. Once things are in place, he'll relax a bit more. Being here has helped, and you …'

April went to protest but Martha shot her a knowing look. 'You have helped him, just as much as he's helped you.' She added a stiff nod to her words, and April found herself dipping her head in agreement. Either that, or she was scared of getting a lecture. She felt a bit fragile at it was. 'He's had a lot of stress. Like you. Tina is a little chaotic, but she won't be around forever. Not this version of her anyway. People change. Things will work out in the end.'

'Sometimes they don't,' April said coldly, thinking of Cillian's hard stare, his ex, their child. It was far too messy to get involved in. She thought of Duncan, swinging his dick around his office, the big man about town with his new family to look forward to. The barren wife with the puppy fat he once loved cast out like an old soggy teabag. *Be happy, April.* Those three words were, as Cillian might say, a fecking insult. She brushed an angry tear away. 'The man I loved second most in this world broke my heart into so many different pieces, I don't know how he ever fooled me in the first place. The man he is now is nothing like the groom who signed our marriage certificate. I hate him, I think.' She paused, taking a deep breath and thinking about it honestly. 'Maybe that was it. Maybe this place is my new goal in life. That should be enough.'

She looked at the box, thinking of what could be inside, what Martha wanted to share. 'And yes, I really think I hate him. How can anything after that, after Tina, work out? It won't, and not everyone gets a happy ever after, Martha.'

'No, they don't, but it's worth a shot.' She shifted in her seat, lifting the lid and pulling out a letter from the neat stack of cream envelopes. She opened the letter up, read a few lines and passed it over.

'Start with this one, but read them in order, okay?' Her hands were shaking, and it wasn't the April weather. It was rather beautiful now, warm air fragrant with the smells of the fresh bark and the wild flowers around them. Even the grass smelled amazing, making April feel just a little less wretched. She went to open the letter, but Martha stopped her.

'Not now, please. Wait till you have a minute, read them on your own.' Martha smiled at her, the straggled mess that she was, and she realised that they'd bonded, in an odd way. Hell, if they had been the same age they would probably have been friends back then. April would have liked that, and she realised it applied now too. She saw so much of herself in Martha, and she wondered

145

if Martha thought the same, in an odd way. When she had started drawing her that day on the porch, it had seemed to wake Martha up a little. Maybe rage was good for the creative juices. April found herself hoping that by doing this, by trusting someone else with her secrets, Martha could finally free herself. Paint once more. She knew she'd been trying. The splotches of paint were like breadcrumbs.

'Not everyone gets a happy ever after, you're right there, but it doesn't mean a life ill spent.' Martha looked across the expanse of the park, back towards town. 'When I was a girl, my family were friends with another family, and they had a son. My Charlie.' She smiled then, and April wondered once more why just thinking of a person could change another person from the inside out in an instant. 'We holidayed here, not having much money for travelling in those days. We weren't bothered. Cornwall was where people travelled for miles to see, still is, and we had it on our doorstep for free. We liked to spend time with the other family, and Charlie and I grew close. In truth, he didn't set my heart alight, but I loved him just the same.'

April couldn't help but think of how different Cillian felt to Duncan. It wasn't just the first stirrings of lust that differed between the two men; she knew that.

'One night, I met a young man here, and it changed my life.' A single tear escaped down Martha's cheek, and she welled up further. 'I didn't do what you did April – I didn't follow my heart. Not until it was too late, and I've lived a half-lived life ever since. No children to occupy me, I painted instead. He loved art, and books, and music, just like me. We would spend hours talking about things. I loved my Charlie dearly, but he wasn't the one. We can love more than one person in our lives, fiercely. Remember that when you open the box. After Charlie passed, I needed to be somewhere familiar. Somewhere that wasn't just him and I, because that time was gone. This place was where *we* met, all those years ago. It just felt right, and then you came ...'

'And it all hit the fan?' April quipped, her usual attempt at awkward humour this time hitting the bull's eye.

Martha laughed, but then her face fell. The noise of a delivery truck came from the entrance, a low rumble as it drove closer. 'Er … not quite, but …'

She reached for the letter still in April's hand and placed it at the very front of the box.

'Is your door unlocked?' she asked, her eyes darting from the truck to the chalets to April like pinballs. 'I'll just put these safe.'

'Oh, okay.' April watched Martha stuff the box under her arm like a thick-thighed winger would a rugby ball, and take off, her paint-splattered clothing making her look like a kind of rainbow. A sweaty one.

'What got into her, I wonder,' she said to herself, as she went to meet the truck. A young lad jumped out of the passenger side, jogging over and handing her a clipboard with a smile. 'All ready for you, as discussed. You ready?' The van was back end facing the playground area now, waiting for the slide that April had managed to find online and get restored at a fraction of the cost. These things were built to last, and the firm worked to code. She just couldn't wait to see Orla's face. She was like a big kid herself. On the back of the van was a large shape, covered in tarpaulin.

'I can't wait! Do it!' She bounced up and down on the spot. It was a slide, set into a little hill setting around the slide itself. On the sides were painted trees and bushes, and little sheep and pigs sat in various poses around the corner. She couldn't help but gravitate to little pink animals lately. Orla's influence was rubbing off on her already. The young bloke grinned, and with help from the driver, they slowly pulled back the tarpaulin.

'Oooooo-hhhhhhhh-arrrgghhhh! What the hell is that?' Her excited whoop gave way to disbelief as she looked at the slide. Instead of being set in a wonderful green hill, it was seemingly being held up by two of the ugliest-looking things ever. They looked like something you might find moaning about trip-trapping under bridges. The colours were more moss-green, dirt-brown, and not a cute little oinker in sight. 'I didn't order this!'

The two men looked bemused, and she glanced down at the clipboard.

'I mean, I can't sign for it, obviously. It's not what I ordered.'

She looked at the order form, and it was all there in black and white. Just as Martha came into view, she saw the point of contact for the change of order, placed a day after her original order. M Rodgers. Looking at Martha, the old woman laughed sheepishly.

'I might have another little confession to make. I forgot, to be honest, but I might have had a little revenge on my ghastly new landlady a little prematurely.' April stared at her open-mouthed as the two men, both twice the size of Martha, shuffled their feet nearby.

April looked back at the trolls and started to laugh. A real belly laugh that made Martha jump in surprise.

April pointed at the trolls. 'One of them me, is it?'

Martha winced. 'I did think there was a likeness, at first glance.' She put her hands together. 'I'm so sorry, April. I'll pay to get it sorted out.'

April held up a hand, cutting her off.

'It's okay,' she said, signing the order and thanking the stunned men. Pulling a black sharpie from her pocket, she walked over to the trolls and scratched away.

'Er ... it's all paid for, miss, and we don't do refunds for deface-ment.'

April turned around, clicking the top back on the pen and grinning from ear to ear.

'It's okay,' she said, looking at the trolls who now had names written across their foreheads. 'I rather like them. Good job, Martha.'

With a wink, she headed off to the chalet, leaving the three staring dumbly after her. Behind them, the trolls, Duncan and Tim, looked quite amused themselves.

Chapter 14

Cillian couldn't stop his foot from tapping, so he crossed his legs and started flicking his pen instead. He'd been so mad since his fight with April that he couldn't believe he was sitting here having to deal with this too. He'd dropped her off at the chalet park and left her for dust, not bothering to say goodbye. Not that she seemed that bothered anyway. She'd jumped out of the van like it was on fire. It was such a bad idea, such a terrible mistake. Those lips of hers on his. *Stop it.*

This job was supposed to be a new start for him and Orla, and now it felt like he'd blotted his copybook with the boss and screwed everything up. They'd not even got to the good bits. Playing the couple had been fun earlier, natural even, and he couldn't help but linger on the thought of kissing her in that shop doorway. He hadn't felt like that in a lifetime, and strangely it had got him thinking of Tina. They were never like that, not even in the beginning and, knowing that, he wondered how Tina had felt. Maybe he hadn't seen it from her point of view as well as he could. All he could focus on at the time was earning the money to provide for his young family back home, and missing his baby daughter. Perhaps it was harder to be left behind than it was to be the one to leave, however noble the intentions were.

Even with Orla being older now, Cillian still struggled some-times with the sheer number of tasks parenthood involved, and that was before he had factored in a woman he kissed in doorways and fought with regularly. He was hard pushed to find the time to run a comb through his hair most mornings, and contrary to what women thought, men did need a little grooming now and then. He had to admit, though, that he might just have made that bit more effort since he got to know his boss.

'Good afternoon, Hendricks and Abbott,' a disembodied voice from behind the reception desk in front of him trilled. 'Putting you through.' The woman looked up at him, her eyebrows saluting him hello. 'Mr O'Leary, he can see you now.'

This was it. This is what the last few months had all led to. What kept him awake at night, the memory of coming home to Orla home alone and hungry. He looked back at the front door and nodded slowly. No backing out now. He rose to his feet, document wallet in hand and carrying a heavy heart.

'Thanks.' He was almost at the end of the corridor when the front door opened again. Turning around, Cillian turned to see Paddy standing there with Tina.

'Paddy? What—'

Tina took a step forward. 'He found me in the pub.'

Cillian's face darkened, and he turned to continue on his way.

'Cillian, stop! I didn't drink.' Something in her voice sounded different this time, sincere. Desperate even. 'Paddy saw me sat with a vodka. I didn't drink it, but I wanted to. I need help, Cillian. I can't do it by myself anymore. He told me about today, and I wanted to come.'

The top of the receptionist's black hair was positively twitching now as she tried to make herself fully invisible.

'I'm glad you're getting help, T, I really am, but this is about Orla. And me.'

'I know, and Paddy has told me you've moved on.' Cillian

frowned at Paddy, but he just winked at him. 'I'm glad for you.' She looked so beaten down, Cillian found his shock and anger subsiding a little. Maybe the social media stuff she posted was just a brave face. It's not like people didn't lie on there, to themselves. He thought of April then, and her fear of going online. Trial by keyboard warriors.

'I just want to make this right. I want to be right – the guilt is crippling me. I know she's better off with you. I came here to say that. I won't cause a scene anymore.'

'No, she won't,' Paddy said, shooting her a friendly glance that told her she was on thin ice with him too. Paddy was a big man with a big heart, and Orla was as close a niece to him as his own flesh and blood. 'Come on, mate, what's the harm? If it goes bad in there, we can do your plan.'

He had been thinking similarly himself, if he admitted it. No matter what struggles Tina had had, she wasn't the person she used to be, and he had to admit that to himself. He sure wasn't. Less than a month with April in his life had changed him again, and he knew what she would say. She'd asked that question, and it had rattled around in his brain ever since.

Does Orla want her mother in her life? Tina was getting help and doing well. One day, when she was grown, she would understand that parents are people with addictions, and problems, and flaws. He knew then what his decision was. He wanted to be able to look an adult Orla in the eye, and tell her he did everything he could to be a good father. That included looking after her mother too.

'And the nursery visit?'

Tina's head snapped down to the floor, and he saw how ashamed she was now. Maybe she really was trying. He thought of Orla, and that strengthened his resolve. He looked down the corridor at the waiting door and turned back to the mother of his child.

'I'll give it a shot, but the turning up drunk stops now. Tina, you understand me? We go in there, and we make a plan for Orla. No more fighting. Last chance.'

Paddy was stood at Tina's side, smiling and nodding at him as he spoke. Cillian narrowed his eyes at him for interfering, but Paddy just laughed. He knew he would be getting a pint when this was all resolved, and Cillian had calmed down his bullish ways and realised how he was trying to help.

'We good? Want me to wait?' he asked his Irish buddy. Cillian walked back across to him and shook his hand.

'I'll take her back there, thanks, mate.' Paddy didn't wait. He stepped forward and wrapped his massive arms around his best friend.

'Good luck, pal,' he said earnestly. Paddy loved Orla to bits, had since the day she was born and he came to hold her in the hospital. Another man who couldn't forgive himself for not being there when things went bad. 'Do it for our girl, eh?'

The two men hugged each other tight, slapping each other on the back and grunting at each other at the end, while they turned away and wiped the tears from their eyes. Paddy gave a nod to Tina, who smiled at him weakly, and he was gone. Leaving them with silence and the twitching top of the receptionist's head.

'Shall we?' Cillian asked. 'Let's go make a plan for Orla.'

Tina, a tear spilling down her cheek as she looked back at the man who was caring for their daughter, uttered the word 'yes' and reached out her hand.

After the troll debacle, April had run an errand and then kept herself scarce. Martha had been in her chalet all day; Cillian had returned to work in the laundry room, staying out of her way till it was time to knock off and pick Orla up. She'd heard his van come back, but she had been busy making sure everything was finished. She had even put an advert in the local shop window in town looking for a receptionist to start immediately, with the park's details on it.

She'd also splashed out on another mobile phone, complete with new number. It still sat in the box. The bloke had set it all up for her, but she'd made him turn it off before she'd left the shop.

When she thought of the sonogram on Duncan's #smuggit post, she felt sick to her stomach. Duncan's fiancée had probably been pregnant at the baby shower, and that made her humiliation complete. How could Duncan have done that? Every so often, April had waited back home, wondering when, even if, Duncan would notice how upset she was, how lost she felt. She'd told him the best she could, but he wasn't there for her. To Duncan, it was a complication. An annoyance, if anything. When he spoke of children, and what them having a child could mean, it was always in terms of family events at work, or what clubs they could join together, which private school he would send their small charges to. Whenever April thought of their child, she would imagine walks in the park in autumn days, sleepless nights alone while Duncan slept in the guest room to get his beauty rest.

Would their baby have been loved like she wanted? A designer fashion accessory wasn't exactly what she had in mind when she thought of her own future children, back when she was married. She was better off knowing the truth, the truth about their relationship, her own body, and the life she was meant to have.

She was sitting on her couch now, her chalet smelling of cleaning products to the point of nausea, because she had been unable to get the dark, panicky thoughts out of her head. It had been a hell of a day, and she found herself sitting now staring at the coffee table as though two live grenades were perched there. Her mobile phone was one, and the box from Martha was the other. As she went to make herself a cup of tea and a sandwich, suddenly realising how famished she was, she looked outside and saw Martha in her own window. She was washing something in the sink, but her face was different somehow. She looked brighter, and from where April was standing, it looked like she was happy.

Taking her supper back through to the living room, she placed her things on the side table and picked up her phone. She downloaded the apps she could stomach. Logging in, she forced herself to bring up the relevant app and look again at the photo. Reading the comments, April scrolled down as she saw former friends, family, and colleagues all wish Duncan and his new bride-to-be best wishes on their impending new arrival. Some people were already calling the baby Mini Dunc, and April's sadness began to dissipate. It was happy news, she could see that, but it didn't hurt any less that people had seemingly moved on so quickly.

The truth was, it was always a case of two worlds coming together with her and Duncan, and now their worlds were further apart than ever. She didn't leave a comment – she didn't trust herself not to gush or sound bitter or 'too okay' about the situation. She had feelings. She didn't need to lay them bare and exposed for people to feed on. Clicking on the profile, she hit the block button and going through her phone, she unfriended and blocked until she could look at her social media pages without wanting to vomit. She'd asked for someone with computer experience for reception, so as soon as she could, she would get the Shady Pines pages up and running properly, up-to-date photographs and information on collaborations with other local businesses, and delete everything else that made her sad. She shouldn't be hiding from her phone, she knew that now, and she needed to claim her life back piece by piece. Satisfied, she put the phone to one side, and opened the box.

Right at the front of the large wooden box was a letter, tatty and well worn. Looking at the date, she could see that it was dated decades before, and addressed to Martha, at the same chalet she lived at now. No postmark though. Hand delivered. Intrigued, she took a sip of tea and carefully covering herself over with a throw from the back of the couch, she opened the letter and started to read.

To the girl who caught my eye,

I've had the best night of my life, thanks to you. I hope that you get this letter and feel the same. I'm not one for declaring my feelings with paper and pen, and my pals would only make fun of me, but I couldn't wait to talk to you again. I was sitting in the games room tonight, waiting for the dance hall to open when you came past. You didn't see me, but my mate Stuart elbowed me in the ribs and we followed you to the beach. Your mate Stella caught his eye the other day, but she had nothing on you for me. It all meant I got to meet you. Being in that water with you, I never loved the sea more, and I never thought I would say that.

My dad always said that I would know when I found someone special, and by God, did I feel it for you. Watching you paddle on that beach, laughing with your girl pals, I fell in love. I am a man in love, and I had to tell you. Will you write me? Will you write and put a young man's poor heart out of its torment?

I beg you, write to me. We have all summer.

Wow. April read the letter three times, reading the nervous declarations of a young man and wondering what else would be in the box. If this was the first letter, what would the rest contain? They knew how to write letters back then. Romantic, heartfelt, painstaking time taken over each word, every sign-off. Getting poked on Facebook didn't have quite the same effect somehow.

The box was full of them. Words of love, all in little cream and white parcels of outpouring and emotion. She ran her hands along them all, in awe at the treasures in the chest.

Looking through the envelopes, she saw that the handwriting changed after a while, to Martha's hand. She had written hundreds of letters, all addressed to G. That was it, no address or name on the envelopes. Just the date of writing, and the letter G. There were no letters back though, not after a certain date, which was almost two years after the first letter. Two years of writing letters to each other, and then nothing. Just one-sided conversations. Pushing her hands through the contents of the box, April saw that the last letter was dated this month. She took a risk, and tore it open carefully. It felt like she was reading the last page of a novel before starting it, but she needed to know. She had had enough secrets and puzzles for a lifetime.

To G,

The gallery is up for sale. I almost bought it, but what would be the point of that? It'd be like a teetotaller buying a pub, and I'm not up to the job. They managed to sell the rest of my paintings, so I should be grateful for that. I don't have anything to show yet, but lately, this place has been coming back to life. Just a little, but I can't wait to see what happens.

April read Martha's words, her handwriting less neat than in her younger years, but still full of emotion. She felt like she was poking around in Martha's head a little bit, and it didn't sit right. Here she was, talking about Shady Pines, and the two of them had butted heads earlier over the trolls.

The new owner is still annoying, of course.

'Cheeky cow,' April muttered under her breath. 'She ruined my play area theme.' It wasn't so much cute little farm now. More Little Shop of Horrors with a big dollop of Brothers Grimm thrown in. She was dreading to think what Orla and the visiting kids would think of it. It was funny.

She is interesting though, and it's lovely to have little Orla around. I wish Cillian could relax a bit more. He has such worries on his shoulders.

156

April's stomach flipped when she thought of Cillian. Angry, toddler-tantrum-throwing Cillian, who made her head spin with his emotions. That was saying something too, given the amount of hormones that had been flowing through her over the last few weeks.

I've finished the sketch that I have been working on, and then it grew to four more. It's a bigger project than I thought, so it's taking me a while to pluck up the courage. I have nowhere to show it now, not one place to sell my art, and that's fine with me for now. When I heard the name of the new owner, I had thought it might be you. I came to look. I couldn't stop myself. I even thought I heard you, but I'm just a silly old fool. Clinging to the past like it will suddenly change before my eyes. We both know that's not going to happen, and I am just talking to myself again. I write you far too often now, but I find I can't stop. Maybe it's nostalgia, but it feels right. Maybe it's the smell of hope in the air. The article said Beaumont, and my heart thought of you. I told you I was silly, dear G. Silly old You, eh. Maybe one day, I'll find the reasons behind it all. Perhaps you'll be there to tell me.

April put the letter to the back of the pile and read them in order. She read about their meeting, one long hot summer at Shady Pines. Martha had been there to enjoy the time with her family and a neighbouring family. They had visited for years, staying close to home. The start of the letters heralded something new though. Young love, and obligations. Over nearly two years, the pair had fallen in love hard and fast, sending each other love letters and passionate declarations, each tied back from the other by family, and the way life was supposed to go. The last letter from G was the worst.

You

*I heard the church bells today. Your church bells. Don't ask
me how. Being in the middle of the ocean thousands of miles
from everything, I thought I would be safe. I swear, as I was
attending to my ship duties, I felt the clock strike one o'clock,
and my heart almost snapped in two. I heard those church
bells as clear as day, and my whole body shook with the tolls.
I know we said we wouldn't write anymore, and this will be
the last letter you will receive. I can promise that to you at
least. My final parting gift, a wedding present from me to you.*

*I hope that he will make you as happy as you make him,
and that he works hard to keep that perfect smile going. If I
were with you today, I would work for the rest of my days
just to have you smile at me like you did. I don't blame our
families; the anger has gone now. All I feel is loss and pain.
So I will tell you one last time, dear You, how much you mean
to me. Consider this my parting vows, so much less than the
vows I would have loved to have said to you.*

*That summer in Shady Pines was the best summer of my
life, and I will love you from afar for the rest of my days. You
are it for me, and I vow never to regret the time we spent
together. If I die tomorrow, my last thoughts will be of you,
so do not grieve for me. They say till death do us part, but
not even that would dim my feelings for you. Every moment,
I will be there, cheering you on in spirit.*

*Don't give up the painting. I know he loves it too. Don't
let yourself be dimmed by life – that would kill me. Go out
there and make the world a brighter place, my sweet. You are
my star, my moon, my guiding light. I'll love you till the very
end.*

G

He didn't write again. True to his word to the last. Martha
Rodgers, resident bad-ass and artist, all this time was loved by

two men. The letters from him were of torment, awe, and fear. A young man, all set for the Navy, meeting a woman already betrothed to another. Two families who were close, and a future wedding at the pinnacle to look forward to. She thought of how wretched Martha must have felt, how torn apart they were.

Nowadays, it would have been easier. People broke commitments all the time, walked away from families and loved ones for a new love, or the next shiny thing. She thought of Duncan and his fancy piece, who was the opposite of her in every way from knicker elastic strength to views on feminism. She couldn't imagine being in love with another and walking down the aisle knowing that your heart wasn't in it, but hundreds of miles away on the high seas. When she had walked down that aisle, not recognising most of the guests, she had felt it too. She realised now, just how many alarm bells she had ignored, and how it had ended.

Martha was still tormented by her last love, and April didn't fancy taking up letter writing any time soon. They had loved each other from the first day they met, till the day she took her vows. Then the letters were all her, talking to him but never sending the letters. Sharing her life, her highs and lows. All written to a man who she had never seen again.

Reaching into the box for the next letter, she pulled out a photo instead. It was of Martha, but it wasn't a traditional wedding shot. This one made April tear up all over again. She knew just by looking at it why it was in the box. Why it wasn't sitting in a gilded frame somewhere, or between the crinkly pages of a photo album. Martha was sitting at the end of a big hall, the black and white of the photo making the scene look all the more dramatic, and stark. The white of her dress as it billowed out beautifully beneath her. Her little white cotton gloves covered her face as she cried. Turning the photo over, she saw that a young Martha had written on the back.

Saying goodbye, it said simply. Nothing else was needed, and April was back there in her own wedding venue, clear as day. She could almost feel the movement of the fitted designer material around her body, her hunger pains gnawing at her empty belly as she said in the side room. Her mother had just left, wishing her all the best and wiping at her mascara-streaked face. She'd sat in just such a chair, waiting to be wed. She could still remember crying her eyes out, petrified and certain that she was making a mistake.

Looking back at the photo of Martha, she wondered what would have happened if they had met that day, on their most confusing days. Maybe the two women would have kicked off their heels and shimmied out of the window together, dresses and veils fanning out behind them as they escaped. Maybe pain would have been avoided, but it was pointless to think about. They had both sat there, in their dresses, wishing to God their veils were capes instead so they could fly away, disappear. As she sat there, staring at the photo, she heard a noise from outside. Recognising it, she grabbed her keys and phone, locking up behind her and running outside.

'Hello,' she said as Cillian returned from the bins. He turned to look at her, and she pushed her keys into her pocket.

'Hi,' he said, standing there in just a pair of jeans and a pair of black socks. The man was shirtless, and it took a moment for April to tear herself away from his porch-light-lit body, which looked like something Martha might have sculpted once upon a time. Maybe even now, judging by the passion April could still feel in her words from her latest letters.

He kept walking up to his chalet door, and April found herself scrambling after him.

'Cillian,' she said when she was standing right behind him. 'I'm sorry, I didn't want to fight.'

He sagged then, and turned to face her properly.

'It was me, my stuff. It's okay.' He spotted the phone in her hand. 'Back in the land of the living finally?' She looked at the handset, then back at him.

'My ex-husband is getting married as you know, but I found out today they're having a baby.'

Cillian's jaws flexed and he stepped forward, pulling her into his arms and turning them both till they were sitting on his porch seat.

'Well, that's awful.' He stroked her arm with his hand as he wrapped his arm around her. She nestled closer, turning till she was resting her cheek on his chest. She could smell soap, and mouthwash and she took a slow breath in to savour his scent. 'My mate Paddy brought Tina to the solicitor's today and told me to sort it out.'

'Wow. How did you dispose of him? Not the bins, I hope.'

Cillian snorted, and she rested her hand on his chest, pulling his shirt in close with her fingers. He lay against the wooden back, bringing her with him.

'I can't tell you that.' He tapped the tip of her nose with his index finger as he looked down at her. 'Top secret.' She looked up at him, and he dropped a kiss where his finger had just touched her skin. She moved her head up, taking his mouth with her own. They kissed for a long time, her lying on him, him wrapping his arms around her and kissing her bad mood away.

Eventually, when they pulled apart, she swallowed hard, and bit the bullet.

'Cillian, I—'

She was about to tell him about Martha, about the letters, and the wailing, heartbroken women in their wedding dresses. She was about to tell him that she was feeling things for him, and she wanted to—

'I'm sorry about earlier.' He seemed to want to talk, and she found herself biting her tongue. She wanted to hear what he had to say. 'It's been awful the last few months, and I took it out on you. Tina wasn't exactly loyal, and with everything else, it's just a lot. I didn't expect you. It's hard to trust, you know? I've got it pretty wrong before.'

She nodded, looking him in the eye now as their hands clasped around each other. He moved his hands further down her wrists, stroking her skin as he went.

'I can't seem to stop touching you, April, or thinking about you.' He tilted his head, taking her lips once more and kissing her like it meant everything to him. 'We got it sorted today. Tina agreed to everything, and I can't help but think that this could be something. I'm not an easy man to get along with—'

'Or live and work with,' she added, giving him a sneaky smile.

'Stay with me, tonight?' He wasn't laughing now; he looked a little scared even. 'I don't mean anything funny, I promise. Orla's asleep. I have a lock on my bedroom door now. We can wake up early. I'm not trying to complicate things, and I know you're still working through some stuff, but—'

He kept talking, softly into her ear while they sat together on that porch. Here was a man with baggage, emotional and real, and he was pouring his heart out to her about how he'd worked through his issues with Tina, how Orla was staying with him now, and how grateful he was that she offered him a job and a place to live. How it was more than that for him now, but he didn't know just what it was. All without a hint of bruised masculinity, and him talking about his wants and needs over others. The differences between him and Duncan were legion, and once more she found herself wondering whether Shady Pines was a place of lost souls after all.

'I'll stay,' she told him, without thought or fear. 'I'll go get some bits, and I'll stay.'

Cillian's nervous features melted into a relaxed and very sexy grin. 'Really?' He looked the happiest she'd seen him since they met, and she couldn't help but grin back. Today, it was as if something had shifted in Shady Pines, and everything was coming to a head.

'Really,' she replied, kissing him again. 'We take this slow, no labels. Okay?'

He was nibbling at the corner of his mouth now, and she frowned. 'What?' She was panicking, panicking that he had changed his mind. 'Cillian?'

He stood up, taking her with him and leading her over to her chalet.

'Okay, but I do need to tell Orla, once we figure it out. I don't like lying to her.' April beamed. Her whole heart swelling at the care and love he showed his child. She couldn't help but think of the sonogram she'd seen, and wonder if the father of that little one would be as selfless. She doubted it somehow, but chose to hope anyway.

'Deal,' she said, heading into the chalet and grabbing a few bits to shove into a bag. On the table sat the box full of letters, and that's when it hit her.

'Cillian,' she called from the bedroom, as he waited in the doorway. 'What was the name of that gallery owner we met? Luke?' She'd had an idea, and once the park was officially open and the dust had settled, she wanted to help both Judith and Martha.

'Beaumont,' he said easily. 'Luke Beaumont. His family bought the gallery. I think they live here now.'

Beaumont. Beaumont. The name rattled around and around in her head, but it wasn't clicking together. Where had she heard that name before? Hell, she was probably just slightly deranged from all the upheaval of the last few months. It was probably one of Duncan's pit bulls from work. That was it. It had to be. Packing the rest of her bits and pieces, and looking around at her little home, she linked arms with Cillian, and the pair of them headed to Cillian's house, her bag slung over his broad shoulders as she headed indoors for a night together.

Chapter 15

'I do love those eggs,' Mr Prince said as he came to settle up his bill. 'Don't suppose you have a dozen more, to take home?'

April, dressed for the late May weather in a maxi dress and pumps, nodded and reached under the counter for a box of Judith's finest.

'No problem, Mr Prince, here you go.'

He slipped some coins into her hand, and she ran the payment through the till, grinning again as she saw the healthy drawer full of cash. Now she wasn't afraid of technology and her phone, she had sorted the website out and the bookings were coming in steadily. A young college student named Amy was the weekend receptionist now, leaving April with some time off bar any arising problems.

Shady Pines was getting into its groove and April found herself optimistic for the future.

'Bye, Mr Prince.' Cillian waved to the Prince family as they drove away to travel home. He thumbed over his shoulder at her. 'Good bloke, eh? Lovely family.'

'Yep, and he took a fair bit home from the shop, and they've booked again for August, same chalet.'

She high-fived him when he raised his hand. Coming behind

the reception desk, he wrapped his arms around her waist and dropped a kiss onto her neck before scrambling away when Orla walked in a second later.

'Morning, April!' Orla was far chattier now, and she loved the troll slide. Duncan was her favourite, which always made April chuckle. Especially since she'd seen Cillian giving it a swift kick when he thought no one was looking. The big lummox was hopping around, and limping half the afternoon.

'I'm going to big school today!'

The nursery children were transitioning into full-time school in September, and Orla couldn't wait. She'd been up since the crack of dawn, even before Kenneth, Judith's punctual cockerel. Cillian walked back around the counter, squeezing April's arm as he passed. When he was standing at the other side of Orla, he winked at April. An image of him half naked, helping her get out of his bedroom window that morning came into mind, and she knew that Cillian would know what she was thinking about, her blush yet again giving it away. They'd barely spent a night apart since their fight, grabbing moments alone when they could once Orla was asleep.

'I know, I'm so excited for you!' She reached under the counter again and pulled out a pencil case. It was bright pink, just like Pinky, with Orla's name embroidered onto it. Lately, she had been walking into the village on the weekends, getting to know her new home and picking up a few bits along the way. She'd not been able to walk past this one in the window, and the shop owner was able to personalise it for her. 'I got you a little something, for luck.'

Orla's eyes widened as April came and knelt by her side, the case in her hands.

'It looks like Pinky!' she squealed, and April and Cillian laughed. Orla took the case and held out a little hand for April to shake. April shook it, pulling a funny face and pretending that Orla was squeezing her a bit tight. The phone rang in the office, and April dropped a kiss on Orla's cheek, whispered good luck to her and ran to answer it.

'Good morning, Shady Pines Chalet Park, April speaking. How may I help?'

'Morning, April, Henry here. The riders all set?'

To say that April had been busy the last few weeks was a bit of an understatement. She didn't throw an official reopening party or anything like that. She didn't have the money, and the woman who woke up in Cillian's arms every morning was a very different creature to the rattled, gibbering wreck she'd been when she arrived in Cornwall. She'd been working her magic ever since, and she wasn't done yet.

'Morning, Henry, all set here.' She could see the Batten family coming across the chalet park, kids and adults alike excited and chattering away as they enjoyed their holiday. Henry, Judith, and April had started to link the businesses together further, and Judith was even hoping to open up her grounds next season, with a view to the donations and fees going towards the animals' upkeep. Henry, with his horses and livery yard, was offering riding lessons to the guests, and the uptake so far had been amazing. April's personal bank account was still low, but she needed less. Her ex-husband would probably faint at the figure, but the truth was, she was spending less. She didn't need to spend £200 on her hair anymore to fit in with the other wives; her nails were painted by either Orla or covered in mud, paint or some other cleaning product; and her wardrobe was definitely more on the casual side these days.

The other day, she'd slept in one of Cillian's flannel shirts and it had felt better than any cashmere on her skin. Cillian had thought it looked rather nice too, as she recalled. Their late-night meet-ups were trickier now with guests milling about the place, but they did manage it. Since that first night, they hadn't spent more than a couple of nights apart, and even then that was only due to working late or one night when Orla was up with toothache half the night. Cillian, ever the doting dad, always put Orla first, never letting her find anything that might confuse her. Their late-night kisses and caresses were as far as it went, and they never discussed anything past the bookings for next week and their next project or update to the park that needed to be dealt with. She was making it work, the park was making money, the repairs and supplier bills less eye-wateringly high. April was living in the moment, barely spending anything, and she was as peaceful as she had been in such a long time.

Henry rang off, eager to get everything perfect for the guests' arrival. April shot off a text to Judith, and before too long, she pulled up in a large and rather battered Land Rover Defender to collect the guests and take them to Henry. April waved them all off as Orla and Cillian looked on.

'She'll suss it out, you know,' Cillian said, leaning on the counter and looking at her in such a way that her knees started to knock. He looked dead-drop gorgeous these days, the haunted look slowly fading away from his features. He looked his most relaxed when they were lying in each other's arms at night, she thought, but she didn't like to take the credit. She knew where her happy place was, and it wasn't her own lonely chalet bed.

Beyond that, she didn't want to tempt fate. Besides, she had plenty to occupy her mind, and the guests were always on hand to keep her from dwelling on things. She was here, she was open, she was doing it. Her new life. She'd even put a photo on social media, though it was a little tongue-in-cheek. A picture of Elvis, leaning against the blue gate and curling his lip. Underneath she'd written *'Elvis is in the garden.'*

A few of her work colleagues had messaged her, and she'd been able to talk to them without feeling shame and embarrassment about her life here. She'd not mentioned Cillian to any of them, not wanting them to be asking questions about where it was going, whether she would remarry, whether she'd be having any bundles of Cornish-bred joy in her future. She didn't want to verbalise it to anyone else, when she couldn't even have the talk with Cillian. *It's going well,* she kept repeating on a loop. *It's going well. That's enough. I'm happy.*

'All good?' Cillian asked, as though he was reading the thoughts right out of her head.

'Good.' She grinned at him. 'You all ready for school, Orla?'

'Yes!' she announced loudly, brandishing her new pencil case. 'Let's go, Daddy!'

The school was giving the kids an extra transition day, while the year six students were away at camp, and Orla couldn't wait. She wasn't as skittish as before, but she still got nervous when Cillian drove her to nursery. She could feel the tension in him as he thought of what his daughter was thinking and worrying about every morning. Most children would laugh or smile at the thought of their mother shouting to them from the school gates. Orla's memory was much less shiny, and April wished she could help them both, but it wasn't her place. They didn't belong to her. She knew deep down, this could only be temporary.

Cillian was fussing around his daughter, making sure everything she needed was ready in her backpack. By the way he was packing, you would think Orla had been recruited by the SAS. April was pretty sure she'd seen him shove a compass and a can of bear spray in the back pockets.

'Cillian, she's fine. You'll be late if you don't get a move on.' She reached for a box of homemade biscuits from the shelf. 'Here, Orla, give these to your new teacher to hand out to everyone.' Orla's mouth dropped open as she looked at the box of gorgeous sugar cookies, all in the shape of shells and sea creatures. She ran to grab them, her backpack and Cillian both strapped to her. Cillian took the biscuits and zipped up her backpack.

'Come on then, poppet.' He passed by April on their way to the exit, and he leaned in, dropping a peck on her lips. 'Thanks, babe. Back in a bit.' Pulling back, he had the biggest, happiest smile on his face. April, however, had frozen in place. Seeing her panicked expression, his face fell. The pair of them looked across at Orla, but she was laughing behind her hands at the pair of them.

April whispered from the side of her mouth as Orla continued to giggle and belly laugh. 'What do we do?'

Cillian, speaking from one corner of his, didn't offer much help.

'I've no idea. I forgot ...' He leaned down in front of Orla. 'Daddy's just being silly, button. Let's go. Say goodbye to April!'

Orla came forward and beckoned for April to lean in. When she did, Orla kissed her on the lips, a fast little touch, and shouted, 'Bye, baby! I'm off to big school!'

She marched out, biscuits and backpack with her, and the pair were left looking at each other aghast. April started to speak, to apologise even, but he cut her off.

'That was close.' It wasn't a warning, but his face was closed off. He didn't look at her in his usual way, his secret looks that told her he was thinking about her when they were working on something for the chalet park, or when they were serving customers, or taking Orla and the others to play in the playground. 'Won't be long.' He didn't look at her again, and she followed him with her eyes as he scooped Orla up and put her into the van. Normally he would turn his head, but he kept his eyes on the road this time. She could tell by the set of his jaw that he was upset, and she felt the stirring in her stomach.

Orla had shrugged it off this time, but it was getting harder to act normal around everyone. She found herself correcting her own body language whenever he was around. A couple of the holidaymakers had even thought them to be a husband and wife team, and April had wanted the ground to swallow her up when Mrs Adamson had left a comment card in her chalet, thanking *'Mr Cillian Statham for repairing the table leg at such short notice'*. She'd hidden it right at the bottom of the file she was making for reception. Even seeing the name Mr Statham made her feel odd, let alone involving the Cillian awkwardness.

Once the van was gone out of sight, and she'd made sure everything was ready for the day, she went to the store room at the back to start the orders she'd had come in for baskets from Judith. They helped each other out, and Cillian had been taking Orla up to help with the animals too, which April loved to hear about later, from both the O'Learys. Orla's stories were short and sweet, but even a few words from her were unheard of just a short time ago. Everything was changing.

Turning around to pack a fresh basket into a cardboard shipping box, her leg hit something hard. A huge box of painting materials, one of three that had been delivered in recent weeks. Sighing, she looked across at Martha's chalet and, picking up the box, she headed over, flicking the five-minute break sign across as she went.

Chapter 16

'Martha?' April tapped on the door of her chalet, heavy box in hand. There was no answer, which wasn't surprising given the last few weeks. Since she had passed on the box, Martha was like a different person. Night after night, while April was reading the letters she'd written to a faraway love, Martha was in her chalet, painting. A few days after the troll slide incident, the original slide had turned up, paid in full. The deliverymen brought more equipment too, and now the Shady Pines playground was a sight to behold. Even Duncan and Tim the trolls looked happier alongside the extended bark-strewn area, swings and roundabouts around them.

The kids who had visited the park so far loved it, and Orla in particular was a regular visitor. Every day after her dad brought her home, he would go back to work, make her tea, and she would sit and play on the porch or in the park. April found herself always aware of where Orla was. It comforted her to know that she was safe, and she knew Cillian never missed a trick either. Between them, they were watching Orla grow into a more confident, happier and chattier girl. The only person missing from the scene was Martha, who had seemingly locked herself away.

She tried again, knocking harder with her elbow as she juggled the box from arm to arm.

'Martha?' Almost dropping the box, she tried the door handle and it opened easily. From inside she could hear voices. The radio. A jingle rang out in the otherwise silent space.

'Martha? You okay?'

'Yes, I'm fine,' a voice said from the side of her, and April shrieked and jumped, the box flipping into Martha's arms like an excited lap dog. 'Ah!' She grabbed the box excitedly, putting it down onto the coffee table and ripping into it with gusto, using a craft knife she pulled from her multi-pocketed apron. 'Finally!'

Reaching into her grey loose bun, Martha pulled out a pencil and started rooting through the box, pulling out a delivery note and frantically ticking off each item.

'Martha, have you eaten?' Looking at her and the chalet, it appeared that the woman had done nothing but paint. Over every surface there were pencil drawings, discarded cups, plates with little bits of cheese and bread crusts sitting discarded, brushes of every size and shape sitting in various pots and crevices all around the space.

'Yes, I ate yesterday.' She pointed in the vague direction of a plate, frowning when she saw the beginnings of mould forming on the top of a little rind of Edam. 'Well, maybe not yesterday.' She waved her arms, reaching for April's hand and yanking her through the chalet to the back room.

'Look,' she said as they reached the entrance to the back bedroom. 'Tell me what you think,' she said, pushing April forward with a nervous grimace. April, still focusing on the fact that the place looked like a hellhole, gently opened the door.

Martha had been painting all right; she had seemingly done little else. Judging by the pile of canvases, all wrapped in cloth, which were leaning against the far wall, she was well and truly free of her block. Lifting the cover from the first one in the pile, April saw a painting of Lizard Point, a couple silhouetted against the setting sun. The colours brushed onto the canvas made the sunset come to life. April looked closer at the couple, who were standing, holding hands and looking out to sea. It reminded her of Cillian, and she wondered if they would ever get to that point. They were there already in some ways.

'It's beautiful,' she said to Martha, who had returned to the frame she was working on. 'Are you okay though?' She didn't want to mention the box, but to be honest, when she wasn't working or spending time with Cillian, the letters were how she spent her time. The love and longing she read in those letters had told her exactly what kind of woman Martha was, and she couldn't help but want to help. She'd been doing her research, through the letters, but even now, she was scared to make a move. She didn't want the fragile calm they were all enjoying to break. They'd come so far. She didn't want to ruin everything and end up with everyone being alone again. It's why keeping Cillian secret was so important. She had to protect it as long as she could. 'I'm still reading them.'

Martha stopped, turning to her and giving April her full attention for once.

'And what do you think?'

April looked back at the paintings, pulling out the next one, which was a landscape of the chalets. The new colours were on there; even the bogey hut was captured in perfectly coloured brush strokes.

'I think that you should find him and take these pieces to the gallery. They would love them, I'm sure.'

'Well, easy to say for a hard woman who packed up her life and came here all alone. Started again. I can't do that. Drink?'

April said yes to coffee, following Martha through to the kitchen. 'I didn't do that, Martha, I ran. I sold everything I owned, I took my late mother's ashes, and my bits and pieces, and I ran. I ran here, and it worked out. *Almost.* Why don't you get your life back, instead of hiding out here?'

173

Martha was filling mugs from a coffee maker on the side, and April took the offering gratefully. The two women stood at the counter, adding sugar and milk to their brews. 'I'm trying, but … I'm scared. I don't know where he is. I know he didn't die in service. I kept a check on that much but since …' She sighed, taking a deep swig of her strong coffee. 'He probably married and forgot all about me. God knows it's what I should have done. The guilt since Charlie passed, I don't like it.' She looked at April with watery eyes, her pale skin not touched by the sun of late, but by the secrets of her past. It was now or never, she realised. Martha needed to know. Hopefully, the answers would be something that she wanted to hear.

'Get dressed,' she said forcefully. 'Martha, get dressed. We are going to pick five pieces from these and take them down to the gallery. Cillian will help us if you like.' She could tell from Martha's worried face that putting her prized and rare paintings in the back of her old Volvo was just not going to cut it somehow. 'I'll call him now.'

Martha was biting the skin around her thumbnail, staring into space.

'Martha? Martha?' She didn't answer, and April worried that she might have broken one of her favourite residents. Not that she would ever tell her that. 'Martha!'

'What!' Martha came to, looking at her as though she was the one acting strangely. 'I'm trying to think what to wear!'

'Hello?'

Cillian's van phone kicked in, his ringing mobile phone cutting through his early morning radio sing-a-long. He'd just dropped an extremely excited pre-schooler off for the day, and he found himself eager to get back to the chalet park, and to April. He wanted to explain why he was odd earlier. She didn't deserve him lying to her. They needed to talk.

'Cillian!' April's happy voice sang out in the cab of the van, and he found himself putting his foot down a little bit harder on the gas pedal. 'I need you!'

'Well, finally,' he quipped, slowing down for a set of red lights. 'I was waiting till you caved.' She laughed, and his heart soared with the sound. 'I'm sorry for earlier. I need to explain.'

'It's okay, it can wait a minute. We have a mission, and I think "baby" was big enough for our relationship today.' She paused, but didn't take it back. Relationship. Having her come and sleep over at his every night had been for comfort initially. An experiment in curiosity and loneliness. Now it was something else entirely, and Cillian himself had been shielding it from the light of day in case it was too much to bear. The truth was, life was almost perfect at the Pines, but they wouldn't be perfect because of what wasn't spoken about.

'I need you to come back home and take Martha and me to the gallery. She's going to sell her work there hopefully.'

It sounded innocent enough, and great news, but Cillian wasn't stupid. His beautiful boss woman was up to something.

'This got anything to do with those letters I keep seeing you crying over?' His gut lurched at the memory as he drove back to Lizard Point. A few nights ago, he had woken up to find April missing from her side of the bed. *Her side, listen to me.* He slept on the side that Tina used to when they were together, and April slept closest to the window.

'April?' he'd whispered, seeing that the lock on the inside of the door was still in place. 'Come back to bed.' She turned from the window, a wad of white paper in her hand. She was crying, the drops of water dripping onto his white T-shirt that she wore. She'd never looked so stunning, or so sad. He made a mental note to punch Duncan in the face if he ever saw him in the flesh. 'Duncan?' he'd forced himself to ask, and her bemused expression made him feel like the king of the world. She shook her head, putting the paper back into her bag and sliding back under the covers with him. The light from the window lit the room dimly, and he'd kissed her tears away, one by one.

'Can you tell me?'

She smiled at him, moving her body closer to his and kissing him once, slowly on the lips.

'I love that you asked me that way,' she said, kissing him again as if she couldn't resist. He loved it when she did that. They were getting closer, and it was getting harder to be around her without telling her how he felt. 'It's not my secret to tell, and the letters aren't about me. Or my stupid ex-husband. He can't hurt me anymore, not now. I promise, I'll tell you when I can.'

Cillian knew she was speaking the truth. Over time, April had grown into her own skin here. She took care of everyone and required no fanfare or thanks. She fitted into his world perfectly, and he couldn't remember ever feeling quite so content. It was enough for now – he would make sure of that. He didn't want to see this woman get hurt again, and it was that fear that had kept him from telling her his own truths.

Her voice filled the van again. 'Yes, it does sound weird, but I—'

'You can't tell me, but it's not about you. I heard you, baby.' He parroted her own words back to her, tooting at a car that was trying to reverse-park into a side road, oblivious of the people walking behind him. 'Okay, okay. I trust you, I'm on my way.'

She rang off, and he drove to Lizard Point, thinking to himself about what the women in his life were going to get up to today, and how good April would feel in his arms later that night. Anything further than that was just not on his radar now. No need to rock the boat. That was when people fell out, and things were lost forever. It could wait just a little longer.

Martha sat in the van and looked out of the window in complete silence. She'd been feeling better lately, and she knew that handing the letters to April had helped. Somehow, the fact that April was reading the letters, and still wanted something to do with her, it helped. She felt lighter than she had in years. The love that she hadn't spoken out loud was known to another now, another who wasn't already gone. Charlie had been a good confidant in death, but the guilt she felt for talking to one man about the other wasn't something that she had banked on. She'd made her choice, that fateful day, and she couldn't bring herself to regret it. She could have walked away from Charlie. Maybe she would have done, if her life had started now. Perhaps she would have been the one to run to the Pines as a single young woman. Perhaps, perhaps, perhaps.

Regrets were slippery little buggers, always sneaking up on people and biting them in the arse. Everyone always spoke of living your life once, and living it well. Without regrets, or doubts, but the truth was, life just wasn't that simple. How could it be? We are all the stars of our own life stories, but to others, we can also be the villain in theirs. Duncan and Tina, the villains of her favourite awkward couple for example. They still dictated the lives of Cillian and April, whether they knew it or not. It was all very vexing to Martha, and what was worse? She cared now. She'd always had a soft spot for Cillian. When he was an excited, expectant dad she had cheered him on, but then the chalet park had gone downhill, and he'd had to leave. She'd never imagined he would be back, let alone as a stressed-out single dad. He felt guilt too; she knew it. They all had it in spades, and the van air seemed to be choked with it.

The White Stripes were playing low on the radio, one of Martha's favourites. She did love the deep bass. Cillian went to touch the radio but she slapped his hand away.

'Leave it,' she said stubbornly. 'I like this one.'

The three of them stayed sitting in silence, April stuck in the middle of the van with Orla's car seat by her feet, the back filled with some of the pieces April had picked out of the stacks of finished creations. The ones Martha had let her see, anyway. She had another stack, and she wasn't going to part with them just yet. Heading to the gallery, they parked up nearby, Cillian jogging off to get a parking ticket. April, seemingly intent on keeping her talking, was rattling on about art and rates to her as they got out of the van in as dignified a way as you can manage when reversing your pleated skirt down a deep step. Cillian was there by her side before her feet even touched the ground, and although Martha did her usual thing of batting him away and telling him she didn't need any help, she was grateful just the same.

'I'll follow you in,' he said, opening the van doors and busying himself with carefully unpacking her creations from the van. She was terrified now, seeing those fabric-wrapped packages and knowing that someone was going to be looking at them soon. *Wake up, Martha, this is the job! You make art, you sell it. Move your feet, woman. He's not here. He's not here. Don't be disappointed, just make something good come of it.*

April was standing by her side on the pavement, and Martha linked her arm through hers.

'Come on,' April said, her face set to determined. 'Let's go meet the new owner.' Martha tensed, and she knew April had noticed by the way she slipped her fingers through hers, holding her hand for dear life. They walked down the street, past the other shops and people doing their early morning routines, looking through the shop windows at all the trinkets and treasures they could buy and take home as souvenirs. They walked right up to the main display window, and Martha gasped.

In the window, was a large painting of Lizard Point. The lighthouse was in the background, and the tops of the chalet huts could be seen peeking through. What the painting focused on though, was the beach. The path to the beach from the chalet park was drawn and painted so perfectly, Martha felt as though she could step into the painting and run through the sand. She knew it as well as she knew her own heart.

'It's … breathtaking.' April, still holding her hand, was gripping it a little tighter now. She didn't take her eyes from the canvas, her gaze roving over every detail, exclaiming here and there as she found another little painted treasure within the frame.

'Thank you,' Martha said with a smile. 'It's mine.' Her face fell into a frown. 'They said they'd sold them.'

All fear replaced by curiosity now, she stepped forward and the two women entered the gallery together. Luke, writing something into a large ledger, looked up at them and smiled.

'Hello, and welcome to the gallery. Oh hi, welcome back!'

'Hello,' April said, gently releasing her friend's arm and walking over to the desk. The two of them started chatting and Martha didn't hear what they were talking about. At that moment, she doubted that she would have been able to pick April out of a line-up. All she could see was her work. All of the paintings that she had had in the gallery were here, all for sale and proudly displayed. Her portraits of some of the past guests, sitting and eating and chatting outside their chalets, her drawings of the birds that nested nearby, or the swell of the sea on the beach. Every art of Lizard Point was here, and it gave her an odd feeling.

'Martha? You okay?' April was looking at her and she spoke calmly, but one look at her and Martha could tell she was nervous about something. She thought back to the timing, the gallery being closed up, and the park being bought.

'Did you buy them?' she asked, not wanting the answer to be yes. It would be too cruel if it had been her all along.

'Yes.' Luke, thinking she was talking to him, stepped forward. 'Well, rather my family did. My father used to holiday round here, once upon a time. We just moved back here.' He was grinning now, looking around the place. 'I was an art major, and Dad's always loved art. When we saw this place for sale, we figured it was perfect.'

April was looking at Martha oddly, but she didn't want to

179

seem rude to the young man. She'd come to lay old ghosts to rest, and that wasn't his cross to bear.

'It is a lovely space,' Martha agreed. 'I've always loved it. I had come to show you some art, but—' She moved her hands around the gallery, gesturing at her many pieces on show. 'I think you might have enough, for now.'

Luke's mouth dropped. 'You're not. Are you?'

Martha chuckled as Cillian walked in with his arms full. April went to help him, and the two seemed as thick as thieves in the corner. Once again, Martha found herself wanting to bang their blinking heads together. Life was too short to be so unsure of things, and she should know. 'I'm the artist, yes. Martha Rodgers. I see you've got some pieces of mine.' She looked at the man, who was olive-skinned and well dressed, and smiled. 'Did you buy them from the old owner?'

April stepped forward, and Cillian wasn't far behind. 'Martha, this is Luke.'

Martha rolled her eyes.

'I know dear, I remember you saying.' She glanced at Cillian, but he was looking intently at one of the new paintings. A painting of Orla, sitting with a little pink teddy on the reception hut steps, laughing. It was from a photo that April had taken, a rare moment of joy snapped and kept forever. April had given it to Martha, and she'd brought it to life. 'Luke dear, I'm so pleased to meet you.'

Just before Luke put his hand into hers, April spoke again.

'He's called Luke Beaumont, Martha. He came to live here with his family.'

Martha's hand paused in mid-air, the oxygen in her lungs pushing out of her in one big, deep expelling movement. 'Beaumont?' she checked, looking at Luke as though he had changed identity before her very eyes. Luke bridged the gap, standing forward and wrapping his hands around hers.

'Mrs Rodgers, I'm honoured to meet you. I've been looking at your work for years.'

'Have you?' she said, in shock and disbelief. 'I … I … It's a bit of a surprise, all this.'

Luke and April looked at each other, and the cogs began to turn. The letters, the desperation to get her work down here to the gallery. It was April, trying to help. She looked again at Luke, not seeing any resemblance at all to the man she'd once known. Other than the name.

'Tell me, Luke, does your mother share your love of art?'

Luke blushed a little, before shaking his head. 'I didn't know my mother, I'm afraid. My dad has a good eye though.'

'I'm sorry,' Martha apologised profusely for her clumsy question. 'I didn't mean to pry. We should go.' She could feel the pricking tears of disappointment and shame as she turned to leave. It was a bad idea, coming here. 'I'll leave my work for a day or two. I can collect it later once you've had a chance to look. Cillian, can we—'

She wanted to run to the van, to home, but her feet were rooted to the floor when a door opened at the back of the gallery, and she heard the voice from the other night once more.

'Martha?'

In that minute, she knew. It was him. This was it. All the last few months had led her here, and she didn't dare breathe or move. She didn't want it to not be true. It would be just too cruel after this. The girl in the housecoat all those years ago was still inside her, still a part of her. Age didn't change emotion, or love. It just made it all the more vital to cherish.

'Martha,' he breathed, and the room stopped dead. 'Is that really you?'

Martha took a shaky step forward, staring at the man wide-eyed, the blood draining from her face.

'George?' The word came out as a whisper, and Martha swallowed hard, trying again. 'George Beaumont?'

George was stunningly handsome. He was standing there in a pair of navy-blue trousers, his shirt and tie a crisp white and pastel blue. He had a stick in his right hand, but when he stepped forward, he discarded it onto the floor.

'Yes!' he half shouted, striding across the room now as Martha gravitated towards him. 'It's me, Martha! It's me.'

They reached each other, and after a second or two of staring at each other, one reached for the other and they met in each other's arms. Martha started to cry softly, a muted sound that made George, the boy from the chalet park, weep at the sound right along with her.

'Let's give them a bit of time.' Luke was already ushering the others out of the shop, and Martha couldn't bear to loosen her grip enough to tell them that she was okay. She would be fine here; she didn't need a lift. Hell, she would probably float home.

'Luke?' she heard George say in question. Luke was practically shoving April and Cillian out of the gallery doors, and Martha caught a glimpse of them looking at each other before walking away down the street. For a couple of meddling folk, they sure were rubbish at sorting out their own lives. She couldn't think about them now, but she wasn't giving up on them. 'Luke, come here.'

Luke came and stood at the side of his father, making George look a little smaller at the side of his child. George's grey hair made his eyes look all the brighter, and Martha couldn't help but stare at him. Record every change in every contour of his skin. She'd dreamed of his face many times over the years, and now here he was. Changed, altered, aged, but still her darling George.

'Luke, this is Martha. The girl from the box.'

Luke was beaming, looking at his dad with such pride and affection. 'I can't believe it,' he said to Martha. 'I've been hearing about you for years. Dad has a lot to tell you, don't you, Dad?' Luke nudged his father, making him laugh and blush at the same time.

'Okay, okay, give me a minute,' he begged and his son left them alone, promising to bring back sandwiches and drinks while they

182

caught up on the last few decades of their lives apart. As they sat down in the gallery, Martha's work hanging on the walls, she gave up a silent word of thanks to her Charlie. She hoped that this meeting would have sat well with him. She felt complete now, for the first time in forever. She couldn't help but think that Charlie would have been happy at the thought.

Chapter 17

'Do you think Luke knew?' April was standing behind Cillian's van, pacing and pacing as she walked from one end to the other, peeping her head out from each end to see if she could see anything happening in the gallery. 'I know I've been sniffing around the place, but he didn't seem at all surprised that his dad was crying in the arms of a stranger.' Cillian was sitting on the pavement behind his vehicle, watching her pace back and forth in front of him. As usual, her curves were filling out her cute outfit, and Cillian couldn't quite tear his eyes away. He shrugged, pulling his phone out of his pocket and checking the time. 'Looked that way.' She was rambling now. 'And what did his dad call him back for? Must be for something like that, right?' He gave another shrug.

'I don't know, maybe it's a painting thing.' They gave each other a long look, both wanting the other to speak first, to clear the air. To snog the other ruddy senseless.

Cillian spoke first. 'Give them a minute.'

'Shall we go back?'

'Back?' Cillian motioned towards the large glass windows of the art gallery. 'If you go back in there now you're likely to have a Martha original inserted somewhere. Let's go grab some lunch,

184

head over after.' He looked back towards the gallery, where he could just make out the pair of them sitting together, chatting like they couldn't get their words out fast enough. Funny, how time and distance didn't dull some things, but shattered others. *Perhaps it's down to the strength of the love in the first place,* he thought. *We just weren't strong enough from the beginning.*

'Do you fancy fish and chips?' April asked, eyeing the little restaurant not too far away and licking her lips. 'I'm actually really hungry.'

Minutes later, they were sitting in a quiet dining area, away from the main hustle and bustle. The Cornish Seafarer Restaurant had a great takeaway counter too, which seemed to be servicing most of the early lunchtime rush. April put her bag off to the side of her seat, which was essentially a circular table deep set in a green leather upholstered booth. The seating bench ran in a circle too, and Cillian and she found themselves slowly moving ever closer to each other. They ordered fish and chips and thick white door-step slices of white bread, slathered in butter. It wouldn't do any good for April's low carb diet, but Cillian always frowned when she didn't eat. He went quiet when she nibbled on lettuce too, and fiddled with the food on his own plate.

He loved her wobbly bits, it seemed. He'd never once criticised her as Duncan had before him. She felt seen by him, and not in a way that made her cringe. She felt … pretty, for want of a better word. Desirable even, and that gave her a confidence that lasted when he wasn't around. She socialised like she never had before, and even enjoyed it. All the while longing for the moment when he would text her, telling her the coast was clear. Wanting her to come to him immediately. The sense of urgency was clear. *Come now. All clear. Can't wait.*

On my way. Die Hard *marathon?*

Woman, you are on. Come quick. Lock up. Waiting at the door to see you over.

It was getting harder and harder not to slip deep into lust every night. They would walk to bed, hand in hand, each turning away from the other to undress. He'd watched her, she knew. The turn of his head as she stealthily peeked was confirmation. Not that she could exactly call him on it. He wasn't being prudish, she knew. It was just savouring the moment.

Tucking into their bread, laughing at each other's butter-covered noses, it was the perfect date. Cillian couldn't have been happier, but then he should have known better.

'So fish and chips, twice right?'

The waitress had a name badge, but Cillian didn't need to look at it. 'Hi, Tina. Yes, thanks.'

April's head was already turned to the server, her manners as polite as ever, but Cillian could see her jaw drop from the corner of his eye. He blinked twice, trying to buy time and process just how bad this was going to get.

Tina smiled, a nervous smile. The one that she'd had that day in his solicitor's office. She placed the plates down in front of them, April moving back to give her room.

'Thank you,' she said once her plate was in front of her. 'Do you need a moment?' She turned to Cillian as she said this, and he shook his head.

'No it's fine. Right, Tina?'

He kept his voice low, not wanting to cause a scene when the ink was barely dry on their agreements. If anything, he was impressed that she was working. Proof she really was trying to make a life for herself. Glancing at April, he was surprised to see that she looked scared. He wondered whether she was expecting a scene.

'Yep, all fine.' Tina was looking between the two of them, frowning. 'Is this your girlfriend?'

'Tina,' Cillian warned. 'That's none of your business.'

Tina bit her lip, looking behind her to see if her work colleagues were watching. Satisfied, she turned back around. 'Actually, I am Orla's mother.' Lip biting again. 'Not a great mother, granted, but …' She looked to April now, and Cillian braced himself for what came next. 'I just want the next … figure in her life to be a good one.' She looked down at her hands. 'One that won't leave her. Cillian and Orla, they're a package deal.'

'This isn't the time or the place,' Cillian muttered back.

'It is, actually,' April said, picking up her knife and fork and cutting off a slice of battered fish. Leaving it on the fork, she looked at Tina and smiled.

'I'm April, I own the Shady Pines Chalet Park.'

She paused to take a sip of water, smacking her lips together. 'Cillian and Orla are very important to me. I can promise you that.'

Tina looked at Cillian, and back to April, and nodded slowly. 'Thank you,' she said. 'I'll leave you to your meal.'

She was gone, out through some double doors, and they were left to stare at each other, their food cooling on their oversized platters.

'I'm sorry about that, I didn't know she was working here.' He swallowed a quick mouthful of food. 'Did you mean that?'

April scanned the room before she answered. 'Orla is very special, of course.'

'About me, I meant. Us.' His words came out sounding grumpy, but he didn't mean them to. It was the frustration humming through his body coupled with the nervous, tentative joy he felt in his heart. 'Our future.'

April kept eating, and Cillian huffed through his lips. She laughed.

'You really are a petulant little thing sometimes, aren't you, for an alpha male?' She raised one brow at him before dipping a chip in ketchup and popping it into her mouth. *His Girl Next Door.*

'I am not an "alpha male",' he retorted, air quoting 'alpha male'

187

and flicking a bit of fish onto her top. She flicked it back at him, missing him entirely and landing it expertly on a young boy from the next table.

'Sorry,' she said, flushing as the mother of the boy looked at her as though she was deciding how to ensure she was dispatched from the earth. 'Really sorry.' She hunched down in the booth, moving closer so that the boy and his family were out of her view. She began eating her food with gusto, and Cillian noticed the change in her.

'It was an accident,' he said, a little louder than needed. 'Don't beat yourself up about it.' He said this quieter, leaning in towards her till their lips were almost touching. April smiled sadly and moved away till their bodies were just out of reach. She started eating her food again, but the moment was irrevocably lost. Cillian scrambled to save it.

'On Sunday, when we are both off for the afternoon, what are you doing?'

She frowned, just for a moment before recovering. 'I have two staff interviews in the morning, but other than that …' She thought for a moment. 'I was pretty much planning to update the bookings diary and then read a few books. Why?'

She looked at him, and the tension was there once more. 'Come to the beach with me.' Just the word beach and April's features lit up. 'And Orla.'

To her credit, she didn't run for the hills, or grimace, but the look was still a tell. He felt as though his heart had stopped for a second, and then it raced to get back into rhythm. It made him feel lightheaded. *What happened?*

'I don't think so Cillian.' She shook her head, only stopping when she saw how upset he looked. It sounded perfect, but God knew, it wouldn't end well. What if she face-planted onto the beach, or worse? Face-planting into the sand, with Orla underneath. She was a bumbling idiot around kids, and she had been feeling more relaxed but look at today. She was a bumbling idiot once more, and now so much was at stake. They'd been so close. If she messed with Orla's life, with Tina getting herself together and obviously still harbouring something for Cillian? How could it end well? She loved being in their family home, with Orla's things around and Cillian's little notes for her on the bathroom mirror.

Brush your teeth, kid
You can do it, Orla
Love you, love Daddy xxx

She loved the domesticity of their home, but more than that, she loved how he was with her. She'd sometimes wake in the night, and before April had had a chance to rouse him, he was already up and out the door, heading to Orla's side. April would lie in the dark, listening to him settle her back to sleep. Always patient, never rushing or getting cross with her. He'd sing The Killers and Robbie Williams to her, and April would giggle into the pillow, or lie back silent, listening to something that was simple and beautiful. A father singing his daughter back to sleep.

Then the pangs would come, but not for a child of her own. She'd tried and sobbed too many times for that now. The pang of longing was to get out of bed and help, to take over or make hot milk. Help Orla settle, and then kiss Cillian better back in bed. Soothing his worries over his daughter. She did that part now, but the disconnect was getting wider. How long till Cillian realised that no matter how hard she tried, life would never go right for her? Duncan had always joked in the early days about getting their strapping sons and porcelain princesses fitted at birth with armour, so their Calamity Jane mother wouldn't bungle their early years with her awkward foolish ways. The joke soon ran thin, and then cut with a knife-like level of cruelty in the end, when they realised it would just be the two of them, and Duncan's eyes looked anywhere but in her direction.

'Why not?' he asked, his face set in a closed-off expression. He was mad; she got it. So was she. She was about to walk away from something that she really wanted, and it made her feel so wretched. 'It's only a day out. I know we said that we were going to keep things as they are, but we can't really. Can we? Come on, April, we've both been feeling a lot more.'

The food was almost gone now, and April wanted the whole day to be over. She'd managed to get Martha to the gallery, and now look what had happened. Cillian was a maelstrom of emotions, and saying all the right things, but all April wanted to do was slip out. All she could see was a lifetime of awkwardly patting heads and fending off questions about whether Orla was going to get a little brother or sister. Cillian deserved a woman who loved him, who could give him more children. More importantly, Orla deserved a mother. A proper one, and April just didn't feel that she could bear ever upsetting that little girl. She deserved better, they both did. She realised belatedly that Cillian had asked her a question and was waiting for an answer.

'I don't think I can do it,' she said, as honestly as she could. 'Sorry, Cillian.' Putting her knife and fork together in the middle of her plate, she sat back, further away from him. 'The park's really busy, and—'

He raised a hand to cut her off and shook his head.

'I wasn't just asking about the beach, and you know it. It's okay, no problem.' He looked at the food left on his plate and pushed it away, pulling some notes from his wallet. April went to object, but he picked the tab up at the counter, paying while she gathered her things together. And her errant thoughts. She felt as though she was spinning like a top.

'Cillian?' she tried as they left the restaurant, seeing his head down and stance determined. He would give Mo Farah a run for his money, he was heading to the van with such determination. 'Can you wait, just for a minute?'

'No!' he shouted, turning back to her. 'I can't!' April looked behind her into the restaurant windows, but no one was watching them. Tina was nowhere to be seen, thankfully. She didn't know what this was, but it was not something that she wanted Tina to be a front-row viewer for. 'I don't get you, April.'

Well, that felt like a slap to the face with a wet fish. A ten-ton wet fish, to be exact. Hearing those words from a man who she had been spending so much time with felt like the ultimate blow.

'What? What don't you get?'

He was still walking away, her following just behind while they stomped to the van. Once they both got inside, Cillian took the ticket off the dashboard and passed it to an elderly couple who were just coming into the car park.

'It's got a good hour left on it,' he said and the couple thanked him, the woman nodding to April as though to acknowledge her gratitude to her partner. This was just it, this is what they would get all the time. Imagine if Orla was there? He waved them off, leaving the car park and heading in the opposite direction to the chalet park.

'Cill, I have to get back. What about Martha?'

'Judith and Henry are stepping in at the park. I texted them from the gallery.' She looked across at him in disbelief. 'Martha has my number.'

'Why would you do that?' she asked crossly. It was her park; she should sort the staffing out. Pig-headed man. 'I do need to be there.'

'Tough,' he countered, and she fell silent. There was no speaking to him when he was this way. His temper could give hers a run for its money, but she didn't feel threatened. She felt quite angry herself, truth be told. 'We won't be long and they know what they're doing.' April couldn't argue against this; she knew that her neighbours were more than capable. Between them they had houses, thriving small businesses, and enough animals to fill an ark. They could handle an afternoon on the reception desk between them. The chalet park was a relaxed place to unplug and that's what people did when they arrived. They didn't ask for much, and April had tweaked the business to fit the guests she had attracted. Her livelihood would be fine. Turning off into a side road, Cillian pulled up in front of a small neat block of flats. It wasn't as nice as Lizard Point, or even as nice as the buildings that ran next to it. It looked dull, a little unkempt. Boxy.

'When Orla came, we were all living here.' He looked up at the flats as though he had a bad taste in his mouth. 'It was just supposed to be a stopgap, till we saved enough to buy somewhere. I'd been saving since I arrived over here, and Tina was working. She stopped when Orla was born. The childcare just didn't make her wage worth having, and I was happier to be honest.'

He looked across at April, who was looking straight at the flats, her hands clasped tight across her lap. 'Do you want to hear this?' he asked her, a little softer now. His anger seemed to be dissipating.

'Yes,' she replied. She did want to hear this. Even in those late, whispered conversations, he'd never really opened up about when his family were together and just starting out.

'We didn't get on, Tina and I. Orla coming was a … surprise. She hated being pregnant, and with money being tight, she didn't like staying home waiting for me.' He looked back up at the flats, one window holding his gaze. 'I started working away, and I thought we would be okay.' His voice broke a little, but he kept going. 'I kept calling, sending money, but things weren't right. Orla looked sad or wasn't there at all half the time when I called. I asked Paddy to check on them, but he couldn't get an answer.'

Even though April knew that Orla was fine, and happy now, her heart raced as he told his story. He didn't look at her once, and she knew he was trying to keep it together. He was trying to make her see his truth, but he didn't know hers yet. This was pointless; it wouldn't change a thing. It would just make it worse. He was pouring his heart out, but it wouldn't stop what was about to happen.

'What did you do?' she asked, putting her hand on his leg when she couldn't resist it for another moment. He covered it with his immediately, giving it a little squeeze and bringing it up to his lips to drop a kiss on each finger.

'I went home. I was working away in London, on a huge site. I just got the next train home, and spent the rest of the journey trying to get hold of Tina. Her phone was on silent or something – it just rang out and rang out.'

He looked back up to the window, seeing something there that April's eyes could never register.

'When I got home, I couldn't believe it. The whole place was in darkness. It was cold. The water was off, and Tina was out. I thought Orla had gone with her at first, and maybe there'd been a power cut but …'

'You don't have to tell me this. It's not my business.' She tried to cut him off, but he frowned at her, his deep brows furrowing together.

'It *is* your business. I want it to be. Tina was with another bloke." He started talking, and it came out in a torrent. He needed her to get it. 'She'd left Orla at home, while she went drinking with some other fella. He didn't even know she had a kid. He'd been to the flat, April. He never even saw my daughter. She left her alone, with emergency credit on for the gas and electric. It didn't last long of course, so Orla was sitting on her own in the dark when I came home. The girl was petrified, and all she kept saying was that Mummy left her at home, and she talked about the other man. She'd seen him, but she'd stayed in her room. She did all that, April, and now after all this, just when I thought everything was utter shit, you came along.'

'Exactly.' She seized on the pause in his speech to try to make him stop. 'I have baggage, and the park to run. We're just going to confuse her, and I don't want to hurt her.'

Cillian banged his hands against the steering wheel in frustration.

'I know you won't hurt her. She likes you! I'm not asking you for anything. It's just a day on the beach. That's it.'

'And what then?' she countered, feeling her own fists clench now as she fought the urge to jump out of the van and run home. Just looking at the flat made her feel angry with Tina, her actions so at odds to anything that April would have done as a mother. Easy to say with an empty womb and no chance to make mistakes, but wasn't that half the point? These issues would come up time and time again, and how could she be involved? It wasn't her business. She would always be the one with no stake in the argument, but dragged in she would be. She'd have to, to protect Orla and Cillian. It was too scary. Too much would go wrong.

'It's not just one afternoon of paddling, is it? It's spending time with your daughter, and acknowledging we're not just working together anymore.'

'I think that the fact you've woken up in my arms for the last solid month should tell you that we're not just work colleagues. Don't see me top and tailing with Henry, do you?' His answer was grumpy, a boy with his lip out. In other circumstances, she would have found it adorable. 'It's changing because we're changing. Orla won't get hurt – you'd never do that.'

'How do you know?' April thought of the girl she was, all those years ago, coming to Cornwall on that back seat. Things changed then, but it was for the better. She could remember so many happy times when they'd come home from Cornwall, settling in Yorkshire again. A different place, a different front door to be photographed in a different school uniform. Those times, just the two of them, were the best times of her childhood, and Shady Pines was the start. She didn't want to derail the magic of the Pines. 'We've only known each other a short time. We haven't even slept together yet. This could all end, and then what? I'm doing this for Orla, and you. I think we should just stay how we were.'

She knew even as she said it that he wouldn't accept it.

'I don't think I can.' He started the engine, motioning for her to put her seatbelt back on before he indicated and pulled back onto the main road. 'I can't lie to Orla. I hate it. It feels wrong.' He looked across at her, her hand still in his, and he released her. With both hands on the wheel, he stared straight ahead. 'I'd rather be out of this altogether.'

'Fine, that's what we'll do then,' April said to the passenger-side window as she stared out of it, not wanting Cillian to see her shocked face. She could see his in the reflection of the window, and it was enough to make her hate herself for being so weak, so beaten down. She could reach out, right now, and grab him. She could tell him how much she cared for him, how his late-night kisses and sleepy chats had made her feel alive and seen. He'd kissed every silvery stretch mark on her body, and declared them all beautiful. He made her feel whole, without ever asking her for a thing. Till now, and look where it had gotten them.

'Fine,' she heard him say as they headed back to the chalet park. Keeping to the speed limit the entire way home, he didn't speak to her again for the rest of the day, other than for work. Even then, it was a very different Cillian who looked her in the eye now, and she couldn't bear to see the hurt and confusion on his face any more than she had to.

Chapter 18

'Elvis, tell me what to do.' A slightly squiffy April was sitting on Judith's back step, a cigarette in one hand and a glass of bubbly in the other. She didn't smoke anymore, hadn't since Lisa Wallaker had given her a puff of her Lambert & Butler at the back of the science block. She hadn't liked it then, but given that she was at a celebration of love, and a packet had been offered in her direction, she went with it. Smokers had the perfect excuse for things like this. The smoking ban in pubs probably helped a lot of introverted people, to be fair. Any excuse to nip off for a bit of nicotine, and mentally regroup. She could have had her own declaration of love earlier, but instead she'd managed to completely fuck everything up. Martha had had a much better day.

When Martha had arrived back at the park, she'd come with George, and he seemingly didn't want to leave her side for the foreseeable. They were like magnets around each other. If Martha moved to the left, George went with her. When Martha went to the toilet earlier, she'd thought that George was going to cry. He even went and stood outside the bathroom door, and Martha emerged looking thrilled to have an escort. Her whole body was lit up from the inside, and the pair of them kept talking to each other secretly, little snippets of information passing from one to

196

the other. They looked like love birds, plain and simple. It made April want to cry tears of joy and vomit all over them at the same time. When one of Judith's mates had offered around the pack, she'd clung to it like a lifeline.

'Cillian left early, didn't he?' she said glumly to Elvis, who was tied to a long post nearby, blanket on his back and happily munching away on the grass. 'I know he wanted to get Orla home, but still.' She took another swig of her champagne glass, putting the unlit cigarette on top of the fence post, out of the reach of greedy goats. It was her third glass, and she was already feeling the effects. She hadn't eaten anything since their disastrous fish and chip lunch, and she'd vomited that back up in her own toilet as soon as they got back.

Cillian had been there at the impromptu little shindig Judith had organised once the jungle drums had gone round that Martha had met up with a lost love. One who people accepted and embraced. Luke, adopted by George from Spain while he was serving over there with the Navy, had heard tales of the girl on the beach every bedtime. He was delighted when we found the gallery and, given his love of art, George had been easy to convince. Luke was delighted with his work and had given April a grateful squeeze as soon as she had arrived.

'I know I have you to thank. You certainly made my little plan easier.' He'd stopped a passing waiter, hired by Henry, who was currently canoodling with Judith in the corner, while a very tired-looking ginger cat sat sleeping on his lap. Taking two glasses of champagne and thanking the waiter, Luke passed her one and beamed as they both watched the happy couple. Martha was giggling like a schoolgirl as George whispered something to her, his own delight plain as day across his face. 'Look at them,' he said proudly. 'I'm so happy that they found each other.'

'Eurk!' April tried to say something, to agree, but it came out as a startled sob. *Oh God, not now!* 'Err, eughhh,' she tried again, but all that came out was the desperate threat of an ugly cry.

197

'I'm—' She pointed to the side door and ran off. Bursting through the thick wooden door, she ran hell for leather down the steps and out onto the grass lawns at the back of the house. Running so fast her legs felt as though they would catch fire, she sobbed till she collapsed at the side of a large empty cage. It was half covered with a tarpaulin, and she sank behind it, grateful that she could only see the blue canvas material before her tear-filled eyes.

'Dad, come on!' A little voice broke through her sobbing, and the otherwise still of the night. April pinned herself against the cage, covering her mouth and wiping ineffectually at her own eyes. 'Come on, slowpoke!' *Orla.*

'I'm coming. Slow down, my little cherub,' Cillian had affection in his voice, but it sounded different. Dull. 'What are we looking at?'

'The rabbits, silly! Judith said that I can name one. I'm going to call it Matilda, like the book.'

April smiled at the little girl's words. She was flowering here. It was so nice to see. Her smile dropped. *From a distance.*

'That's a lovely name,' Cillian said, sounding closer. April risked a peek over her shoulder, and could just see two pairs of feet, near the long pen a short distance away. Half a dozen rabbits were eating, sleeping and running around in there on the grass, the odd squeak of excitement from Orla making April's heart beat that tiny bit faster. But not as fast as when Cillian spoke next.

'Orla, are you happy?'

The emotion behind the words almost felled April where she crouched. She looked across, but the feet hadn't moved.

'Yes, Daddy,' she said sweetly. 'I like it here. Can we stay?'

Yes. Orla, this is your home. And your dad's. Forever. She wanted to jump out and declare her intentions, but she'd had her chance there and bungled it as usual. Now she was back hiding. Go figure.

'I think we can. I hope so. Orla, what do you think of April?'

198

Holy loaded question, Batman.

'She's nice. She likes farm animals, and she knows Henry and Martha and Judith. She sings too, but she's not very good.' April rolled her eyes. She knew the little tyke had been sniggering at her rendition of 'Love Me Tender' the other day in the office. Granted, the twerking wasn't up to muster, but still, she thought it was rather good. She smiled at the memory. She had a bunch of them with Orla now: fixing her plait the other morning while her dad came in all flustered looking for a snack. April had started stocking cereal bars to help him out.

'I'll give you the singing.' He laughed softly, just once and she cringed as she remembered he'd heard her too. In a rather more romantic moment, snuggled up on the sofa watching *Dirty Dancing* with the sound down low for Orla. 'Hungry Eyes' was always a favourite of hers. 'Daddy likes April too. A little differently though.'

'Like you liked Mummy?' she said, so innocently as if she had just asked for a biscuit, not recognised a person who had caused them such torment.

'No,' Cillian said, a little too quickly. 'Yes, and no. I like Mummy because she gave me you, and you are my bud, right?'

'Right,' Orla shouted, and April heard the sound of palms clapping together.

'Right. Daddy likes April as a friend, but as maybe more and I wanted to ask you what you thought.'

Nothing was said for a moment, and April rubbed her leg to ease the cramp that had seized it. She couldn't move now; she'd give herself away and that would be far worse than eavesdropping. Which was bad enough. Ever the interloper.

'I like her, Daddy. She's nice. You know Sarah Jenkins, from nursery?'

'Yeah?'

'Her mummy went away, and then her daddy met another lady.'

April could feel the gasp from Cillian in her bones, let alone hear it.

'Yeah?' It was barely audible.

'Yep,' Orla said, making a few little nibbling noises at the rabbits. 'Sarah likes her, and she goes places with them.'

'Would you like April to go places with us sometime, like that?' Cillian's voice sounded calm, and chilled but April knew what this question meant. She knew he needed this answer, because she did too. She knew as soon as it was asked, that this was the thing holding her back from taking that next step. From telling Cillian that he had fixed her business, and her shattered heart.

'Dur, Dad, that's what I'm saying!' As ever, Orla was straight to the point, and April had to stick her hands under her armpits to stop herself from throwing an air punch or two. 'We should do that!'

Cillian grunted a little, and when April looked the feet were gone, and the two of them were dancing up the garden, singing Meatloaf's finest as Orla sat astride Cillian's shoulders. He had his hands tight around her legs, wiggling his bum as he sang his heart out. She watched them till they were out of sight, and then slowly made her way back up to the house too. Waiting a decent amount of time, she crept back inside, soon swallowed up by the joviality. Martha's eyes narrowed when she looked at her, and then she flicked her head to the right. Cillian was sitting on one of the sofas, Orla chatting away about rabbits to one of the other children at the party. She locked eyes with him instantly, his head turning as soon as hers searched his, but his face was passive. He looked at her a beat longer and then looked away. Saying something to Orla, they started to say their goodbyes and Cillian pretty much hoicked her over his shoulder and ran out of the place.

April stood there, stunned, staring at the door. She must have done that for ten minutes before Martha nudged her arm, George's face mirroring hers with care and concern. *Great, everyone knows.* She felt the sting of tears threaten to come and she made her fake, 'happy happy don't worry about me' goodbyes to the couple, waved distractedly at Judith and Henry, and went to leave. Judith and Henry were still very much exploring their newfound relationship, and only had eyes for each other so they didn't even notice.

Elvis had listened to all of this in a seemingly interested way, only trying to eat her glass once or twice. Given that she'd left the party, she couldn't very well go back in for another glass, or bottle, and it probably wouldn't be a good idea anyway.

'Are you okay, April?'

George was walking down the path towards her, dipping his head to Elvis by way of greeting.

April wiped at her tear-stained, make-up-smeared face and tried to smile at him, but she was pretty sure she looked like an Alice Cooper tribute singer, and that made her think of Cillian again, because everything did. That's when the snot bubble came, and April gave up altogether on looking dignified. George, to his credit, remained utterly unflustered. Passing her a cotton handkerchief, he sat down a little way away from her and Elvis, who kept eyeing him as he did every new person. The ultimate guard goat.

'I met Martha at your chalet park, when I was just about to go into the Navy.' He smiled then, which made him look rather boyish. 'I know Martha gave you the letters, but there's always two sides to the story. Martha was always meant for Charlie, and their families were hinged around that for years. When Martha and I met, we tried, but we just missed our chance.' He turned back to the house, looking around as if he couldn't quite believe where he was. 'Truth was, I should have fought harder. I left, and the love of my life married another man. I always regretted that. I should never have got on that train.'

April's memory sparked at his words, and she remembered one of the letters, one that he hadn't seen. The one where Martha told him that she went to get him; she chose him. He didn't know.

201

'What are you saying?' she said, as politely as she could. She needed to think about this. Martha hadn't told him about the letters, so should she tell him? Would it matter anyway? The past was something that couldn't be changed. She knew that only too well. 'Are you not happy now?'

George chuckled, as though it was absurd. 'I'm the happiest I've ever been, but what else could we have had? How much more time together? They say youth is wasted on the young, but I rather think that's a load of old bull.' April laughed, and he leaned forward, closer to her. 'It's wasted on the things we dare not hope to have, so we never try at all. You decided to help Martha, and here I am. What do you want, for your life, April? You only get the one, after all.'

'George? Where are you, dear?'

Martha's wifely tones came from the now-open front door, the party seemingly still quite lively behind her.

'Read the letters,' April said, urgently, half whispering in the dark. 'You should read the letters. I'll bring them over tomorrow. If Martha agrees, of course.'

George frowned for a moment, unsure of her meaning but then he patted her shoulder, turning towards Judith's.

'The answer to that question, Martha dear, from this day forth, is always—' he sidled up to the side of her, linking her arm through this and dropping a kiss onto her lips '—right by your side.'

The two of them walked back inside, George obviously filling her in about the night's events. The sounds of the evening surrounded her once more.

'Well, Elvis,' April said, hauling herself up and heading for home, the odd misstep occurring as the night air mixed with the champagne in her system. 'April has left the building. Peace out.'

Chapter 19

Cillian looked at the text message on his screen, gutted that it wasn't the person he wanted to hear from. It was Tina. He braced himself, but the anger and hurt didn't raise its head as before. He just felt tired now, and sad about how things had turned out. They were never right for each other, but hindsight was a wonderful thing that bit you in the bottom weeks, months, years later.

I'm glad things are working out. For you and for me. I'm sorry, Cillian. Look after Orla. Both of you. Tina. It was the old Tina, a glimpse of the generous and caring friend he'd once had. Trying to make it more hadn't worked because it wasn't meant to.

As he tidied up the dinner things from the table, he tried to apply the same logic to April. Maybe they just weren't meant to be either. Perhaps this was why they hadn't taken things further than they had. Had he been trying to force something that wasn't there? Everything in him told him that this wasn't the case. He was hooked. Line, sinker – all his eggs in one big basket of April-filled love. He didn't care that it was fast this time; it felt so different. They both had a lot to lose still, but he'd been willing to try. Orla's approval had sealed it for him. He had wanted that. He still did. He'd frozen at the party when he saw her. She looked beautiful, standing there talking to everyone. Luke loved her already and they'd only met a couple of times. Fresh from his father-daughter heart to heart, he'd been happy. Till he'd seen her and realised that it didn't matter what Orla wanted. April didn't want this at all.

He typed back, *We will,* at first, but it was a lie, and sounded a little cruel even. They had made peace, and Orla came first over grudges any day of the week. *Thanks, am glad too.* He added a photo to his response, a snap of Orla in her big girl uniform. He didn't expect a reply, and he didn't get one. That would be enough, for now.

Looking round the neat chalet, he glanced across at the television, the bookshelf. Nothing interested him, and he had hours to kill before he could go to bed. His phone beeped in his hand.

Can we talk? April. Thank God. He went to start typing, but he saw the three dots on the bottom of the screen and waited. Maybe it wasn't good news. He waited, and waited. He heard a faint scraping sound from under the front door, and turned just in time to see a flash of white disappear under the doormat. As he picked it up, a text came through again. *Read it before you open the door.*

His hand was already on the door handle, but he didn't turn the key. Instead, he took a bottle of beer out of his fridge and sat on the sofa. The envelope was cream, pretty. The lettering unmistakably April's, her spider-like scrawls webbing across the paper.

Dear Cillian

I decided to take a tip from one of Shady Pines' finest resident letter writers for this one, so please excuse my ramblings. The truth is, I struggle to get my words out some-times, even around you, and I didn't want to mess this up. When I came here, I was hiding from my old life, because it had outgrown me, or I thought it had. I came here to start again, but I didn't have a clue what I was doing. You, and everyone here, helped me in so many ways to hang in there.

When you asked me to go on a day trip with Orla today, as more than just the weird lady who runs the place and draws on trolls, I panicked. I don't want to cause Orla any upset, but I know now it's not what scared me. All my life I have felt a bit like an outsider, the kids at school not understanding my family life, being the new kid. When I married Duncan, I thought that was it, but it wasn't right either. Now, I finally feel like I am starting to have a life, and that includes you.

The truth is, I do want to come to the beach. I'm just scared of what comes after. I want you to really think about what us taking the next step means. We can't get this wrong, Cillian, but with me, you just get me. That's it. With you and Orla, it's a no-brainer. Like Tina said, you are a package deal, and I want both. I just don't know what that will look like, but for once I want to stay and try. I'll try not to drop her like I did my first pet rabbit, Mr Frisky the Third (he lived another two years after that, and he was fine).

Meet me out the back.

April

April was halfway down the path to the moonlit beach when she heard footsteps behind her. Turning, she saw Cillian walking towards her, the letter in his hand. She went to walk back to him, but he stopped her.

'Let's go to the beach,' he said, leading the way.

'Orla?' she checked, looking back at the chalet.

He took her in his arms and she felt her body relax as it came into contact with his. She'd missed him, body and soul. Arguing with him earlier had been horrific, and he obviously wasn't going to go there again. Neither did she though, that was the problem.

'She's sleeping at Paddy's. She used to go before. First time she'd asked in a while. Paddy flew round here to pick her up.' He turned her chin with his hand till he was focused on her, on them once more. 'You worry about being around Orla, but you love each other already. You thought of her first then. How can that be a bad thing?'

She knew what he was saying, but she still couldn't shake the feeling that it could all go so very wrong. They walked down to the beach together, each lost in their own thoughts, till they reached the shoreline. Taking off her sandals, she dipped her toes in the water, Cillian joining her.

'So, what were you going to do tonight?' she asked him after a while, his hands reaching for hers as they stood at the water's edge. He turned to her, brushing the hair back from her face with one hand, and putting her letter into his back pocket.

'Well, I had a bit of laundry to do, and the book I'm reading is quite good.' He moved closer, kissing her with everything he had left to show her. 'Also, I'm sweet on the woman who lives next door, and I missed seeing her in my house.'

'Oh really,' she exclaimed. 'Cute, is she?'

'Yep.' He ran his stubble slowly along the length of her jawline, making her shiver. 'She's also very stubborn.' He leaned in close to her ear, nibbling it lightly. 'She's insanely fecking hot too.'

They walked the beach that night, strolling and talking. The whole world went on without them, and they were happy to be together, away from it all. By the time they unlocked Cillian's door, both of them not even considering being anywhere else, they were together. When they were half asleep that night, much much later that night, in each other's arms, Cillian laughed in the darkness.

April, half asleep and pretty sure she had been about to drool and dribble on his muscular forearm, stiffened.

'Laughing after what we just did might be considered bad form in some parts you know.'

He laughed again, and she reached for something to tweak.

'Arggh,' he said, dodging her nippy fingers and wrapping his whole body over hers, pinning her there. 'That's enough. I'm not laughing at that. I'm just glad my night off involved more than washing my smalls.' He kissed her again, and she kissed him right back. Happy to be here, finally. After everything that had brought her here, she couldn't help but marvel at how things had worked out.

'I'm glad too.' She kissed against his skin, moving under him to get closer. He held her tight.

'I wish we could stay here forever,' she said sadly. 'Shame we'll have to get up soon.'

He looked at the clock. Barely 4 a.m. His smile grew devilish.

'We have a bit of time – your interviews aren't that early.'

She looked at the handsome Irish man who had come to her rescue, daughter and moody aura with him, but she'd found a home with him too.

'I know,' she said, teasing him now. 'But I have a date on the beach with my boyfriend and his gorgeous kid. I have a lot to get done, so I can enjoy the day.' Cillian kissed her again, and they didn't speak again. They didn't need to. They were home.

I was there. On the platform that day, THE day. I was there.

I know I've never told you, but the day you left, I came. I came for you.

I woke early that morning and crept out of my bedroom window. The same one I crept through to meet you those nights on the beach. I was coming to you again, for good this time.

I didn't even pack. I just threw on my housecoat and ran.

I couldn't let you go. I felt so scared, so sick. I feared you wouldn't have me, the real me, standing in front of you, with my wild hair, chest heaving from my escape, but my feet kept me moving, fast, fast, so fast I felt like I was flying. We had nowhere to go, no life to speak of, but I knew in that moment that I would rather be nowhere with you than anywhere with someone else.

When I got to the platform and saw the lights from the train fade into the dark of the night, I knew I was too late. You were gone, leaving me alone in the crowd. My heart broke that day, and by the time your next letter came, I knew it was hopeless. We had missed our chance. Perhaps in another life, we will be together. Happy, in love. I envy that girl so much. I'd give anything to run like I was flying again.

I dare not even send you this letter, or the others. I will probably write to you for the rest of my life, and that thought both serves to depress me entirely and to provide me hope. Hope is essential in life, even if the odds are stacked against that much wished for life. I was the girl on the platform, but I missed my chance. You left, and you have your duties. I hope you have a life full of value, and love. I hope that when you look out to the water, you think of me. The girl from the sand dunes who will adore you forever. The girl who wished she'd never let you leave.

That girl is still here, and I think she will always regret that day, but I have to pack her away now. I have to start my life. Whatever you think of me, today or years from now, just know that I shall endeavour to be happy. I hope you will too, till we meet again.

Y

xx

Reading the letter, Martha shakily sitting next to him, George's eyes welled up. 'You came. I left you. I always thought you just made your choice that day. You chose Charlie. Why didn't you tell me? We wrote till you wed.'

Martha took the letter from him, rereading it herself, her glasses wet with her tears. 'I was too late. When you wrote next, you were scared and sad. I hadn't called off my wedding, and I just went along with it. I loved Charlie, don't get that wrong.' She bit her lip, but he just smiled at her.

'I know you did. I don't begrudge you that. From your paintings, I knew he was making you happy.'

'I do hope Cillian and April get it sorted out,' she said, sighing as he pulled her in close and they sank back into the couch together. 'I think the time is just right.'

George chuckled. 'I think they'll be fine. Besides, I have a lot of reading to do.' He kissed her then, and she sank into his embrace. 'So do you. I have a Navy chest full of treasures from lands afar. I wrote you all the time, Martha. You'll see, it's at my house. Come tomorrow.'

Martha cried then, and George shushed her. 'None of that, we have our lives together. Don't you see?' He pulled his wallet out, and a photo of her winning an art competition was sticking out from a wad of notes. 'We've been together, all this time. No tears now, we have a lot to be doing together, my love.' Martha cuddled him close, glancing across at Cillian's chalet through the window. His porch light was on, and April's was in darkness. She smiled to herself and settled in for an evening with her beloved.

Chapter 20

Lizard Point looked gloriously beautiful from April's bedroom window. The September sun was shining, the weather was still warm, and she had awoken to the sound of the sea and birdsong. Today was the day. She'd put down roots here, the second season was coming to a close, and she felt like they'd laid all of their ghosts to rest.

'Morning,' a sleepy voice rumbled next to her. Cillian dropped a kiss onto her collarbone, grazing her with his stubble and making her insides melt.

'Good morning.' She smiled, dropping a kiss onto his forehead as he laid tucked into her side.

'Morning!' a far too cheerful voice sounded outside. 'It's breakfast time!'

Cillian looked at the alarm clock on the bedside table and groaned.

'It's only six, button. You not tired?'

The doorknob turned, and the pair scrambled to cover over their naked bits with the quilt.

'Nope, and April said we could have pancakes. With strawberries *and* whipped cream. She promised.' Her eyes were as wide as saucers now as she gave her dad her very best butter-wouldn't-melt angelic look. 'Right, April?'

'Right!' April pinched Cillian under the duvet, making him squeak as she reached for her fluffy dressing gown and got up. 'Let's get some coffee on, and the pancakes. Pancakes, baby?'

Cillian beamed at her, and Orla gasped.

'You getting soppy on me?' His eyes were full of adoration, and once again she resisted the urge to jump back into bed and hold the pair of them close. She felt like her happiness well was a lot fuller these days, and it cheered her up no end. Especially today. 'Orla, you think April is getting soppy?'

Orla giggled, covering her tittering mouth with her cute little hands. They had the same sparkly nail polish on them as April had on hers, left over from their little trip into town the weekend before. Sometimes, Tina would come and meet them for coffee, or a quick lunch at the soft play centre, Leaping Lizards. Cillian couldn't fully be a part of it, still not able to totally forgive and forget the Tina of the past, but April knew what it was like to miss a mother and she knew it would get easier over time. In the meantime, she was happy to meet with her, give their relationship a chance. Maybe they wouldn't ever have the traditional mother and daughter relationship, but it was better than nothing at all. Orla deserved all of the people who loved her getting along and helping to make her life happy.

'She called you baby,' Orla sang, erupting into a fit of high-pitched giggles again.

April rolled her eyes, laughing as she headed to the kitchen.

'Yeah yeah, whatever, dude. You'll never domesticate me. I'm too much of an independent woman now.' She snapped her fingers in the air in front of him as she left, tossing her hair and trying her best to look fierce and sassy. Not an easy feat to pull off in a fluffy dressing gown that made her look like a polar bear, but she did it anyway. It had been a while since she'd cared about

211

her body and its wobbly bits, or what people made of it. Judging by Cillian's appreciative eyes, she was doing just fine, and she felt great.

'We'll see about that,' he called gruffly from the bedroom. 'Still time to make Mrs O'Leary out of you. Eh, Orla?'

Orla nodded studiously, all thoughts of pancakes gone as she reached out and locked fingers with April.

'That would be so cool,' she said earnestly. 'Now, pancakes? Dad has something to go with it, don't you, Dad?'

April looked back at Cillian, and he was smiling at her from the bedroom doorway. Down on one bended knee. He looked at her shocked face, and his jaw tensed.

'Don't panic,' he said softly, turning to Orla as though they were both hunters, and April was the startled faun. 'Orla, keep holding her hand.' He looked back at the woman he loved as his daughter squeezed her hand tight, her little Mary-Jane-clad feet bouncing up and down on the spot with excitement. 'You can't run now,' he said to April, nodding towards the door. April laughed and relaxed.

'You're an idiot,' she said, awe and shock tinting her words.

'An idiot in love,' he retorted. 'April Elizabeth Statham, nee Wagstaff, will you do Orla and I the honour of becoming an O'Leary, and promise to keep us in check forever more?'

'I don't want to be in check! I like spots!' Orla boomed, affronted by an image of them all dressed like a Burberry advert presumably. *She definitely got her dress sense from her mother,* April thought to herself, smiling.

'No check, Orla, slip of the tongue. Go see Martha, eh? Tell her the pancakes are on!'

Orla grabbed Pinky from her room, leaving the pair of them in limbo. Cillian on one knee looking adorably vulnerable, April rooted to the spot. She came running back out, backpack on her shoulders, Pinky sticking out and staring dead-eyed at them both.

'Good luck, Daddy, make her stay forever!' she urged as she

belted out of the doors. 'Nana Martha, Nana Martha, Daddy's doing it! He's asking April to marry us all!' Her voice retreated as she moved further from the chalet.

'Wow.' April breathed a nervous half laugh out. She was shaking with nerves, and she clasped her hands together to root herself to the floor. To tether her to the moment. 'No pressure there then.'

Cillian's green eyes flashed as he laughed softly.

'No pressure at all. We do things our way, as always.' He looked down at the beautiful diamond ring in the little black box, and his mouth turned up into a half-smile. 'I just fight for what I want to keep. For who I love.' He took the ring out of the box slowly, placing the container open on the floor beside him. The ring flashed in the early morning sun in the window, casting off tiny prisms of light around them. 'This,' he said, his words like velvet to her ears, 'means that you belong to me, like I belong to you, and Orla. We were meant to be a family, April, and I love you so much, I feel like being your husband is my final fight in life. I want you, forever. Just you.'

April felt a single tear trickle down her cheek, and she left it there unchecked.

'What about kids though? You love Orla so much, but is that really enough?'

'You are enough April, don't you get that?' He sighed, ruffling his hair in frustration. 'I love Orla, but she's not just mine. You brought us here, and she is a different kid now. She loves you so much, and I know you love her too. She's our daughter, ours and Tina's. She's the luckiest girl in the world, and she takes after her dad. Because if you say yes, I promise you, April, I will be the best husband you ever asked for. I'll be the husband you deserved the first time, and I'll love you forever. Whether we're a family of three or thirty-three, it's us. This—' he pointed between them both, and pulled out a hankie from his pocket, passing it to her '—is my world.'

April wiped her eyes on the handkerchief that smelled like him, and looked into the nervous eyes of the man she adored.

'Yes,' she said, starting to laugh with happiness. 'Cillian, I love you both. So it's yes.'

'Yes?' Cillian checked, shock and bemusement evident on his face. 'Yes, for real?'

April held out her bare left hand, wiggling her fingers at him. 'Yes!' She laughed.

'Wow,' he said, reaching for her hand and kissing it from wrist to fingertip. 'I thought you'd put up a bit of a fight. Paddy got me kneepads and a cup for my jewels.'

April rolled her eyes, and Cillian blushed.

'I'm not kidding,' he said bashfully, rapping his knuckles on his groin area. April gasped when she heard a series of knocks. 'See, safe and sound.'

April shook her head at him, and he kissed her hand again. His eyes turning serious, he slowly placed the ring on her finger.

'It fits,' he breathed, his face lit up with happiness. 'This ring is from a long line of O'Learys. My ma sent it over for me. She's going to want to come over very soon, I warn you now.'

Before she had a chance to panic, he had bounded forward and she suddenly found herself laid in his arms as he half ran to the front door. Shielding her from the doorframe, he walked out onto the porch and roared like Tarzan.

'Oooooohhh-wi-oooooooo-wi-ooooooo!'

'Stop it you daft pillock, I'm not Jane,' she laughed, squirming to get out of his arms. He held her tighter, brushing his lips on hers and making her stop dead to kiss him back.

'I don't care. I'm happy.' He was grinning like an idiot, and April knew she looked just the same.

'So Tarzan,' Martha's voice called out. 'Are you going to carry the poor woman off into the trees or what?'

The pair of them looked across and saw Orla munching on a piece of toast, covered in chocolate spread that April and Cillian

214

didn't let her have for breakfast. Martha and George were sitting together on a new love seat that George had bought her, arm in arm.

'She said yes!' Cillian shouted, jiggling up and down with excitement. April squealed in his arms.

'Cillian, you're going to drop me!'

He twirled her close to the ground, showing off before standing again and hugging her tighter.

'Shut up, woman, you're as light as a feather.' He dropped another hungry kiss on her lips before pulling away. 'We have to stop, or we'll never get any work done.'

She waggled her eyebrows at him, leaning into his neck innocently before running her tongue along his skin. He growled a little, and she laughed.

'Lunchtime,' she said. 'We can celebrate our engagement then.'

Cillian dropped a kiss onto her lips once more, looking at her with such deep affection April couldn't hold him tight enough.

'I can't believe I get to kiss you every day,' he said, colouring a little. 'All of this, it's just … you, April. You brought this place back to life. Hell, you brought us all back to life.'

April looked at their neighbours, playing with Orla. George was taking a photo of the pair of them dancing along to the radio, the occasional whoop from them both as they chatted about the upcoming Lizard Point wedding. Judith would be here soon, and they would all eat pancakes together, spilling out of each other's chalets and houses as the holidaymakers all awoke and started their day in this beautiful corner of the world. They did things like this all the time, swopping goods, helping with the animals, spending time with Orla and the guests who all came for a holiday, to spend time together and to make memories together. It was more like a community than a chalet park, and the guest books and bookings log were full of repeat customers, thrilled with their stay and booking their next visit before they even left Lizard Point.

She shook her head, looking back at her future husband. She couldn't wait to be Mrs O'Leary, but she still had something to do before she could truly enjoy the moment. The last part of her past to lay to rest. It didn't feel like an ending now though, but more a beginning.

'Cillian, I could say just the same about you. Hiring you was the best thing I ever did.'

'I rather thought the night in the laundry room was the best,' he whispered in her ear, making her whole body tingle. 'Need a reminder?'

April smiled at him broadly. 'Speaking of reminders, aren't you supposed to be making breakfast?'

Cillian narrowed his eyes, his dimple showing in his cheek as he grinned at her.

'I was, was I? Bossy wife already, I like it.' Turning his head to the others, he called across. 'Pancakes on the way people, over at the O'Learys'!' He pulled his tongue out at her as she winced at his loud declaration. 'Shut it, or you get porridge.'

Kissing her again, he turned around and walked her over the threshold, wiggling his bum all the way as Orla shot in and copied him, making April guffaw with laughter.

As Martha and George made their way over, minus the bum wiggles, George turned to Martha, and she frowned at his slight limp.

'What's wrong, your dodgy hip again?' she asked him.

George rolled his eyes, and Martha saw the boy he was, and the man he had become, all at once. A face she had pictured for years, and could now kiss and touch and see any time she wanted.

'My hip is fine, I told you. I banged it on the bedside table, remember?'

Martha blushed.

'I was thinking though, we should do it too. Get married.'

Martha looked at him open-mouthed. He stood there, probably waiting for her to shoot him down, to point out the madness of it all, but she didn't speak. She couldn't get her brain to work.

'Martha?' he asked, the colour draining from his face. 'Too soon? I knew it, trust me to bloody well cock this up after all this time. I knew it!' He tutted at himself, something he used to do as a young man. The little action catapulted her back to that day all those years ago, when he had asked her out. She'd said no because of Charlie, and he'd tutted at himself then. He was nervous; she knew it as well as she knew her own feelings.

'George,' she said softly, seeing April's face looking at them from the window. Orla's face popped up in front of them, and she started screaming excitedly. Bouncing up and down, she whispered something into April's ear, and April joined in. After a moment or two, when Martha was just about to ask the earth to open up and swallow her, a pair of strong arms came from nowhere, wrapping around the two screeching females and pulling the curtains shut behind them. She smiled to herself. Cillian was a true gent. She couldn't be happier for him. He deserved it – they all did.

George flinched, but he didn't meet her eyes. The confident grown man he had become wasn't the driving force behind his eyes at the moment, and Martha felt it too. She had to keep from looking down at herself, half expecting to see her party dress and high heels, rather than her comfortable painting clothes.

'George,' she said again. 'It could never be too soon. I didn't get to marry you yesterday, but I'd marry you tomorrow over and over again. Yes.'

George swallowed hard and reached for her. Pulling her into his arms, he kissed away the years and distance between them. They were still on that beach, wrapped around each other. This time though, they were together. It was finally their time.

Over George's shoulder, Martha saw the curtains twitch and

spied April looking out at her, her face full of tears. A hand came from nowhere, passing her a white handkerchief and disappearing again. She looked at April and nodded, and April gave her a snotty double thumbs up before running off. Probably to dance around with her excited little family. A family that they were both a part of now, more than ever. She was a nana, and a friend, and now a bride-to-be again. Mrs Martha Beaumont. She thought of Charlie, and sent up a silent thank you to him, for loving her for her best years. She couldn't bring herself to regret them, not even with George producing a ring from his jacket pocket. The truth was, she'd loved two men, in very different ways. Her life was full of art and pain, but the love had been there too, all along.

As they headed indoors, Martha marvelling at the ring on her finger, they heard the excited dance party from within. Martha pushed open the door with a shove.

'Eugh, I forgot my earplugs,' she said loudly, causing the trio to stop dead. 'We Are Family' was playing on the radio, and Cillian was half mounting the back of the sofa, an inflatable guitar from the gift shop in his hands. Orla was mid bum wiggle, and April was doing what looked like a bad version of the robot. 'What on earth are you lot doing?'

She gently let go of George's arm and then stomped over to the radio, clicking the CD player on and shoving a CD in. Her face was set like thunder, but then the music started and suddenly she was moving.

Beyoncé was playing and Martha sang along, dipping her hands and moving her legs to the music. Everyone was staring at her open-mouthed. She laughed, her face dropping her old rather dour expression, and she beckoned with her hand before flashing her ring hand from side to side to the music of the Queen. 'Come on, girls, we have two engagements to celebrate!'

The room erupted, the lot of them doing their best dance moves. Cillian had Orla in his arms, and she was doing her best not to laugh as he danced like the biggest idiot in the room. April, dancing along with them, reached for Martha and hugged her tight.

'We did it,' she said. 'We survived another season.'

She felt Martha's body move as she chuckled.

'We sure did. Ready to do it all again next year?' The two women looked at each other and grinned.

'Bring it on!' They both whooped, and they joined back in with the dancing. They had a lot to celebrate, the ladies of Lizard Point, and they couldn't wait to get started. They knew what waiting for life to begin felt like now, and they wouldn't waste a moment.

Clutching candles wrapped in card collars, Judith and Henry, the O'Leary to-be-three, Martha and George all walked silently down the beach path to the point where the shore met the sand. The sun was just setting, and it was still quite warm. April looked out at the sea, feeling her bare feet sink into the sand, and she knew. This was it. It was perfect. Her mother would always be with her, and now she would always be here, at Lizard Point. At the place where years and near lifetimes apart, the women's lives had changed forever. It wasn't lost on each and every one of them how precious this place was. How they would always treasure being a part of it.

They all gathered in a semi-circle of light, one candle being much lower, Orla carrying a battery-powered lamp of her dad's. Ever the cautious parent. It made April love him all the more, seeing how he cared for the women in his life. He was truly good, and she counted her lucky stars that Duncan had led her here. Looking back, she knew it wasn't real love. It couldn't be, because she had that now and it was a world apart. Duncan was happy now it seemed, the last time she had heard. She wished them well.

'You okay, darling?' Cillian nudged her gently, his side staying close to hers. 'You don't have to do this if you're not ready.'

She smiled, giving him a kiss and touching her forehead to his.

'I'm fine. Will you take my candle? It's perfect to do this now.'

He nodded, trusting her but obviously not enjoying seeing her in pain.

'I love you,' she told him, and he relaxed, as she knew he would. She turned to the small crowd, grateful for each and every person there. 'My mother loved this place, and she brought me here as a girl to start a new life. When I grew up, I always felt connected, and it was here I found my new life too, with you all.'

They all looked at each other, smiling as they let the moment wash over them.

'So, Mum, I made it. You don't have to worry about me anymore. I have family, and you will always be a part of this place. You can rest now.'

In her hands sat an urn shell. Cillian had researched for hours once he'd heard that April wanted to set her mother to rest on that beach. It contained her ashes, with some placed into a necklace that April now wore around her neck. The shell sat on the surface of the sea, April's tanned hands around it tight.

'I love you, Mum. Goodbye.'

She released the shell, and it slowly starting to float further from the shore. They watched till the candles burned down, and the shell was out of sight. April waited for the sense of panic or regret to sink in, but it never came. Her mother was a free woman when she died, full of life till illness struck. She deserved to be out there, in the world. It comforted April to think of her that way. The sea seemed to sparkle all the more.

Turning to her new husband to be and growing stepdaughter, she opened her arms, and they came together.

'Family hug!' Orla yelled. 'Everybody in!'

The others laughed, and they all held each other tight while Orla giggled in the middle.

'So,' Cillian said when the others started to head back, Orla chattering away to them all the way. 'Happy?' He was still concerned, a telltale furrow in his brow that gave him away. He didn't have a great poker face either, which she loved.

'Happy,' she breathed, looking one last time out to sea and blowing a kiss to the waves. 'Now let's get indoors and get tea sorted. When Orla's asleep we can test out that new hot tub we got sent. We should check they're up to muster before we commit to one for each chalet.'

Cillian's eyebrows shot up to his hairline, and he growled at her, pretending to bite at her neck.

'Mrs O'Leary, did anyone ever tell you that you are a slave driver of a boss?'

She thought for a moment, before shaking her head and pulling him close.

'Yes, but the job has its perks too.' She gave him one last lingering kiss, before walking away, teasing him with the curves he loved. She'd come to love them too. She was happy with who she was now, and she would never make herself small again. Here, at Lizard Point, she'd found the room to breathe, to heal, to grow. She'd found her happy place, and she would never hide again.

Swept away by April's story and the residents at Shady Pines? Don't miss *The Flower Shop on Foxley Street*, another uplifting romance from Rachel Dove. Available now!

Acknowledgements

As ever, a book is more than one person eating snacks and looking up Gerard Butler on the internet. Huge thanks to Belinda Toor, Abi and the team at HQ – this cover is my best yet. Can't wait to see what the next one will be like!

To the team at The Kate Nash Literacy Agency, and my agent Lina Langlee – thanks for the support, the brainstorming, all your hard work behind the scenes and the gentle nudging to stop googling Gerard and actually get some work done.

To all my writer buddies, especially my Yorkshire writers. I can't wait till we can meet at Pret again and work together. We didn't make the Ivy, but we will one day soon to celebrate.

Love to you all, and everyone at the Romantic Novelists' Association. Proud to be a part of your organisation.

At the biggest thanks go to my readers, who keep buying my books and fall in love with the characters. All this is because of you, so thank you.

And to my family and friends, thanks for being there. I love you all, even more than toilet roll.

Rachel

Dear Reader,

Thank you for taking the time to read my book. I hope you enjoyed it as much as I enjoyed writing it and, like me, fell in love just a little bit. I love to engage with readers, so feel free to contact me on Twitter, Instagram and Facebook and let me know what you think, and to find out what else I might have written that tickles your fancy. I am already hard at work on the next book, so look out for the next book release very soon.

If you do get a moment, popping a review onto Amazon/iBooks/Kobo would be much appreciated. It not only brightens my day, but also helps other readers who might enjoy my stories to find me and take a chance on my books, and that's just brilliant all round!

Twitter: @writerdove

FB: https://www.facebook.com/RachelDoveauthor/

Instagram: @writerdove

Dear Reader,

We hope you enjoyed reading this book. If you did, we'd be so appreciative if you left a review. It really helps us and the author to bring more books like this to you.

Here at HQ Digital we are dedicated to publishing fiction that will keep you turning the pages into the early hours. Don't want to miss a thing? To find out more about our books, promotions, discover exclusive content and enter competitions you can keep in touch in the following ways:

JOIN OUR COMMUNITY:
Sign up to our new email newsletter: hyperurl.co/hqnewsletter
Read our new blog www.hqstories.co.uk
🐦 : https://twitter.com/HQDigitalUK
📘 : www.facebook.com/HQStories

BUDDING WRITER?
We're also looking for authors to join the HQ Digital family!
Find out more here:
https://www.hqstories.co.uk/want-to-write-for-us/
Thanks for reading, from the HQ Digital team

DIGITAL HQ

If you enjoyed *The Second Chance Hotel*, then why not try another delightfully uplifting romance from HQ Digital?

If you enjoyed the Second Chance Hotel, then why not try another delightful uplifting fortune from HQ Digital.